ON SPEC
THE FIRST FIVE YEARS

On Spec

The First Five Years

The ON SPEC
Editorial Collective

Tesseract Books

an imprint of
The Books Collective

This edition is published by
> Tesseract Books, an imprint of The Books Collective
> 214-21, 10405 Jasper Avenue
> Edmonton AB Canada T5J 3S2

with financial assistance from the Canada Council and the Alberta Foundation for the Arts

Canadian Cataloguing in Publication Data

Main entry under title:

On spec : the first five years

Selections from: On spec : the Canadian magazine of speculative writing.
ISBN 1-895836-12-3 (bound) -- ISBN 1-895836-08-5 (pbk.)

1. Fantastic fiction, Canadian (English).* 2. Science fiction, Canadian (English).* 3. Canadian fiction (English)--20th century.*
PS8323.F305 1995   C813'.087608054   C95-910434-8
PR9197.35.F3505 1995

Cover art: Steve Fahnestalk & Lynne Taylor Fahnestalk
Page design & typesetting: Jena Snyder, Clear Lake Ltd.

The body of this book was set in 9.5 point New Century Schoolbook, with titles in Delphian.

Printed in Canada

To all of you
who asked

"What if...?"

From all of us
who said

"Why not?"

ACKNOWLEDGMENTS

Acknowledgment is made for permission to print the following material (all work reprinted by permission of the authors):

"Those First Five Years" © 1994 by Barry Hammond; a longer version entitled *"ON SPEC* History" first appeared in *ON SPEC* Volume 6 #3 (Fall 1994).

"Carpe Diem" © 1989 by Eileen Kernaghan; first appeared in *ON SPEC* Volume 1 #2 (Fall 1989).

"Muffin Explains Teleology to the World at Large" © 1990 by James Alan Gardner; first appeared in *ON SPEC* Volume 2 #1 (Spring 1990).

"Just Like Old Times" © 1993 by Robert J. Sawyer; first appeared in *ON SPEC* Volume 5 #2 (Summer 1993).

"Hopscotch" © 1992 by Karl Schroeder; first appeared in *ON SPEC* Volume 4 #1 (Spring 1992).

"Sommelier" © 1993 by Catherine MacLeod; first appeared in *ON SPEC* Volume 5 #4 (Winter 1993).

"Frosty" © 1992 by Jason Kapalka; first appeared in *ON SPEC* Volume 4 #3 (Winter 1992).

"Crossroads" © 1992 by Wesley Herbert ; first appeared in *ON SPEC* Volume 4 #2 (Fall 1992).

"What Happened to the Girl?" © 1990 by Wade Bell; first appeared in *ON SPEC* Volume 2 #1 (Spring 1990).

"Circle Dance" © 1993 by Eileen Kernaghan; first appeared in *ON SPEC* Volume 5 #1 (Spring 1993).

"Three Moral Tales" © 1993 by Dirk L. Schaeffer; first appeared in *ON SPEC* Volume 5 #1 (Spring 1993).

ON SPEC: THE FIRST FIVE YEARS

ON SPEC
EDITORIAL COLLECTIVE

CONTENTS

THOSE FIRST FIVE YEARS...

Barry Hammond

If someone wrote that a stack of rejection letters, a piggy bank, a bold experiment, and a University English class taught by **Rudy Wiebe** combined to change the course of English Speculative Fiction History in Canada, you might think you were reading science fiction, fantasy, magic realism, or even a horror story.

This would be absolutely fitting because you'd be reading the history of *ON SPEC*, the magazine in whose pages the stories in this collection were originally published.

Back in the late '80s there was a group of adult students who'd been attending writing classes together at the University of Alberta, first from Rudy Wiebe and later from Katerina Edwards. They decided, once classes were over, to continue to meet and workshop stories, the way they'd been doing in class.

The core of this group were: **Marianne O. Nielsen**, a local speculative fiction fan and aspiring writer who was studying for a PhD in Criminology; **Hazel Sangster,** a transplanted Scot and freelance writer with an MA in English and German from the University of Edinburgh; and **Karen Grant**, a British Columbia Master's student in English, who came to Alberta because the U of A would allow her to do a creative thesis. A bit later, after Karen moved back to BC to continue her academic career, they dragged in **Lyle Weis**, a poet, short story and children's writer, who was then Executive Director of the Writers Guild of Alberta. Lyle and Hazel recruited **Phyllis Schuell**, a writer, Edmonton Public School teacher and Writers Guild Treasurer. **Diane Walton**, a long time SF fan, writer, and systems analyst, began submitting stories to the group as well. More people came and went, but with these six, the basics were in place.

As Karen Grant recalled: "Writers match up with each other on many levels. Besides having come to a certain level of trust and appreciation of each other's feedback and despite drastically different styles, they shared a degree of commitment, ambition, time schedules, and maybe even a sense of humor."

The humor was displayed in the name the group chose: The Copper Pig Writers' Society. It was derived from an ornament Karen had in her study for several years—a piggy bank. To keep themselves motivated and producing work the group agreed that if a member didn't have a story for each meeting, they had to forfeit first twenty-five cents and, later, a dollar to the pig. The money was used to finance group dinners and parties.

Because of the ambitious goals they'd set, the pig did well. The parties were good.

The story output of the group was high, too. The stories were finished, workshopped, revised, and rewritten, then sent out to markets.

At this point the speculative fiction writers began to realize something: there were no magazine markets for their kind of writing in Canada. Sure, there were two French periodicals, *Solaris* and *imagine...*, but nothing in English except the *Tesseracts* anthologies every couple of years.

When they submitted to British and American markets, the rejection letters said things like: "situation too alien to American readers," "locale too exotic," "needs an upbeat ending." Obviously, something was different about the type of SF being written in Canada, even if it was hard to define. The Copper Pigs decided something had to be done.

The answer, of course, was to create an English speculative fiction magazine for Canada. That answer was *ON SPEC*.

The title was decided on as a play on Speculative Fiction, and the writing term "on spec." Although there was some early criticism that this was a term used by editors when they didn't want to pay contributors, the magazine would put that one to rest by being a paying market. But the whole venture was "on spec," on the speculation that there was an audience for this kind of writing and that someone would buy it.

The format the Copper Pigs decided on was, I think, uniquely Canadian. Marianne conjectured that, "Canadian literature and Canadians in general seem to have a respect for and an acknowledgment of different cultures and their mythologies. Mythology and archetype is the basis of much literature, speculative or otherwise. Lyle went even further, suggesting that so-called mainstream literature really has two components—one designed for the general public and one produced by the Universities. The first plays to the lowest common denominator and tends to be as formulaic as pulp magazines, the second claims to be general but is really aimed at a small esoteric group. Neither of these gives the general audience anything fresh. By contrast, a good genre writer will try to give his/her audience something new, shaking the boundaries, constantly renewing the genre, and the result is a truly popular literature. "We felt very strongly that we didn't want to produce another dry, literary magazine read by only a hundred people. We wanted something more..."

The potential *ON SPEC* editors agreed that the key to *ON SPEC* would be good writing, and the base—through science fiction, fantasy, magic realism, and horror—would be broad.

Now, they just had to do it.

"Doing it" began to look like a very real possibility when Lyle recruited writer and Writers Guild newsletter editor **Jena Snyder**, who had a background in weekly newspaper production. Not only did she know how to lay out a publication, she had the computer to do it on—and the willingness to tackle the task.

All the Copper Pigs seemed, in retrospect, well-suited to the job. While none of them will admit to being anything but foolhardy neophytes, nearly all had some experience in writing, editing, and small press production and they were all committed. What they lacked in experience for finance, public relations, and distribution, they figured they could learn. Marianne was elected General Editor "while I was in the washroom" and Lyle helpfully volunteered Jena as Production Editor because of her background in desktop publishing. Artist **Tim Hammell** was recruited to be Art Director: his job was to find artists to produce the full-color cover art and black and white interior illustrations for the stories.

The group decided on some basic principles: contributors were to be paid for their work—even if the staff was not. Submissions would be read "blind" without the authors' names attached, so the only criterion for acceptance would be the quality of the material. This gave everyone, novice and professional, an equal chance. Since the speculative community in Canada is relatively small, and since the editors themselves would be contributing, it also took away the possibility of accepting people only because they were friends or colleagues. The stories would be screened by an Editorial Advisory Board of established writers and critics. The Editorial Board for the first issue consisted of **Douglas Barbour, J. Brian Clarke, Candas Jane Dorsey, Pauline Gedge,** and **Monica Hughes**.

The first issue was published in the spring of 1989. The initial print run of 500 copies sold out in three weeks. The ecstatic Copper Pigs ordered another 500 and decided they had a going concern.

Since then, *ON SPEC* has continued to grow and evolve. The format has changed from saddle-stitched to perfect bound, and the page count has increased from 84 to 96 pages (up to 112 for the special Worldcon issue, Fall 1994). The publication frequency has increased from biannual to quarterly and pay rates have quadrupled, while the cover price has gone *down* 5 cents to $4.95. New features have included theme issues, articles on each year's Aurora Award winners, novel excerpts, French/English transla- tion exchanges, columns, cartoons and essays.

There have been personnel changes over the years. Karen Grant and some of the other original Copper Pigs moved away or left the group before the magazine even came out; Phyllis Schuell went back to teaching; and Lyle Weis, after a few issues, decided to pursue writing full time.

Cath Jackel, who had just finished a degree in Physics and was looking around for something to do next, joined the magazine in 1989. She had been active in fandom organizing conventions and was President of the Edmonton Science Fiction and Comic Arts Society. She knew the milieu and had the necessary organizational skills. In short order, Cath became the magazine's administrator and "Jackel of All Trades," taking care of finances, paperwork, mailings, subscriptions, publicity, advertising, planning and many other details. If Marianne was "The Figurehead and General Sharkbait" of the magazine, Cath was and is its heart and guts.

After both of us had stories published in the magazine, **Susan MacGregor**, a freelance writer who worked for the University, and myself, **Barry Hammond**, came on board in 1991.

In the fall of 1992, **Lynne Taylor Fahnestalk** replaced Tim Hammell as Art Director. She has pursued the same high artistic standards Tim set forth, and has expanded that tradition. Lynne and her husband, Steve Fahnestalk, collaborated to produce the striking cover of this anthology.

Marianne left in the fall of 1992 to pursue her career teaching Criminology in Flagstaff, Arizona. Instead of appointing another General Editor, we became an editorial collective in her honor.

Hazel Sangster now lives in Duluth, Minnesota, having moved in the Fall of 1993, but we still have her on the revolving Editorial Board.

Many others have contributed to the magazine's production: please see the list on page 255, where we hope we have thanked everyone we didn't have the space to mention here.

ON SPEC is very proud to have both been a part of, and spurred on, the burgeoning field of Canadian speculative writing. Nominated every year since our inception for Canadian Science Fiction and Fantasy (Aurora) awards, we took the "Best Work in English (other)" award in both 1990 and 1991.

For three out of our first five years, we published the Aurora-winning short stories: **Eileen Kernaghan**'s "Carpe Diem" (1990); **James Alan Gardner**'s "Muffin

Explains Teleology to the World at Large" (1991); and **Robert J. Sawyer**'s "Just Like Old Times" (1994). Many of our writers have been Aurora nominees, or have picked up Honorable Mentions in such collections as *The Year's Best Fantasy and Horror* and *The Year's Best Science Fiction*.

This anthology features some of the best writing in *ON SPEC*, as chosen by members of the editorial collective and advisory board. I wish we had more space to devote to the artwork that has been an integral part of the magazine since its beginning. The wonderful color covers chosen for us by both Tim and Lynne have gained us critical and reader acclaim for years. The interior illustrations have allowed dozens of Canadian artists to present their work in a national forum. Every year since the category was created in 1991, our artists have been nominated for Auroras for Artistic Achievement, and every winning artist has had some connection with our magazine. In particular, art director Lynne Taylor Fahnestalk has twice won, in both 1991 and 1993.

When people ask, "Why Edmonton?" as a location for this magazine, the answers range from: "synchronicity," "serendipity," and even "I don't know." I think Marianne was onto something when she said: "Critical Mass."

"You need a certain number of people with a certain kind of talent and a certain inclination to get involved in things all at the same place at the same time to sort of egg each other on..."

And we're still going strong. Check the ad on the inside back cover, and join us. There's a future out there and we're exploring it. •

packs of cigarettes, half a quart of whiskey after supper..."

Dorothy, turning a page of *Christian Health*, allows herself a ladylike snort. Martha hopes this unfortunate piece of history has not been recorded in June's file.

"Mind you," says June cheerfully, "that wasn't what killed him. When he died, he was drunk as a newt in bed with Sally Rogers from next door, who wasn't a day over eighteen."

Martha laughs. It's hard to stay depressed with June in the next bed. "Gather ye rosebuds while ye may," Martha says.

"Come again?"

"A poem. 'To the Virgins, to Make Much of Time.' By Herrick, I think—one of those fellows, anyway. Second-year English. It was a catch-phrase around our dorm." Martha closes her eyes, drawing the lines bit by bit out of the deep well of the past.

> *Gather ye rosebuds while ye may.*
> *Old time is still a-flying:*
> *And this same flower that smiles today,*
> *Tomorrow will be dying...*

She falters. "Damn. I wish I could remember the rest of it."

"Well, I never was much of a one for poetry," June says. "Though I didn't mind a good Harlequin once in a while. But that, what you just said, makes good sense to me."

"It did to us, too," says Martha, remembering, with affection and astonishment, her eighteen year old self.

At three a.m., Martha wakes from an uneasy doze. She has not slept well since she came here; and tomorrow she faces a battery of tests. She tells herself there is no need to worry. She hasn't touched sweets for fifteen years, or butter, or cream, or cigarettes. Nor, in spite of her joke about the Bushmills, alcohol. Seven years ago she gave up meat. She is only slightly overweight—better than being underweight, according to her doctor, who keeps up on the latest studies. She walks everywhere, takes megavitamins,

exercises, practices biofeedback and meditation, checks
her blood pressure daily; is as scrupulous as Angela in the
use of U-V shield and air monitor. There is, perhaps, a
little breathlessness on the stairs; a trace of stiffness in
her finger-joints. An occasional absent-mindedness. Normal enough, surely, for a woman of sixty. Nothing to worry
about. Certainly nothing to warrant Reassignment.

Her throat is dry, and her heart is beating faster than it
should. She repeats a mantra in her head: *Health. Joy.
Peace. Sleep.* Other words, unsummoned, creep into her
mind.

> *That age is best which is the first,*
> *When youth and blood are warmer;*
> *But being spent, the worse, and worst*
> *Times still succeed the former.*

She wants a drink. She wants a cigarette. She wants to
get out of this place. Lying wide awake and fearful in the
aseptic dark, she listens to the small, mouselike rustle of
candy wrappers.

Martha lies back on her pillows, staring at the posters on
the opposite wall. They remind her of the samplers in her
grandmother's drawing room. "Healthiness is Next to God-
liness." "A Healthy Mind in a Healthy Body." "A Mega-
vitamin a Day Keeps the Doctor Away." She is exhausted
by the day-long pokings and proddings and pryings, the
sometimes painful and frequently embarrassing invasions
of her person. She admires, without daring to imitate,
June's cheerful rudeness to counselors and examiners; her
steadfast refusal to cooperate. Only Dorothy seems unaf-
fected by the tests. She wears the smug and slightly relieved look of a schoolgirl who knows she has done well on
her math final.

June turns on the TV. Martha realizes, with some surprise, that it is New Year's Eve. A pair of talking heads is
discussing The Year 2000. With the end of the millen-
nium only twelve months away, the media are obsessed
with predictions, retrospectives. It is hard for Martha to

imagine what may lie around that thousand-year corner.
She finds it odd—and in a curious way exciting—that by
a mere accident of birth, she may live to see the next mil-
lennium.

"The biggest New Year's Eve Party in a thousand years,"
says June, when the commercial comes on. Her voice is
wistful. "I always did like a good party."

Martha smiles at her, remembering that she was fond of
parties too, when she was younger. There seems so little
point in them now.

"Perhaps," she says, "we will be allowed a glass of champagne."

June chuckles. "Maybe one small glass. The last for a
thousand years."

That's enough to set them off. They take turns describing what they will eat and drink on the Eve of the Millen-
nium—a stream of consciousness recitation of forbidden
delights.

"Chocolate mints," says June. "Pecan pie. Truffles."

"Amaretto cheesecake," Martha adds. "Christmas pud-
ding with rum sauce. Tawny port."

Pointedly, Dorothy puts on earphones. Martha and
June, caught up in their game, ignore her.

"Fish and chips. Bangers and mash."

"Guinness stout. Roast suckling pig."

"Crab croquettes and oyster stew."

It's so long since Martha has eaten anything unwhole-
some, she has to stop and think. "Sour cream and hot
mango chutney." Then—an inspiration— "Sex-in-the-
Pan."

"Sex in anything," says June, and howls with laughter.

Dorothy seems to take their foolishness as a personal
affront. Lips pressed into a thin line, she thumbs rapidly
through a fresh copy of *Christian Health*.

They sit up to see the New Year in, and afterwards Martha
sleeps soundly, even though there are tests scheduled for
the morning. These ones don't sound too awful. Blood
sugar again, cholesterol check, an eye and ear exam; and—
absurdly, it seems to Martha—tests for the various sorts

of social diseases.

Still, she is awake hours before the first robots rumble down the hall with breakfast. She knows, instantly, that something is wrong. She sits up, switches on her overhead light. In the far bed, Dorothy is heavily asleep. The other bed, June's bed, is empty.

The bathroom, Martha thinks; but no, the door is ajar and the light is out. Could June have been taken ill in the night? A sudden heart attack, like her father? Has Martha somehow slept through lights, buzzers, running feet, the clatter of emergency equipment? But when that happens, don't they always draw the bed curtains?

Dorothy is awake. "Where's June?" she asks immediately, smelling trouble.

Martha shakes her head. She feels on the edge of panic. Should she push her bell? Call for a counselor? Go out and search the corridor?

And then suddenly June is back, waltzing into the room in boots, hat, coat, humming gently to herself. The cloud of cheap perfume that surrounds her is not strong enough to drown out the smell of liquor.

"June, where have you been?" Martha realizes, to her dismay, that she sounds like a mother interrogating a wayward teenaged daughter.

June grins and pulls off her toque. "Should old acquaintance be forgot," she sings, "and never brought to mind... I went to a New Year's party."

Dorothy gives a snort of disbelief. "How could you have gotten out of the building?"

"Who was to stop me? Only robots on night shift, and one duty counselor. Only reason nobody walks out of here is nobody thinks to try."

She flops across her bed, arms outflung, short skirt riding up over pale, plump knees. After a moment she sits up and tries, unsuccessfully, to pull off her boots. "Oh, shit, Martha, can you give me a hand?"

She slides down on the mattress so that both feet are dangling over the edge. Kneeling on the cold tiles at June's feet, Martha takes hold of the left boot and tugs hard. It's a frivolous boot—spike-heeled, fur-cuffed, too tight in the calf. Dorothy watches in outraged silence.

Martha rocks back on her heels as the boot comes off with a sudden jerk. She hears June give a small, contented sigh.

"Oh, Christ, Martha, what a ball I had! There's this little club on Davie... I wish you'd been there too, there were these two guys..." June sighs again, as the other boot comes off. "But I knew you wouldn't come, there was no use asking, you're too afraid of old creepin' Jesus, there..."

Dorothy, white-faced with fury, stalks into the bathroom and slams the door.

"June, what did you *do?*" Martha hears her voice rising, querulously, and thinks, *I sound like my mother did; I sound like an old woman.*

"Christ, honey, what *didn't* I do? I drank. I ate. I danced. I smoked." Her S's are starting to slur. She rolls over, luxuriously, and adds something else which is muffled by her pillow.

"I beg your pardon?" Martha asks.

June sits up. Loudly enough to be heard at the end of the hall, she announces, "I even got laid."

"Shhh," Martha says, instinctively. Then, "June, how could you? All the tests we have to take today—blood sugar, cholesterol—"

"AIDS," says Dorothy grimly, through the bathroom door.

"Oh, June. Oh, my dear." Martha is just now beginning to realize the enormity of what June has done.

There are footsteps in the corridor as the day shift arrives. Martha feels like crying. Instead, she searches through June's bedside drawer for comb, makeup, mouthwash; and silently unbuttons June's coat.

On Wednesday the test results are announced. One at a time they are called to the Chief Examiner's office for their reports. Dorothy returns, smug-faced and unsurprised, and puts on her street clothes. Martha's name is called. Sick and faint with anxiety, she makes her way through the maze of corridors. She has passed, but with a warning.

June is gone for a long time. "I thought from the first,"

Dorothy remarks, as she waits for the Chief Examiner to sign her out, "that June lacked any sense of self-respect."

Martha doesn't often bother to contradict Dorothy's pronouncements, but this time it seems important to set the record straight. "You don't mean self-respect," she says. "You mean self-preservation."

Then the door opens, and June comes in. She has applied her blusher and lipstick with a heavy hand; the bright patches of red look garish as poster paint against the chalk white of her skin. She stares blankly at Martha as though she has forgotten where she is. Gently, Martha touches her arm. "June? What did they say?"

"Nothing I didn't already know." June's voice shakes a little, but her tone is matter-of-fact. "Sugar in the blood—incipient diabetes. Gross overweight. High cholesterol count. Hypertension. Just what you'd expect."

"They can treat all those things. They don't have to Reassign you."

June shrugs. "Not worth it, they say. Bad personal history. And there's my pa."

"Quite right," says Dorothy. How Martha has learned to loathe that prim, self-congratulatory voice. "If people won't take responsibility for their own health..."

"Better to get it over with," June says. "It'd be no fun at all, hanging around for Reassessment."

And then—awkwardly, and oddly, as though it is Martha who is in need of comfort—she pats Martha's shoulder. "Never mind, Martha, love, that was a hell of a good party, the other night. And there's something I want you to remember, when your time comes. Once you know for sure, once you make up your mind to it, then you can spit in their eye, because there's bugger all more they can do to you."

Dorothy pins her hat on her gray curls, and leaves. Martha's papers are signed; she could go too, if she wished, but she has decided to stay with June. She knows she won't have to wait long.

Soon they hear the hum of trolley wheels at the end of the hall. Martha holds June's hand.

"Listen, the news isn't all bad, "June says, with gallows

humor. "The kidneys are still okay, and the lungs, and a few other odd bits. There's quite a lot they can Reassign. Maybe to some pretty young girl. I like that idea a lot."

Then the trolley is wheeled in.

"A short life and a merry one," says June. She winces slightly as the counselor slips the needle into her arm. "Remember to drink a glass of bubbly for me, at the big party."

Martha nods, and squeezes June's hand as June slides away. •

MUFFIN EXPLAINS TELEOLOGY TO THE WORLD AT LARGE

James Alan Gardner

Winner of the 1991 Aurora Award

I told my kid sister Muffin this joke.

> *There was this orchestra, and they were playing music, and all the violins were bowing and moving their fingers, except for this one guy who just played the same note over and over again. Someone asked the guy why he wasn't playing like the others and he said, "They're all looking for the note. I've found it."*

Muffin, who's only six, told me the joke wasn't funny if you understood teleology.

I never know where she gets words like that. I had to go and look it up.

> **teleology** [teli-oloji] *n.* doctrine or theory that all things or processes were designed to fulfill a purpose.

"Okay," I said when I found her again, "now I understand teleology. Why isn't the joke funny?"

"You'll find out next week," she said.

I talked to Uncle Dave that night. He's in university and real smart, even though he's going to be a minister instead of something interesting. "What's so great about teleology?" I said. He looked at me kind of weird so I explained, "Muffin's been talking about it."

"So have my professors," he said. "It's, uhh, you know, God has a purpose for everything, even if we can't understand it. We're all heading towards some goal."

"We took that in Sunday School," I said.

"Well, Jamie, we go into it in a bit more detail."

"Yeah, I guess."

He was quiet for a bit, then asked, "What's Muffin say about it?"

"Something big is happening next week."

"Teleologically speaking?"

"That's what she says."

Muffin was in the next room with her crayons. Uncle Dave called her in to talk and she showed him what she was working on. She'd colored Big Bird black. She has all these crayons and the only ones she ever uses are black and gray.

"What's happening next week?" Uncle Dave asked.

"It's a secret," she said.

"Not even a hint?"

"No."

"Little tiny hint? Please?"

She thought about it a minute, then whispered in his ear. Then she giggled and ran upstairs.

"What did she say?" I asked.

"She said that we'd get where we were going." He shrugged and made a face. We were both pretty used to Muffin saying things we didn't understand.

The next day, I answered the front doorbell and found three guys wearing gray robes. They'd shaved their heads too.

"We are looking for her gloriousness," one of them said with a little bow. He had an accent.

"Uh, Mom's gone down the block to get some bread," I answered.

"It's okay," Muffin said, coming from the TV room. "They're here for me."

All three of the men fell face down on the porch making a kind of high whining sound in their throats.

"You know these guys?" I asked.

"They're here to talk about teleology."

"Oh. Well, take them around to the back yard. Mom doesn't like people in the house when she's not here."

"Okay." She told the guys to get up and they followed her around the side of the house, talking in some foreign language.

When Mom got home, I told her what happened and she half-ran to the kitchen window to see what was going on. Muffin was sitting on the swing set and the guys were cross-legged on the ground in front of her, nodding their heads at every word she spoke. Mom took a deep breath, the way she does just before she's going to yell at one of us, then stomped out the back door. I was sure she was going to shout at Muffin, but she bent over and talked quiet enough that I couldn't hear from inside the house. Muffin talked and Mom talked and one of the bald guys said something, and finally Mom came in all pale-looking.

"They want lemonade," she said. "Take them out some lemonade. And plastic glasses. I'm going to lie down." And she went upstairs.

I took them out a pitcher of lemonade. When I got there, one of the bald guys got up to meet me and asked Muffin, "Is this the boy?"

She said yes.

"Most wondrous, most wondrous!"

He put both hands on my shoulders as if he was going to hug me, but Muffin said, "You'll spill the lemonade." He let me go, but kept staring at me with his big, weepy, white eyes.

"What's going on?" I asked.

"The culmination of a thousand thousand years of aimless wandering," the guy said.

"Not aimless," Muffin cut in.

"Your pardon," he answered, quickly lowering his head. "But at times it seemed so."

"You'll be in the temple when it happens," Muffin said to

him.

"A million praises!" he shouted, throwing himself flat-faced on the ground. "A billion trillion praises!" And he started to cry into our lawn. The other two bowed in the direction of our garage, over and over again.

"You want to pour me a glass of that?" Muffin said to me.

The next day it was a different guy, wearing a red turban and carrying a curvy sword almost as tall as me. When I opened the door, he grabbed the front of my T-shirt and yelled, "Where is the Liar, the Deceiver, the Blasphemer, the She-Whore who Mocks the Most High?"

"She went with Uncle Dave down to the Dairy Queen."

"Thank you," he said, and walked off down the street. Later, I heard on the radio that the cops had arrested him in the parking lot of the mall.

The next day, Muffin told me I had to take her down to the boat yards. I said, "I don't have to do anything."

"Shows how much you know," she answered. "You don't know anything about teleology or fate or anything."

"I know how to cross streets and take buses and all, which is more than I can say for some people."

"I have ten dollars," she said, pulling a bill out of the pocket of her jeans.

That surprised me. I mean, I maybe have ten dollars in my pocket twice a year, just after Christmas and just after my birthday. "Where'd you get the money?" I asked.

"The monks gave it to me."

"Those bald guys?"

"They like me."

"Geez, Muffin, don't let Mom know you took money from strangers. She'd have a fit."

"They aren't strangers. They're the Holy Order of the Imminent Eschaton—the Muffin Chapter."

"Oh, go ahead, lie to me."

"You want the ten dollars or not?"

Which wasn't what I ended up with, because she expected me to pay the bus fare out of it.

•

When we got to the boat yards, I thought we'd head right down to the water, but Muffin just took out a piece of paper and stood there frowning at it. I looked over her shoulder and saw it was torn from a map of the city. There was a small red X drawn in at a place about a block from where we were. "Where'd you get that? The monks?"

"Mm-hm. Is this where we are?" She pointed at a corner. I looked and moved her finger till it pointed the right place. "You should learn to read some time, Muffin."

She shook her head. "Might wreck my insight. Maybe after."

I pointed down the street. "If you want to go where X marks the spot, it's that way."

We walked along with sailboats and yachts and things on one side, and warehouses on the other. The buildings looked pretty run down, with brown smears of rust dripping down from their metal roofs and lots of broken windows covered with plywood or cardboard. It was a pretty narrow street and there was no sidewalk, but the only traffic we saw was a Shell oil truck coming out of the Marina a ways ahead and it turned off before it got to us.

When we reached the X spot, the only thing there was another warehouse. Muffin closed her eyes for a second, then said, "Around the back and up the stairs."

"I bet there are rats around the back," I said.

"I bet there aren't."

"You go first."

"Okay." She started off down an alley between the one warehouse and the next. There was a lot of broken glass lying around and grass growing up through the pavement.

"I bet there are snakes," I said, following her.

"Shut up, Jamie."

The back was only a strip of weeds about two yards wide, stuck between the warehouse and a chain link fence. Halfway along, there was a flight of metal steps like a fire escape leading up to the roof. They creaked a bit when you walked on them, but didn't wobble too badly.

On the roof we found a really weird looking airplane. Or boat. Or train. Or wagon. Anyway, it had wings and tail like an airplane, but its body was built like a boat, a bit like the motorboat up at the cottage, but bigger and with these super-fat padded chairs like maybe astronauts sit in. The whole thing sat on a cart, but the cart's wheels were on the near end of a train track that ran the length of the roof and off the front into the street.

"What is this thing?" I asked.

"The monks made it for me," Muffin said, which didn't answer my question. She climbed up a short metal ladder into the plane and rummaged about in a cupboard in the rear wall. I followed her and watched her going through stuff inside. "Peanut butter. Bread. Kool-Aid. Water. Cheese. Diet Coke. What's this?" she said, handing me back a roll of something in gold plastic wrapping.

I opened one end and sniffed. "Liverwurst," I said.

"Is that like liver?" She made a face.

"No, it's sort of like peanut butter but made from bologna."

"Weird. Do you see any hot dogs?"

I looked in the cupboard. "Nope."

"I should phone the monks. We need hot dogs."

"What for?"

She ignored me. "Is there anything else you'd want if you knew you were going to be away from home for a few days?"

"Cheerios and bacon."

She thought about that. "Yeah, you're right."

"And Big Macs."

She gave me a look like I was a moron. "Of course, dummy, but the monks will bring them just before we leave."

"We're going on a trip?"

"We're on a trip now. We're going to *arrive*."

Early the next morning, Dr. Hariki showed up on our doorstep all excited. He works with my dad at the university. My dad teaches physics; he works with lasers and everything. Dr. Hariki is in charge of the big telescope on the top of the Physics building, and he takes pictures of stars.

"What's up?" Dad asked.

"You tell me," Dr. Hariki said, spreading out a bunch of photographs on the coffee table.

Dad picked up a picture and looked at it. Turned it over to check out the date and time written on the back. Sorted through the stack of photos till he found whatever he was looking for and compared it to the first. Held the two together side by side. Held one above the other. Put them side by side again. Closed his right eye, then quick closed his left and opened his right. Did that a couple of times. Picked up another pair of photos and did the same.

Muffin came into the room with a glass of orange juice in her hand. "Looks more like a dipper now, doesn't it?" she said without looking at the pictures.

Dad and Mr. Hariki stared at her. "Well, it was a bit too spread out before, wasn't it?" she asked. "Don't you think it looks better now?"

"Muffin," Dad said, "we're talking about stars...suns. They don't just move to make a nicer pattern."

"No, but if they're going to stop moving, you might as well make sure they look like a dipper in the end. Anything else is just sloppy. I mean, really."

She walked off into the TV room and a moment later, we heard the Sesame Street theme song.

After a long silence, Dr. Hariki picked up one of the photos and asked, all quiet, "Something to do with entropy?"

"I think it's teleology," I said.

That night Uncle Dave was over for Sunday supper. Mom figures that Uncle Dave doesn't eat so good in residence, so she feeds him a roast of something every Sunday. I think this is a great idea, except that every so often she serves squash because she says it's a delicacy. Lucky for us, it was corn season so we had corn on the cob instead.

After supper we all played Monopoly and I won. Uncle Dave said it made a nice family picture, us all sitting around the table playing a game. "Some day, kids," he said, "you're going to like having times like this to remember. A perfect frozen moment."

"There are all kinds of perfect frozen moments," Muffin said, and she had that tone in her voice like she was eleventy-seven years old instead of six. "Right now, people all over the world are doing all kinds of things. Like in China, it's day now, right Dad?"

"Right, Muffin."

"So there are kids playing tag and stuff, and that's a perfect moment. And maybe there's some bully beating up a little kid, and punching him out right now." She banged her Monopoly piece (the little metal hat) when she said "now." "And that's a perfect moment because that's what really happens. And bus-drivers are driving their buses, and farmers are milking their cows, and mommies are kissing daddies, and maybe a ship is sinking some place. If you could take pictures of everyone right now, you'd see millions of perfect little frozen moments, wouldn't you?"

Uncle Dave patted Muffin's hand. "Out of the mouths of babes... I'm the one who's studying to appreciate the great wonder of Life, and you're the one who reminds me. Everything is perfect all the time, isn't it, Muffin?"

"Of course not, dummy," she answered, looking at Uncle Dave the way she did when he tried to persuade her he'd pulled a dime from her ear. She turned around in her chair and reached over to the buffet to get the photograph they'd taken of her kindergarten class just before summer holidays started. "See?" she said pointing. "This is Bobby and he picks his nose all the time, and he's picking his nose here, so that's good. But this is Wendy, with her eyes closed cuz she was blinking. That's not perfect. Wendy cries every time she doesn't get a gold star in spelling, and she knows three dirty words, and she always gives Matthew the celery from her lunch, but you can't tell that in the picture, can you? She's just someone who blinked at the wrong time. If you want someone who should be blinking, it should be dozy old Peter Morgan who's fat and sweats and laughs funny."

Uncle Dave scratched his head and looked awkward for a bit, then said, "Well Muffin, when you put it like that ...yes, I suppose there are always some things that aren't aesthetically pleasing... I mean, there are always going to be some things that don't fit properly, as you say."

"Not always," she said.

"Not always? Some day things are just suddenly going to be right?" Uncle Dave asked.

Muffin handed me the dice and said, "Your turn, Jamie. Bet you're going to land in jail."

Next morning, Muffin joggled my arm to wake me up. It was so early that the sun was just starting to rise over the lake. "Time to go down to the boat yards."

"Again?"

"Yep. This time for real." So I got up and dressed as quietly as I could. By the time I got down to the kitchen, Muffin had made some peanut butter and jam sandwiches, and was messing around with the waxed paper, trying to wrap them. She had twice as much paper as she needed and was making a botch of things.

"You're really clueless sometimes," I said whispering so Mom and Dad wouldn't hear. I shoved her out of the way and started wrapping the sandwiches myself.

"When I rule the world, there won't be any waxed paper," she sulked.

We were halfway down to the bus stop when Uncle Dave came running up behind us. He had been staying the night in the guest room and I suppose he heard us moving around. "Where do you think you're going?" he asked, and he was a bit mad at us.

"Down to the boat yards," Muffin said.

"No, you aren't. Get back to the house."

"Uncle Dave," Muffin said, "it's time."

"Time for what?"

"The Eschaton."

"Where do you pick up these words, Muffin? You're talking about the end of the world."

"I know." The first bus of the day was just turning onto our street two corners down. "Come to the boat yards with us, Uncle Dave. It'll be okay."

Uncle Dave thought about it. I guess he decided it was easier to give in than to fight with her. That's what I always think too. You can't win an argument with her, and if you try anything else, she bites and scratches and uses her knees. "All right," Uncle Dave said, "but we're going to phone your parents and tell them where you are, the first chance we get."

"So talk to me about the Eschaton," Uncle Dave said on the bus. We were the only ones on it except for a red-haired lady wearing a Donut Queen uniform.

"Well," Muffin said, thinking things over, "you know how Daddy talks about everything moving in astronomy? Like the moon goes around the earth and the earth goes around the sun and the sun moves with the stars in the galaxy and the galaxy is moving too?"

"Yes..."

"Well, where is everything going?"

Uncle Dave shrugged. "The way your father tells it, everything just moves, that's all. It's not going anywhere in particular."

"That's stupid. Daddy doesn't understand teleology. Everything's heading for where it's supposed to end up."

"And what happens when things reach the place where they're supposed to end up."

Muffin made an exasperated face. "They *end up* there."

"They stop?"

"What else would they do?"

"All the planets and the stars and all?"

"Mm-hm."

"People too?"

"Sure."

He thought for a second. "In perfect frozen moments, right?"

"Right."

Uncle Dave leaned his head against the window like he was tired and sad. Maybe he was. The sun was coming up over the housetops now. "Bus drivers driving their buses," he said softly, "and farmers milking their cows...the whole world like a coffee table book."

"I think you'd like to be in a church, Uncle Dave," Muffin said. "Or maybe walking alone along the lake shore."

"Maybe," he smiled, all sad. Then he looked my sister right in the eye and asked, "Who are you, Muffin?"

"I'm me, dummy," she answered, throwing her arms around his neck and giving him a kiss.

He left us in front of the warehouse by the lake. "I'm going to walk down to the Rowing Club and back." He laughed a little. "If I get back, Muffin, you are going to get such a spanking..."

"Bye, Uncle Dave," she said, hugging him.

I hugged him too. "Bye, Uncle Dave."

"Don't let her do anything stupid," he said to me before heading down the street. We watched for a while, but he didn't turn back.

Up on the warehouse roof, there was a monk waiting with a McDonald's bag under his arm. He handed it to Muffin, then kneeled. "Bless me, Holy One."

"You're blessed," she said after looking in the bag. "Now get going to the temple or the airport or something. There's only about ten minutes left."

The monk hurried off, singing what I think was a hymn. We got into the plane-boat and I helped Muffin strap herself into one of the big padded seats. "The thing is," she said, "when the earth stops turning, we're going to keep on going."

"Hey, I know about momentum," I answered. I mean, Dad *is* a physicist.

"And it's going to be real fast, so we have to be sure we don't run into any buildings."

"We're going to shoot out over the lake?"

"We're high enough to clear the tops of the sailboats, then we just fly over the lake until we're slow enough to splash down. The monks got scientists to figure everything out."

I strapped myself in and thought about things for a while. "If we go shooting off real fast, isn't it going to hurt? I mean, the astronauts get all pressed down when they lift off..."

"Geez!" Muffin groaned. "Don't you know the difference between momentum and acceleration? Nothing's happening to us, it's everything else that's doing weird stuff. We don't feel a thing."

"Not even wind?"

"The air has the same momentum we do, dummy."

I thought about it some more. "Aren't the buildings going to get wrecked when the earth stops?"

"They're going to stop too. Everything's just going to freeze except us."

"The air and water are going to freeze too?"

"In spots. But not where we're going."

"We're special?"

"We're special."

Suddenly there was a roar like roller coaster wheels underneath us and for a moment I was pressed up against the straps holding me down on the seat. Then the pressure stopped and there was nothing but the sound of wind a long way off. Over the side of the boat I could see water rushing by beneath us. We were climbing.

"Muffin," I asked, "should one of us maybe be piloting this thing?"

"It's got a gyroscope or something. The monks worked absolutely everything out, okay?"

"Okay."

A long way off to the right, I could see a lake freighter with a curl of smoke coming out of its stack. The smoke didn't move. It looked neat. "Nice warm day," I said.

After a while, we started playing car games to pass the time.

The sun shone but didn't move. "If the sun stays there forever," I asked, "won't it get really hot after a while?"

"Nah," Muffin answered. "It's some kind of special deal. I mean, it's not the same if you set up a nice picture of a park full of kids playing and then it gets hot as Mercury."

"Who's going to know?" I asked.

"It's not the same," she insisted.

"How can we see?"

"What do you mean?"

"Well, is the light moving or what?"

"It's another special deal."

That made sense. From the way dad talked about physics, light was always getting special deals.

The water below us gradually stopped racing away so fast and we could sometimes see frozen whitecaps on the peaks of frozen waves. "Suppose we land on frozen water," I said.

"We won't."

"Oh. Your turn."

"I spy with my little eye something that begins with B." Right away I knew she meant the Big Macs, but I had to pretend it was a toughie. You have to humor little kids.

We splashed down within sight of a city on the far side of the lake. It was a really good splash, like the one on the Zoomba Flume ride when you get to the bottom of the big, long, water chute. Both of us got drenched. I was kind of sad there was no way to do it again.

Then I thought to myself, maybe if we were getting a special deal on air and water and heat and all, maybe we'd get a special deal on the Zoomba Flume too.

We unstrapped ourselves and searched around a bit. Finally, we found a lid that slid back to open up a control panel with a little steering wheel and all. We pushed buttons until an inboard motor started in the water behind us, then took turns driving towards shore. Every now and then we'd see a gull frozen in the sky, wings spread out and looking great.

We put in at a public beach just outside the city. It had been early in the day and the only people in sight were a pair of joggers on a grassy ridge that ran along the edge of the sand. The man wore only track shorts and sunglasses; the woman wore red stretch pants, a T-shirt, and a headband. Both had Walkmans and were stopped mid-stride. Both had deep dark tans, and as Muffin pointed out, a thin covering of sweat.

I wanted to touch one to see what they felt like, but when my finger got close, it bumped up against an invisible layer of frozen air. The air didn't feel like anything, it was just solid stuff.

Down at one end of the beach, a teenage girl was frozen in the act of unlocking the door into a snack stand. We squeezed past her and found out we could open the freezer inside. Muffin had a couple of Popsicles, I had an ice cream sandwich, and then we went swimming.

Lying out in the sun afterward, I asked Muffin what was going to happen next.

"You want to go swimming again?" she said.

"No, I mean after."

"Let's eat," she said, dragging me back towards the boat.

"You can't wiggle out of it that easy," I told her. "Are we the only ones left?"

"I think so."

"Then are we going to freeze too?"

"Nope. We got a special deal."

"But it seems pretty stupid if you ask me. Everything's kind of finished, you know? Show's over. Why are we still hanging around?"

"For a new show, dummy."

"Oh." That made sense. "Same sort of thing?"

"We'll see."

"Oh. Where do *we* fit in?"

Muffin smiled at me. "You're here to keep me company."

"And what are you here for?"

"Everything else. Get me a sandwich."

So I reached down into the basket we'd brought and pulled one out. It was inside a plastic sandwich bag. "Didn't we put these in waxed paper?" I asked.

Muffin smiled. •

JUST LIKE OLD TIMES

Robert J. Sawyer

Winner of the 1994 Aurora Award

The transference went smoothly, like a scalpel slicing into skin.

Cohen was simultaneously excited and disappointed. He was thrilled to be here—perhaps the judge was right, perhaps this was indeed where he really belonged. But the gleaming edge was taken off that thrill because it wasn't accompanied by the usual physiological signs of excitement: no sweaty palms, no racing heart, no rapid breathing. Oh, there was a heartbeat, to be sure, thundering in the background, but it wasn't Cohen's.

It was the dinosaur's.

Everything was the dinosaur's: Cohen saw the world now through tyrannosaur eyes.

The colors seemed all wrong. Surely plant leaves must be the same chlorophyll green here in the Mesozoic, but the dinosaur saw them as navy blue. The sky was lavender; the dirt underfoot ash gray.

Old bones had different cones, thought Cohen. Well, he could get used to it. After all, he had no choice. He would finish his life as an observer inside this tyrannosaur's mind. He'd see what the beast saw, hear what it heard, feel what it felt. He wouldn't be able to control its movements, they had said, but he would be able to experience every sensation.

The rex was marching forward.

Cohen hoped blood would still look red.

It wouldn't be the same if it wasn't red.

"And what, Ms. Cohen, did your husband say before he left your house on the night in question?"

"He said he was going out to hunt humans. But I thought he was making a joke."

"No interpretations, please, Ms. Cohen. Just repeat for the court as precisely as you remember it, exactly what your husband said."

"He said, 'I'm going out to hunt humans.' "

"Thank you, Ms. Cohen. That concludes the Crown's case, my lady."

The needlepoint on the wall of the Honorable Madam Justice Amanda Hoskins's chambers had been made for her by her husband. It was one of her favorite verses from *The Mikado*, and as she was preparing sentencing she would often look up and re-read the words:

> *My object all sublime*
> *I shall achieve in time—*
> *To let the punishment fit the crime—*
> *The punishment fit the crime.*

This was a difficult case, a horrible case. Judge Hoskins continued to think.

It wasn't just colors that were wrong. The view from inside the tyrannosaur's skull was different in other ways, too.

The tyrannosaur had only partial stereoscopic vision. There was an area in the center of Cohen's field of view that showed true depth perception. But because the beast was somewhat walleyed, it had a much wider panorama than normal for a human, a kind of saurian Cinemascope covering 270 degrees.

The wide-angle view panned back and forth as the tyrannosaur scanned along the horizon.

Scanning for prey.

Scanning for something to kill.

The Calgary Herald, Thursday, October 16, 2042, hardcopy edition: Serial killer Rudolph Cohen, 43, was sentenced to death yesterday.

Formerly a prominent member of the Alberta College of Physicians and Surgeons, Dr. Cohen was convicted in August of thirty-seven counts of first-degree murder.

In chilling testimony, Cohen had admitted, without any signs of remorse, to having terrorized each of his victims for hours before slitting their throats with surgical implements.

This is the first time in eighty years that the death penalty has been ordered in this country.

In passing sentence, Madam Justice Amanda Hoskins observed that Cohen was "the most cold-blooded and brutal killer to have stalked Canada's prairies since *Tyrannosaurus rex...*"

From behind a stand of dawn redwoods about ten meters away, a second tyrannosaur appeared. Cohen suspected tyrannosaurs might be fiercely territorial, since each animal would require huge amounts of meat. He wondered if the beast he was in would attack the other individual.

His dinosaur tilted its head to look at the second rex, which was standing in profile. But as it did so, almost all of the dino's mental picture dissolved into a white void, as if when concentrating on details the beast's tiny brain simply lost track of the big picture.

At first Cohen thought his rex was looking at the other dinosaur's head, but soon the top of other's skull, the tip of its muzzle and the back of its powerful neck faded away into snowy nothingness. All that was left was a picture of the throat. Good, thought Cohen. One shearing bite there could kill the animal.

The skin of the other's throat appeared gray-green and the throat itself was smooth. Maddeningly, Cohen's rex did not attack. Rather, it simply swiveled its head and looked out at the horizon again.

In a flash of insight, Cohen realized what had happened. Other kids in his neighborhood had had pet dogs or cats. He'd had lizards and snakes—cold-blooded carnivores, a fact to which expert psychological witnesses had attached great weight. Some kinds of male lizards had dewlap sacks hanging from their necks. The rex he was in—a male, the Tyrrell paleontologists had believed—had looked at this other one and seen that she was smooth-throated and therefore a female. Something to be mated with, perhaps, rather than to attack.

Perhaps they would mate soon. Cohen had never orgasmed except during the act of killing. He wondered what it would feel like.

"We spent a billion dollars developing time travel, and now you tell me the system is useless?"

"Well—"

"That is what you're saying, isn't it, professor? That chronotransference has no practical applications?"

"Not exactly, Minister. The system *does* work. We can project a human being's consciousness back in time, superimposing his or her mind overtop of that of someone who lived in the past."

"With no way to sever the link. *Wonderful*."

"That's not true. The link severs automatically."

"Right. When the historical person you've transferred consciousness into dies, the link is broken."

"Precisely."

"And then the person from our time whose consciousness you've transferred back dies as well."

"I admit that's an unfortunate consequence of linking two brains so closely."

"So I'm right! This whole damn chronotransference thing is useless."

"Oh, not at all, Minister. In fact, I think I've got the perfect application for it."

The rex marched along. Although Cohen's attention had first been arrested by the beast's vision, he slowly became aware of its other senses, too. He could hear the sounds of the rex's footfalls, of twigs and vegetation being crushed, of birds or pterosaurs singing, and, underneath it all, the relentless drone of insects. Still, all the sounds were dull and low; the rex's simple ears were incapable of picking up high-pitched noises, and what sounds they did detect were discerned without richness. Cohen knew the late Cretaceous must have been a symphony of varied tone, but it was as if he was listening to it through earmuffs.

The rex continued along, still searching. Cohen became aware of several more impressions of the world both inside and out, including hot afternoon sun beating down on him and a hungry gnawing in the beast's belly.

Food.

It was the closest thing to a coherent thought that he'd yet detected from the animal, a mental picture of bolts of meat going down its gullet.

Food.

The Social Services Preservation Act of 2022: Canada is built upon the principle of the Social Safety Net, a series of entitlements and programs designed to ensure a high standard of living for every citizen. However, ever-increasing life expectancies coupled with constant lowering of the mandatory retirement age have placed an untenable burden on our social-welfare system and, in particular, its cornerstone program of universal health care. With most taxpayers ceasing to work at the age of 45, and with average Canadians living to be 94 (males) or 97 (females), the system is in danger of complete collapse. Accordingly, all social programs will henceforth be available only to those below the age of 60, with one exception: all Canadians, regardless of age, may take advantage, at no charge to themselves, of government-sponsored euthanasia through chronotransference.

There! Up ahead! Something moving! Big, whatever it was: an indistinct outline only intermittently visible behind a small knot of fir trees.

A quadruped of some sort, its back to him/it/them.

Ah, there. Turning now. Peripheral vision dissolving into albino nothingness as the rex concentrated on the head.

Three horns.

Triceratops.

Glorious! Cohen had spent hours as a boy pouring over books about dinosaurs, looking for scenes of carnage. No

battles were better than those in which *Tyrannosaurus rex*
squared off against *Triceratops*, a four-footed Mesozoic
tank with a trio of horns projecting from its face and a
shield of bone rising from the back of its skull to protect
the neck.

And yet, the rex marched on.

No, thought Cohen. Turn, damn you! Turn and attack!

Cohen remembered when it had all begun, that fateful day
so many years ago, so many years from now. It should
have been a routine operation. The patient had supposedly
been prepped properly. Cohen brought his scalpel down
toward the abdomen, then, with a steady hand, sliced into
the skin. The patient gasped. It had been a *wonderful*
sound, a beautiful sound.

Not enough gas. The anesthetist hurried to make an
adjustment.

Cohen knew he had to hear that sound again. He had to.

The tyrannosaur continued forward. Cohen couldn't see its
legs, but he could feel them moving. Left, right, up, down.

Attack, you bastard!

Left.

Attack!

Right.

Go after it!

Up.

Go after the *Triceratops*.

Dow—

The beast hesitated, its left leg still in the air, balancing
briefly on one foot.

Attack!

Attack!

And then, at last, the rex changed course. The ceratopsian appeared in the three-dimensional central part of
the tyrannosaur's field of view, like a target at the end of
a gun sight.

"Welcome to the Chronotransference Institute. If I can just
see your government benefits card, please? Yup, there's

always a last time for everything, heh heh. Now, I'm sure you want an exciting death. The problem is finding some-body interesting who hasn't been used yet. See, we can only ever superimpose one mind onto a given historical personage. All the really obvious ones have been done al-ready, I'm afraid. We still get about a dozen calls a week asking for Jack Kennedy, but he was one of the first to go, so to speak. If I may make a suggestion, though, we've got thousands of Roman legion officers cataloged. Those tend to be very satisfying deaths. How about a nice something from the Gallic Wars?"

The *Triceratops* looked up, its giant head lifting from the wide flat gunnera leaves it had been chewing on. Now that the rex had focused on the plant-eater, it seemed to com-mit itself.

The tyrannosaur charged.

The hornface was sideways to the rex. It began to turn, to bring its armored head to bear.

The horizon bounced wildly as the rex ran. Cohen could hear the thing's heart thundering loudly, rapidly, a bar-rage of muscular gunfire.

The *Triceratops*, still completing its turn, opened its parrot-like beak, but no sound came out.

Giant strides closed the distance between the two ani-mals. Cohen felt the rex's jaws opening wide, wider still, mandibles popping from their sockets.

The jaws slammed shut on the hornface's back, over the shoulders. Cohen saw two of the rex's own teeth fly into view, knocked out by the impact.

The taste of hot blood, surging out of the wound...

The rex pulled back for another bite.

The *Triceratops* finally got its head swung around. It surged forward, the long spear over its left eye piercing into the rex's leg...

Pain. Exquisite, beautiful pain.

The rex roared. Cohen heard it twice, once reverberat-ing within the animal's own skull, a second time echo-ing back from distant hills. A flock of silver-furred pterosaurs took to the air. Cohen saw them fade from view as the dinosaur's simple mind shut them out of the display. Irrelevant distractions.

The *Triceratops* pulled back, the horn withdrawing from the rex's flesh.

Blood, Cohen was delighted to see, still looked red.

"If Judge Hoskins had ordered the electric chair," said Axworthy, Cohen's lawyer, "we could have fought that on Charter grounds. Cruel and unusual punishment, and all that. But she's authorized full access to the chronotrans–ference euthanasia program for you." Axworthy paused. "She said, bluntly, that she simply wants you dead."

"How thoughtful of her," said Cohen.

Axworthy ignored that. "I'm sure I can get you anything you want," he said. "Who would you like to be transferred into?"

"Not who," said Cohen. "What."

"I beg your pardon?"

"That damned judge said I was the most cold-blooded killer to stalk the Alberta landscape since *Tyrannosaurus rex*." Cohen shook his head. "The idiot. Doesn't she know dinosaurs were warm-blooded? Anyway, that's what I want. I want to be transferred into a *T. rex*."

"You're kidding."

"Kidding is not my forte, John. *Killing* is. I want to know which was better at it, me or the rex."

"I don't even know if they can do that kind of thing," said Axworthy.

"Find out, damn you. What the hell am I paying you for?"

The rex danced to the side, moving with surprising agility for a creature of its bulk, and once again it brought its terrible jaws down on the ceratopsian's shoulder. The planteater was hemorrhaging at an incredible rate, as though a thousand sacrifices had been performed on the altar of its back.

The *Triceratops* tried to lunge forward, but it was weakening quickly. The tyrannosaur, crafty in its own way despite its trifling intellect, simply retreated a dozen giant paces. The hornface took one tentative step toward it, and then another, and, with great and ponderous effort, one more. But then the dinosaurian tank teetered and, eyelids slowly closing, collapsed on its side. Cohen was briefly startled, then thrilled, to hear it fall to the ground with a *splash*—he hadn't realized just how much blood had poured out of the great rent the rex had made in the beast's back.

The tyrannosaur moved in, lifting its left leg up and then smashing it down on the *Triceratops*' belly, the three sharp toe claws tearing open the thing's abdomen, entrails spilling out into the harsh sunlight. Cohen thought the rex would let out a victorious roar, but it didn't. It simply dipped its muzzle into the body cavity, and methodically began yanking out chunks of flesh.

Cohen was disappointed. The battle of the dinosaurs had been fun, the killing had been well engineered, and there had certainly been enough blood, but there was no *terror*. No sense that the *Triceratops* had been quivering with fear, no begging for mercy. No feeling of power, of control. Just dumb, mindless brutes moving in ways preprogrammed by their genes.

It wasn't enough. Not nearly enough.

Judge Hoskins looked across the desk in her chambers at the lawyer.

"A *Tyrannosaurus*, Mr. Axworthy? I was speaking figuratively."

"I understand that, my lady, but it was an appropriate observation, don't you think? I've contacted the Chronotransference people, who say they can do it, if they have a rex specimen to work from. They have to back-propagate from actual physical material in order to get a temporal fix."

Judge Hoskins was as unimpressed by scientific babble as she was by legal jargon. "Make your point, Mr. Axworthy."

"I called the Royal Tyrrell Museum of Paleontology in Drumheller and asked them about the *Tyrannosaurus* fossils available worldwide. Turns out there's only a handful of complete skeletons, but they were able to provide me with an annotated list, giving as much information as they could about the individual probable causes of death." He slid a thin plastic printout sheet across the judge's wide desk.

"Leave this with me, counsel. I'll get back to you."

Axworthy left, and Hoskins scanned the brief list. She then leaned back in her leather chair and began to read the needlepoint on her wall for the thousandth time:

My object all sublime
I shall achieve in time—

She read that line again, her lips moving slightly as she subvocalized the words: "I shall achieve *in time...*"

The judge turned back to the list of tyrannosaur finds. Ah, that one. Yes, that would be perfect. She pushed a button on her phone. "David, see if you can find Mr. Axworthy for me."

There had been a very unusual aspect to the *Triceratops* kill—an aspect that intrigued Cohen. Chronotransference had been performed countless times; it was one of the most popular forms of euthanasia. Sometimes the transferee's original body would give an ongoing commentary about what was going on, as if talking during sleep. It was clear from what they said that transferees couldn't exert any control over the bodies they were transferred into.

Indeed, the physicists had claimed any control was impossible. Chronotransference worked precisely because the transferee could exert no influence, and therefore was simply observing things that had already been observed. Since no new observations were being made, no quantum-mechanical distortions occurred. After all, said the physicists, if one could exert control, one could change the past. And that was impossible.

And yet, when Cohen had willed the rex to alter its course, it eventually had done so.

Could it be that the rex had so little brains that Cohen's thoughts *could* control the beast?

Madness. The ramifications were incredible.

Still...

He had to know if it was true. The rex was torpid, flopped on its belly, gorged on ceratopsian meat. It seemed prepared to lie here for a long time to come, enjoying the early evening breeze.

Get up, thought Cohen. *Get up, damn you!*

Nothing. No response.

Get up!

The rex's lower jaw was resting on the ground. Its upper jaw was lifted high, its mouth wide open. Tiny pterosaurs were flitting in and out of the open maw, their long needle-like beaks apparently yanking gobbets of hornface flesh from between the rex's curved teeth.

Get up, thought Cohen again. *Get up!*

The rex stirred.

Up!

The tyrannosaur used its tiny forelimbs to keep its torso from sliding forward as it pushed with its powerful legs until it was standing.

Forward, thought Cohen. *Forward!*

The beast's body felt different. Its belly was full to bursting. *Forward!*

With ponderous steps, the rex began to march.

It was wonderful. To be in control again! Cohen felt the old thrill of the hunt.

And he knew exactly what he was looking for.

"Judge Hoskins says okay," said Axworthy. "She's authorized for you to be transferred into that new *T. rex* they've got right here in Alberta at the Tyrrell. It's a young adult, they say. Judging by the way the skeleton was found, the rex died falling, probably into a fissure. Both legs and the back were broken, but the skeleton remained almost completely articulated, suggesting that scavengers couldn't get at it. Unfortunately, the chronotransference people say that back-propagating that far into the past they can only plug you in a few hours before the accident occurred. But you'll get your wish: you're going to die as a tyrannosaur. Oh, and here are the books you asked for: a complete library on Cretaceous flora and fauna. You should have time to get through it all; the chronotransference people will need a couple of weeks to set up."

As the prehistoric evening turned to night, Cohen found what he had been looking for, cowering in some under-brush: large brown eyes, long, drawn-out face, and a lithe body covered in fur that, to the tyrannosaur's eyes, looked blue-brown.

A mammal. But not just any mammal. *Purgatorius*, the very first primate, known from Montana and Alberta from right at the end of the Cretaceous. A little guy, only about ten centimeters long, excluding its ratlike tail. Rare creatures, these days. Only a precious few.

The little furball could run quickly for its size, but a single step by the tyrannosaur equaled more than a hundred of the mammal's. There was no way it could escape.

The rex leaned in close, and Cohen saw the furball's face, the nearest thing there would be to a human face for another sixty million years. The animal's eyes went wide in terror.

Naked, raw fear.

Mammalian fear.

Cohen saw the creature scream.

Heard it scream.

It was beautiful.

The rex moved its gaping jaws in toward the little mammal, drawing in breath with such force that it sucked the creature into its maw. Normally the rex would swallow its meals whole, but Cohen prevented the beast from doing that. Instead, he simply had it stand still, with the little primate running around, terrified, inside the great cavern of the dinosaur's mouth, banging into the giant teeth and great fleshy walls, and skittering over the massive, dry tongue.

Cohen savored the terrified squealing. He wallowed in the sensation of the animal, mad with fear, moving inside that living prison.

And at last, with a great, glorious release, Cohen put the animal out of its misery, allowing the rex to swallow it, the furball tickling as it slid down the giant's throat.

It was just like old times.

Just like hunting humans.

And then a wonderful thought occurred to Cohen. Why, if he killed enough of these little screaming balls of fur, they wouldn't have any descendants. There wouldn't ever be any *Homo sapiens*. In a very real sense, Cohen realized he *was* hunting humans—every single human being who would ever exist.

Of course, a few hours wouldn't be enough time to kill many of them. Judge Hoskins no doubt thought it was wonderfully poetic justice, or she wouldn't have allowed the transfer: sending him back to fall into the pit, damned.

Stupid judge. Why, now that he could control the beast, there was no way he was going to let it die young. He'd just—

There it was. The fissure, a long gash in the earth, with a crumbling edge. Damn, it *was* hard to see. The shadows cast by neighboring trees made a confusing gridwork on the ground that obscured the ragged opening. No wonder the dull-witted rex had missed seeing it until it was too late.

But not this time.

Turn left, thought Cohen.

Left.

His rex obeyed.

He'd avoid this particular area in future, just to be on the safe side. Besides, there was plenty of territory to cover. Fortunately, this was a young rex—a juvenile. There would be decades in which to continue his very special hunt. Cohen was sure that Axworthy knew his stuff: once it became apparent that the link had lasted longer than a few hours, he'd keep any attempt to pull the plug tied up in the courts for years.

Cohen felt the old pressure building in himself, and in the rex. The tyrannosaur marched on.

This was *better* than old times, he thought. Much better.

Hunting all of humanity.

The release would be *wonderful.*

He watched intently for any sign of movement in the underbrush. •

HOPSCOTCH

Karl Schroeder

It was raining fish.

Linda gave a whoop of triumph which made him jump. Alan clutched the dashboard and stared. An absurd thought came to him: *lucky we're parked.*

The vista of marshlands outside was drawn in thatches of yellow grass under a perfectly blue sky. Yet, out of the clarity a steady downpour of fish was falling. They were no more than six to eight inches long, silvery and seemingly alive. Three were already flopping on the gold hood of the Honda.

"I don't know my fish," mumbled Alan.

"What?" Linda, bouncing in her seat, turned to him. "Get the camera. It's in the glove compartment under the maps."

"...what kind they are," he half-finished. He was reaching for the glove compartment when she opened her door.

Alan dragged her back and Linda fell across the stick shift. "Ow! What are you doing?"

"Don't go out there! It's crazy."

"The camera! The camera!" She fought past (knocking him in the chin with her bony shoulder) to get it. He made sure he had a good grip on her arm.

"You're not going out there."

"Let go of me." She hastily rolled down the window, and began snapping shots.

"Lens cap!"

"Yeah-yeah." She popped it off and kept shooting.

Thud. Some little mackerel or minnow or other left a smear of ocean on the windshield. He watched it slide down over the wiper. "Jesus, this is weird, you know? I mean, *really* weird."

"I told you I expected it. What did you think, I was crazy?" He shrugged and she, not seeing it, looked back. "You like that in women?"

He gave her a shit-eating grin. Then he sprawled against the door with one arm along the seat-back. "You told me. People tell me a lot of stuff I don't believe."

"Good for you." She poked her head out. "It's slackening off." Before he could react she had the door open and hopped out. He followed with a curse.

Man killed by falling fish. "Christ, Linda. Get in the car. You'll be brained or something."

"Wow! Look at this!" She craned back to take a photo straight up. He banged the roof in frustration.

Then he did look around, and the reality of it finally hit him: the marsh flats, surprised birds huddling in the grass, and everywhere fish, flapping, bloody or dead, lying like the sticks of some fortune-telling operation thrown but never read.

He reached out to touch one of the fish which lay on the roof. It was very cold, with the slick feel of decay. He snatched his hand back. For a moment he was very afraid of Linda, as if she'd just *done* this or something, to impress him.

"We're on the trail of it, you know, Alan? The big *it,* the nameless dread everyone blames when something really *off* happens. We got its scent."

"Yeah." He tried to smile. "Like a fish market."

Later when they were driving back to town, his right leg started to hurt badly, mostly in the calf and knee. It took a bit of thought before he realized that, for a few moments when it all started, he had been pushing at the floor of the car with that foot, like he was trying to put on the brakes.

He lay with his face buried in her hair. Linda was asleep. He was on the comfortable side of awake, most likely to join her. He couldn't stop thinking, though.

About fish, for one thing. About the blank spaces on his bank statement where there should be numbers. About the way summer liked to fall into autumn suddenly, just when he was getting used to things. And about Linda, whom he might never get used to.

Linda was always zipping off in ten different directions at once. Always talking, always thinking even during sex. He tended to be passive except when inspired, so together they evened out, he calming her down, she revving him up.

She was terrified of conforming. "If I got a normal job, Al, settled down, had kids...I'd disappear. Gone. Fade into the background. There's four billion people in the world, and maybe a couple hundred stick out." So she was on a constant hunt for the *outré*. She'd pore over the headlines of some lurid tabloid and crow when she found a particularly strange title. "Rhinoceros delivers woman's baby in zoo!" or "Apparition of Elvis appears on bingo cards!"

She'd get all excited: "What if it were *true*, Al! Say the universe is more twisted than we thought? No one's ever scientifically studied the really weird. Maybe it's real—like it's the natural equivalent of the Big Lie. Think about it!"

Well, he tried. They had met because they shared a love of practical jokes. He'd concluded lately that his jokes were just an attention-getting device. Her nonconformism went deeper than he could follow. Ultimately he still dreamed of a big house, a fast car and a gorgeous wife. Linda wanted to pop out of what she called the "programmed world" like a bubble, unique. He figured it was because her parents had started out as hippies and ended up as right-wing stockbrokers. That would confuse anybody.

Everything she experienced, she tried to re-experience in a new way, as different from the ordinary. They'd seen some kids playing hopscotch once. "That game is three thousand years old," she said as they walked past. "Each square represents a stage on your way to Egyptian heaven or hell. When you play it you're practicing for the afterlife." Simple as that, then she was pointing out the way the windows of the Faculty Club caught the evening light in rose squares, while he gawked back over his shoulder and the kids posed like storks.

But he was broke now and it was August. Linda had her grants and bursaries; whatever she did she was really good at it. Alan hadn't yet told her he didn't have the money to go back to school. The fact was, he was sponging off her, had been all summer, and he no longer wanted to be an engineer.

Linda had this grant and was doing her PhD on statistical studies of irreproducible phenomena. He'd known in a vague sort of way that it had to do with UFOs but he didn't believe in them and couldn't believe she would. When she said why didn't he come along for a couple of weeks while she went into the field, he'd jumped at it.

She went to strange places. Never holiday spots. But the fields in Ohio in July were surreal, faced by soft mists with the faint factory smell of distant cities, and they'd made love there to the buzz of insects and sigh of big trees. The Atlantic, in Maine, was unimpressive, slate gray, somehow unbelievable but he was paying more attention to her than it and even it got pretty romantic.

Alan was prepared to admit he was in love, but love was one of those things Linda didn't believe in—it was another "program"—so he didn't know what to say to her. Yes she cared for him, but she thought it was some kind of betrayal to express love in the normal fashion. While she believed they were freer this way, her attitude was coming between them; and his lack of money was also, and then this afternoon the thing with the fish, was like a wedge to pry her away from him.

He didn't know where that had come from. Really. What was she up to? He didn't know and if he didn't know the really basic things about her, why she was here, how she could be looking for miracles and finding them, while he drowsed and whittled wood on the hood of the car...then, they weren't making it.

"You have to tell me how you're doing this."

In the car again. Hell. And it was dark this time. Linda draped herself over the wheel, staring across a cabbage field at a black line of trees. They had the windows open and a cooler of beer in the back but it didn't help. He was hot.

"Statistics."

"You say we're gonna see a UFO tonight."

She brightened. "If I'm right."

"Like we've graduated from falling fish?"

"Not exactly."

"So explain."

Annoyed, she turned to him, resting her cheek on the wheel. "You never asked before."

"Well, I'm asking now. Getting whacked by a mackerel from space got my attention, okay?"

She chuckled. "Sure. Anyway, I didn't want to talk about it because it was so off the wall and probably wrong.

"The thing is UFOs and things like that've been around since Moses. They're all part of one big stew—UFOs, apparitions of the Virgin Mary, Bigfoot, poltergeists, even visitations by Liberace. You see, all these things appear in the same places, sometimes at the same time. And, say in 1880, they saw dirigibles, not flying saucers. When *we* build flying saucers, we'll be seeing something different, something new."

"How?"

She squinted at him. "Most people ask *why,* you know. They get obsessed with the details. When a UFO lands and gives somebody a starmap, it sets them off for years. But the guy from the UFO is just as likely to give you a plate of pancakes." He laughed, but she sat up and shook her head. "It happens. Scout's honor. The point is, these things are like TV. All form, no content. All picture with no message to it. Try and figure out the *meaning* as a way of getting at origins, and you're fucked. So I'm doing it differently."

"Shit. You really are chasing the things, aren't you?"

"You saw. Alan, you *saw* the fish." Uneasy, he was silent. She had that look in her eye again. "It's a matter of correlating the data on when and where, and ignoring the details of the individual events," she went on. "So I've been doing that. And I found an equation that matched up the incidences of things. I found a *pattern.*"

"Like you know where they're from? Venus, or something?"

"No, that's not what I'm looking for, if it was I wouldn't have got this far. It's the raw pattern I was after. When fish fall in Virginia, something else is going to happen along a sort of line, a space-time line, a measurable distance away. You do the statistics, follow that line through space and time, and, in this case, it winds up here."

"Here. How do you know it's gonna be a UFO?"

"I checked the literature. They've never had fish falls here, but they do see flying saucers now and then."

"Simple as that? No reasons, no clue why?"

"Who cares?" She beamed at him. "That's the beauty of it. Like quantum mechanics, it lets you describe the workings of something without having to deal with the plain impossibility of what you're describing. It's crazy, but it works. A way of getting a handle on all of this without having to believe in the divinity of Liberace. See?"

Fireflies were coming off the fields. He stared at them. "Huh. An equation to catch Elvis? Flying tortillas and little-girl poltergeists? Ha!" He sat back, seeing nothing but the humor in it. He started to laugh.

"Alan!" Oh there she went, pissed off again. But Linda grabbed his arm and pointed, and there, rising behind the black line of trees across the field, was the mother of all fireflies.

And *bang,* she was out of the car again. Him still sitting with his jaw down.

But there, that vision of her as a silhouette, too thin, with this green light like an umbrella over the forest all seen past the rearview, the flyspecked glass and the hood; it froze him up. So she was twenty feet away before he could cut his hand finding the door handle and run after.

Cabbages everywhere. "Get back to the car! Get back to the car, Goddamn it! Now!" but she ran away. Had the camera again. Alan went after but wanted to run the other way; he couldn't look at that big light or he'd stop dead. She was trying to take pictures and run at the same time so she tripped over a cabbage. Great. He did a dog-pile fall on her.

"Get off! Get off!" she shrieked.

Alan found the adrenaline rush astonishing. He was terrified and he'd never been before. She elbowed him in the stomach but he didn't even feel it. "You're not going in those trees," he shouted. "Get back!"

They rolled over and over and then she was up and on her way again. He caught snatches of words: "—see it, right up close—got to get close, catch it—"

It was all the places she was going where he couldn't follow. It was the University, and the corners of her mind where he couldn't fit, all in this green thing so maybe he was just as pissed off as scared now. He was jealous of it.

Wild idea. Funny what you thought when terrified.

He caught her again near the woods and they went down. This time they were both silent but he had her good. Now he was aware of a kind of hiss, more silent like the memory of a sound, but definitely there. They both looked up, her head under his. *We must look pretty stupid,* he thought, floundering in cabbage.

The light went out like it was blown out by a wind; it flickered away over the trees in shreds. For a long time they lay in the dirt, not speaking or even moving. Then she said, "You're heavy."

At a diner under a huge neon stetson, she fidgeted over a sundae and he glared at the camera. "Think you got it?" he asked at last.

"I don't know." She was pissed off but trying not to be. She looked at him, resigned. "You didn't have to knock me down."

"Just trying to keep you from getting killed."

"They're not dangerous."

"How the hell do you know? It's like the nineteen fifties: 'a little radiation never hurt nobody!' None of the people who said that are around anymore, are they?"

"Get this straight," she said tightly. "I know what I'm doing. I'm a scientist, and I'm trying to learn objectively about a phenomenon of nature."

"Nature, hell! We were in gunsights back there!"

She shook her head quickly. "No gunsights. No little green men. Oh, yeah, maybe there would have been some. But they're not *real* aliens. They're real like the Virgin Mary and Liberace. You honestly think Elvis lives in a UFO? Come on." She tapped her spoon on the table.

"Christ, I need a cigarette."

"Then what was it, if it wasn't aliens?"

"I..." She stopped. "Don't know. Don't want to know. That's the point, isn't it? We can't lose our objectivity. Can't go flying off the handle like you did. Like you were Rambo versus the space gooks."

"Come on." But he bit back on the rest of his retort because he remembered so clearly the wild look in her eye when he had her down. Reason gone.

"You ran after it," he accused. "Like it *was* something."

Linda acted casual. "I wanted to get as close as I could. Doesn't that make sense? Have to study it."

"You wanted—" he stopped again. He didn't want to argue; this was where she drew the line, he knew. She would never admit to what she really wanted, and he couldn't think how to stop her wanting it.

But he was sure she'd wanted to be taken up in that flying saucer, if only so she could argue with the aliens.

The old man droned on over the tape recorder. Linda couldn't still be listening and Alan hadn't started out interested anyway. He was too busy thinking about the big two-letter word *us*. There were all these contradictory impulses he wanted to follow, most of them stupid and what she wouldn't laugh at she'd be insulted by.

Hell. He poked at the plastic over the window of this seething hot trailer, and glanced back at the old man, who was telling some incoherent story about hurricanes and walking radio towers. Linda had her eyes on the old guy so Alan's gaze drifted to her and stayed, locked.

A lot of men stayed away from her because she was "too intense." At moments like this she sure looked it, with all her attention going to something he'd given up on already. It was this *focus* that was scary.

It was great when you were the one focused on, and he'd thought that, fundamentally, it was him. But right now she had her eyes fixed like searchlights on the old man, or rather on what the old man was telling her, and Alan was somewhere in the penumbra of shadow around her.

Originally he'd been able to get her attention back, with

tricks and humor. Not any more. In fact, it would feel kind of like cheating to have to be dragging her back with neon signs, instead of letting her go where ever her quick blade of intellect cut.

Later at the car, while Linda unlocked the doors, Alan picked at the weather-stripping on the window then said, "I'm tired."

"Yeah, we're done. Let's go back to the hotel."

"No, I mean tired of all this. This...weirdness. What are you trying to do, anyway?"

She paused, continued unlocking and got in. He half-expected her not to unlock his side but she did. She watched him get in.

"You're scared."

"Bullshit."

"That bit with the UFO scared you. Admit it. It's okay to be scared."

"I'm *not* scared." He hopped a bit in the seat, waving his hands to start talking, getting nowhere. "It's—just—" Brainlock set in. He slumped back. "Just...not what I signed up for."

She stared out stonily, started the engine. "I think you're doing exactly what you keep telling me not to. You're acting out a script of some kind you've made up. 'Daring researcher makes blinding breakthrough.' You're thinking in headlines. Admit it."

"What?" She was getting heated up. "I *know* what I'm doing. I'm the first person to have a handle on this stuff! I've found the answer, this could be as big as discovering electricity, bigger than going to the moon!"

"Sure." He held up his hands. "Sure. You...got the figures. But I think you're turning it into a crusade. I saw you running after the UFO. You've fallen for the mythology, you're not just doing statistics now. You want to *get* the thing behind all this. I mean you believe there is something behind it now, don't you? And you want it."

Linda drove silently for a bit. Then she said, "What do *you* want?"

"I'm just an ordinary guy. I don't want to know what I want. It gets too complicated that way."

Despite herself, she smiled, glanced at him and jigged her eyebrow. "Every time you say something like that, you guarantee you'll never be 'ordinary.' " She turned her eyes back to the road, pensive.

"What are you going to do next?"

"I know where the next anomaly will appear," she said. "Michigan. Are you coming?"

He thought it over. "No. It's not what I came for."

"Fine. I'll draw you a map, in case you change your mind." Her voice had gotten cold. "You want me to drop you off somewhere?"

"Don't chase it, Linda. That's what everybody else does, you said so yourself."

"You want me to drop you off somewhere?"

He wanted to kill something. Killing off a few beer was no substitute. Alan kicked about his friend Murray's apartment for a couple of days. The map she'd drawn, with her calculated date for the next appearance, lay on the kitchen counter. Murray was not happy about having guests, especially nonpaying ones. Alan had two hundred in the bank and no idea where more might come from.

Of course, after a couple of days he decided it had been a stupid idea to run off the way he'd done. She needed him now more than ever. Now that things were happening. But she was such a pig-headed, insensitive bitch sometimes, when she got notions in her head... And this latest stuff was way out of his league. He'd drag her away from it if he just knew how. But it was too strange, he couldn't get a handle on it.

She pretended to be so objective. Ha. He'd held her when she cried over the stupidity of life, when they'd talked about what it would be like to win a lottery, just *make it* some day. She always came down on him for being too unimaginative, for plotting out his life and his relationships according to simple models he got from TV and movies. Linda went too far the other way; she thought she could keep it all up in the air, and some treasure would rain down on her someday. Like the fish...

Drunk and watching something safe—*Dallas*—he was

worrying again about what might be waiting for her in Michigan, feeling futile about being unable to even *know* that, when he remembered something she'd told him. He got up to pace.

She'd said she knew the Ohio thing was going to be a UFO because UFOs had been seen in that area before. Bet she knew the fish would be fish for the same reason. He knew where she did her newspaper-morgue research, had seen her at it. That must be how she knew.

If he just knew what it was going to be, he'd feel better. He kicked the TV off and headed for the door, just as Murray came in.

"Christ, can't you do the dishes for a change?" said Murray.

"When I get back."

"Oh, you're coming back?"

He took the bus down to the newspaper. He hated buses, but they were it from now on. At least till he had a job. He didn't want to get onto that train of thought, better think about something more fun...like the fields at night, and the blanket she kept in the back of the Honda.

Shit. It hurt to remember.

They let him into the morgue and he sat down, feeling useless, at a microfiche of headlines. Thousands of them, fading away in a kind of miniature landscape he cruised over. After an hour or two of blue-gray figure and ground, he was getting nowhere, but somehow felt like he was doing something and so kept at it. It was late afternoon, they were going to kick him out soon, but maybe he'd be back tomorrow. Nothing else to do.

Then the headline popped out at him. The place was right. He stared. *Man vanishes before witnesses.*

The Honda sat in the middle of a broken, tilted concrete lot. Some ex-gas station, he figured as he drove up. This was the middle of nowhere. He couldn't see her at first and felt a pulse of anxiety. He got out of his rented car.

Linda had been checking her tires. She stood up from behind the Honda, surprised. For a moment neither of them spoke.

Then she sort of smiled, and tried to frown at the same time. "I was hoping you'd come, you know. And I was afraid you'd show up right now, just when things should start happening."

He went over. They embraced okay, just like before, and he started to relax. "You're crazy to go for this one," he said, and felt her tense. "Sorry. I was just remembering you're crazy all the time, so why should I object."

"Thanks. I'm glad you're here." She broke from the embrace and went to rifle the car for something. She came up with a battered notebook. "The numbers say a disappearance should happen. So I'm going to keep an eye on *you.*"

"It's scary. That's all. I'd feel safer if you gave this one a miss."

"Can't. I won't know if I'm on the wrong track unless I verify this one." She scribbled something in the notebook.

Alan thought about it. "I don't buy that. If somebody vanishes, first off it probably won't be noticeable for days, and second it'll eventually make the papers. So you don't have to be here."

"Sure I do. This is science in action, Al."

"Now that is bullshit. You're hunting again, that's all. You want to actually be there when it happens. You want to catch the gremlins in the act."

She frowned at the notebook, squinted up at him, and shrugged. "So?"

"Aha! You admit it! You've fallen for the whole paranormal schtick after all."

"That's not it at all," she said hotly. "It's something else. It's something bigger than just 'psychic.' So okay, I admit I want to find out what. Why not? I've taken the first step. I've proven it exists. And this is something I have to do for *me.* Because I know you, and I know you don't believe in any of it. Despite what you've seen. When you left I was thinking all kinds of things, things to say or do to make you stay. But I kept coming back to: *he doesn't believe me. Even after what he's seen.* So I let you go." She put a hand to her forehead quickly like a soap queen, and looked at him under it. "You see what I'm saying?"

Alan opened the driver's door and sat down on the edge.

Heat wafted off the concrete. He smelled hot vinyl. She went around and opened the hatch of the Honda, and rooted around in the back of the car. He stared into the hazy distance.

"It's not you I don't believe in," he said slowly. "It's the idea that you're unlocking the secrets of the universe."

"Maybe that's what I'm doing," she said, her voice muffled. "You wouldn't believe it even if it were true. You have to play the role of the 'rational man.' So you're blind to the things I'm seeing. You don't really see me. Maybe I can't see your way either. We're different, Al. I guess we'll never see eye to eye."

Alan stared at his hands, depressed. "Playing roles," he said. "Like by falling in love. And worrying. And things like that?" He shook his head. "We all do that. We can't not do it. You do it too, you're doing it now with your obsession with these stupid incidents. There's only a few ways to live. I have to follow the way my life is laid out. Even if it's been done a million times before. I'm conventional and I think conventionally, I feel conventionally. You have to see that."

The sounds from the back had stopped. He looked over again but didn't see her. "You can't just break out and look down at yourself," he said more loudly, "to see what's really you and what isn't. —That's what you really want to do. Isn't it?"

But she didn't answer, and he stood up and walked around the car, and found she was really gone. Stepped through some door while he'd been looking the other way.

He walked the big square slabs of concrete calling her name, until it started to get dark. And then he sat down on the hood of her Honda and cried. •

SOMMELIER

Catherine MacLeod

The sign above the door read, simply, *Sommelier*. There was no storefront. The carved wooden door was set in the brick wall between a used-book store and Cerene's music school, and Henry Garret regarded it warily as he approached. Aurelie watched unseen as she unlocked the door, allowing light and warmth and the fragrance of mint to seep into the cool morning. Sommelier was open to the public, even though it was too early to be conducting business.

But then, it was also early enough that no one would see him here. She knew his need for secrecy. For this he'd evaded his bodyguards and carried a briefcase full of greenbacks into a neighborhood where he saw an even chance of being murdered. He glanced over his shoulder to be sure he was alone, and turned back to an open door.

Aurelie Rupert said, "Right on time, Mr. Garret. Come in, won't you?" She stepped back to let him pass.

And he hesitated. Actually paused. Not because he suddenly doubted the worth of his errand here; or because of the sudden dreadful certainty that she could deliver what he wanted. Not even because the eyes that regarded him with professional indifference were a truly unnerving shade of blue. But Henry Garret, native of the boardroom and veteran of countless takeovers, wasn't used to being looked at as if he wasn't God.

Aurelie waited, accustomed to the reaction, gazing out at Cawley Road where no one had ever been murdered, where Victor Ludin was dragging out café furniture and his young wife, Kiri, was brewing coffee. Aurelie raised a hand in greeting, and the acknowledgment of people in the street sent Garret racing past her into the waiting room.

Surroundings more alien than those outside. Small room painted in warm, neutral colors. Comfortable furniture covered with tapestry. No leather, no chrome. No receptionist. Aurelie closed the door and sat in the nearest armchair. "How may I help you, Mr. Garret?" She didn't invite him to sit.

He sat immediately, glad she'd dispensed with courtesies for which he had neither talent nor taste. He pulled a scrap of newspaper from his breast pocket and passed it to her. She took it between two fingers. She didn't wrinkle her thin nose at his odor of vaguely-obtained wealth.

He said, "I want you to make me a brandy from this."

She read the obituary quietly. Andrew Hall, millionaire industrialist. No doubt a fine enemy: Henry Garret was hardly one to request remembrance of a friend, assuming he had one.

She smiled coolly. "This will take a year, Mr. Garret. The work is delicate and time-consuming—and it cannot be done cheaply."

"Fine," he said impatiently. "Anything."

She moved to the squat cabinet sitting beneath the room's only window, and returned with an account ledger. "Anything" was the usual price offered by her customers, but Garret seemed prepared to be taken at his word. She wrote his bill in a swift, spidery hand and gave it to him. One million dollars.

"In advance," she said. He paid in cash.

Then she held the door for him, nodding politely to Cerene's first student of the day. Garret left without goodbyes or unnecessary cheer. She watched him for a long moment, then dropped Andrew Hall's obituary in the trash.

Begin with hatred, Aurelie mused, and plucked a vial from a high shelf.

Essence of anguish. Dreams half-remembered. Dash of pure glee.

Suspicion for color.

She stoppered the beaker and locked it away to age in the dark. She sighed quietly and hummed as she cleaned her workroom. Henry Garret's life would be terribly empty without his cherished foe.

Emptier, she amended, and turned off the lights.

She passed through the wine cellar on her way out, regarding the bottles with an expert eye. Five hundred bottles glowing in the light from the stairwell, containing tangos and carnivals and baby's first smile. Jeweled moments, favorite weeks, entire lives aging slowly and well.

Aurelie climbed the stone steps to her office and brewed mint tea for her next appointment. Business was up. Times might be tough out there, but little changed on Cawley Road, and nothing changed at Sommelier. She laughed softly at the whimsy of the name: wine steward—maker of fine wines and keeper of secrets not hers. Her clients were the very rich, the truly joyous, the criminally insane. Sometimes they were the same person.

They came wanting a glass of autumn; a goblet of May; a chalice of birdsong. There was always a market for memory.

Surely none of them were innocent enough to think she actually pressed grapes.

Tess Edmund said, "Do you have children, Mrs. Rupert?"

Aurelie gazed into eyes filled with shadows and ash. "Yes. Two by my first husband, two by my second." She didn't elaborate. Tess didn't need to know she'd outlived them all, or how long ago. "Their childhood was a wonderful time for me."

"Yes—but did you know it at the time?"

Tess, "a woman of a certain age," faced Aurelie with none of Henry Garret's doubt. She was twice-divorced, mother of three, as dark as Aurelie was fair. According to the polls, the president of Edmund Cosmetics was most-influential, much admired and the best-dressed.

She came to Sommelier and told Aurelie a secret her analyst didn't know.

"I want you to make me a wine." Tess clearly wanted to get up and pace. She didn't. "I was busy building up my company when my children were small. I spent more time in the boardroom than in the nursery. I missed school plays and softball games, and I didn't see any of them take their first steps. They're not resentful—but I am. I know I couldn't always be there."

"But I *wanted* to be there." She laughed sadly. "Can you believe I'm nostalgic for scraped knees and car pools?"

"Why not?" Aurelie smiled: there was something comfortable about this woman. "You want what you've missed. You'll have it a year from today." She wrote the bill and passed it over with a second cup of tea.

"One hundred thousand dollars. In advance."

She mixed the spirit from memory:

Sticky fingerprints on the windows. Jam-flavored kisses. Three sets of first steps. Piano lessons. Halloween. It-followed-me-home-can-I-keep-it? Nights spent battling stubborn fevers. Report cards and early sunlight on little faces. Elusive lightning bugs.

Essence of peanut butter.

She sealed the bottle and set it near the workshop window to absorb the fragrance and mystery of the four winds. It would be bittersweet. It would leave Tess Edmund giddy and breathless, or calm and content.

It would tingle on the palate and leave tears in her throat.

His name was Bram Owen. He was a slight, short man who'd aged quickly in the three months since the death of his wife, Laurel. He came to Sommelier with her photo and letters in her handwriting. Aurelie set them aside and said, "Tell me about her."

He spoke slowly at first, then faster as the memories grew more vivid.

The herbs in her garden. The fragrance of her soap. Her cat, Sphinx, whose eyes were the color of Aurelie's.

The Staunton chessboard he'd given her as a birthday gift, and the way she caressed the wooden chessmen as they played. She loved violets. She cried over old movies. On Sundays they'd gone to the park to feed the swans.

Her slender softness in their old bed, her breath warm on his face, sweet pale rain against the windows.

The afternoon was far gone when he finished. Next door, Cerene's students were playing Bach, a piece of sheer joyous power.

Aurelie thought of her second husband, a misshapen hulk of a man whose voice was a narcotic, and said, "One year from today, Mr. Owen, you'll have your wine." She presented his bill with a small flourish.

His surprise was evident. "One dollar?" he said.

"In advance."

Summer now. Aurelie stepped outside leaving Sommelier's door unlocked. The phone rang in her office. She made no move to answer it. She'd spent a portion of her morning on the phone with Henry Garret's secretary, a curious young man who'd found her name in Garret's personal calendar.

It was kind of him to call her, she said. Yes, she'd read the paper, knew that Garret had died this morning. Peacefully, in his sleep, really?

In his sleep, perhaps. Peacefully, she doubted.

Yes, she admitted, he'd called to confirm their appointment. No, he'd placed no order. She thought he would have preferred to do that in person. Yes, thank you for calling.

And she fetched Henry Garret's wine up to her office. It was a glowing, dark, almost toxic brandy; how sad he would never taste it. She opened the bottle, poured a little. Its surface sparkled vilely. She swirled the wine, inhaled sharply: a clot of hatred rode on her breath, sizzled in her mouth. It was indeed a fine revenge. She lifted her glass to his memory and touched her lips to its rim.

Her head spun. It was the kind of hatred for which the world stops. It was intent, murderous, bizarre. Aurelie had dispatched her own enemies by outliving them, but if Garret's rancor was any gauge, she'd never imagined so magnificent an enemy as Andrew Hall.

She set the glass aside and lifted three tiny vials from a deep skirt pocket. She worked quickly, sitting behind her desk. The brandy gleamed malevolently: she was almost sad to be altering it. She opened the first vial and held it up to the narrow window beside her desk. It contained a century. She poured it slowly and marveled at how the hatred faded. She cracked the second vial: compassion. The brandy turned the color of pearls, the hue of quiet sadness. She opened the third—love—and stopped the bottle immediately. The brandy would release a flow of fine memories. It would also poison the drinker: such love, undiluted, would kill.

She set the bottle in the cupboard beside her account file, locked the workroom door, and went outside.

A warm, spice-scented wind blew through Cawley Road, lifting the hem of her dress. She watched Cerene, in gypsy silks and ribbons, seeing a student to the door. Aurelie thought she'd aged considerably during the winter, when she'd had fewer students and little to fill her time. But now there was less gray in her auburn hair and her step was light. She seemed refreshed and lively, as she always did after teaching class. Her student offered Aurelie a shy smile in passing. Behind him, Cerene closed her door and strode across the street to Victor's café.

Tess Edmund passed her on her way to Sommelier. She was early for her appointment, but her smile was full of such anticipation Aurelie could not think of making her wait: it would be like making children wait for dessert.

"Good morning," she said cheerfully. "Come in."

Tess closed the door and turned to see her bottle held at eye-level. It was a carafe of blue glass, the exact color of the perfect Saturday sky. Tess' mouth twitched as though aching to laugh. Or cry out. Aurelie wrapped the carafe in heavy paper, eased it into her hands.

"If you're not happy with this, please call me."

"Thank you," Tess said absently. Aurelie took her arm, saw to it she didn't stumble over the door sill. She watched her until she turned the corner, still smiling at nothing-in-particular. Aurelie realized her own smile was similar. She noticed the open window in the studio over the bookstore, saw no sign of the young potter who'd taken up residence there. But she heard the faint whir of his wheel and imagined wet clay writhing beneath his hands. She'd never met him. But Victor's Kiri, wondrously pregnant, moving among the customers with heavy grace, served coffee in the cups he'd sold them. Tall mugs glazed in shades of

turquoise and gold, colors that became purple and rose
when hot coffee was poured.

Aurelie wondered if he would make her a wine pitcher.

Aurelie shook Bram Owen's outstretched hand and drew
him inside.

"Would you mind if I left the door open?" she asked.

"Of course not, Mrs. Rupert. You wouldn't want to miss
a moment of such a day."

"Just so."

He smiled as though the worst of his mourning was
done. She brought his wine from her office and set it on the
low table between them. He considered the nondescript
bottle carefully. Guessing at its contents, she thought.
Wondering, *If Laurel were wine, what would she be?*

"Champagne," Aurelie said, and he glanced across the
table at her.

"My God," he said softly.

"Excuse me?"

"Your smile just now was like Laurel's when I missed
the obvious." Aurelie didn't have an answer for that one.
"Mrs. Rupert," he asked suddenly, "do you ever drink with
your customers?"

"No one's ever asked me."

"I'm asking you," he said boldly. "Do you have glasses?"

She found a pair of champagne flutes, the blown glass
almost invisible until the light touched it. She was genu-
inely pleased to share his wine, knowing there were few
people with whom he could share his memories. The cork
exploded from the bottle, bounced off the far wall, and the
wine fizzed lightly, a sound like faint laughter in another
room.

"Will it always fizz like that?"

"Always. Just a little, Mr. Owen—don't waste your wife
on me."

He poured an inch into the bottom of her glass; the flutes
chimed as they toasted Laurel, and he drank. Aurelie
watched curiously, never having seen the first tasting. He
closed his eyes over unexpected tears. The lines on his
brow smoothed themselves out. She noted the exact

moment the memories took him.

She tipped her glass and went with him.

A month in Paris. A year in Vienna. Children grown and gone in the space of minutes. She opened her eyes to look into his. He whispered, "Thank you."

She wrapped the glasses in a narrow box with Laurel's champagne and saw him out. She offered her hand, wasn't surprised when he raised it to his lips. She *was* surprised to see it was evening. The champagne had distorted her timesense, no question of it. She would have to be careful of that.

But it wasn't the worst way to pass the afternoon.

A half-dozen customers lingered at Victor's, drinking coffee beneath paper lanterns. Closing time. She stepped back to shut the door.

"Wait." He was a young man, thin and ragged.

"Yes?"

"I need a bottle of wine."

Need, not *want*. Desperate, she thought. Capable of violence. But—so am I.

"Come in." She heard the door click shut. "What would you like?"

"A...gift for my wife."

This is the one, she thought. He was nondescript, a man who'd go unnoticed in a crowd but for his eyes: warm gray and too-sharply focused. They looked bruised; he was near exhaustion, but made no move to sit down.

"Tell me about her."

His silence was that of a man with much to say and no time to say it all. Finally he said, "Julie's home tonight. Tomorrow she goes back to the hospital. I...we...don't think she'll be coming home again."

She brought Henry Garret's brandy from the cupboard, leaving her ledgers inside. There'd be no discussion of price. Even if he could afford to pay—and he couldn't—he wouldn't be back to settle the bill. Aurelie didn't think he'd let Julie drink alone. He intended to take the bottle by force if necessary, not knowing he couldn't. And if she killed him, Julie would have no release.

She wrapped the bottle in newspaper. "Drink what you

want. Dispose of the rest." He nodded.

And paused. "Thank you."

Not for the wine, Aurelie knew. For her mercy. She watched him struggle for unnecessary words.

But finally he just left: Julie was waiting at home.

Aurelie locked the door behind him, wondering if Bram Owen had ever wished for such a wine. Maybe. She had herself, once. There'd been a time when a stiff drink would have been a kindness.

Kindness.

Yes. She turned out the lights and went downstairs, the steps lit by the glow of five hundred lifetimes anchored in the wine racks. Several would be needed tomorrow. She wondered if anyone would mourn the young couple. *I will remember them. I have a good memory.*

Kindness, she thought. Release for Julie. Release for her husband, who'd shown Aurelie that solace wore many guises. She'd made fortunes from memory's comfort, of course, but perhaps it was time to expand the business. Tonight's visitor had paid in possibilities: there were those who would pay for release.

The burdened, the ill, the terminally alone—she had no doubt that, if they needed to, they'd find her. Hadn't all the others?

Aurelie understood perfectly the law of supply and demand, and she sang sweetly as she worked.

There was a market for mercy out there. •

FROSTY

Jason Kapalka

There must have been some magic in that old silk hat they found, for when they placed it on his head, he began to curse and growl.

But as soon as he noticed all the children staring up at him in wonder, he calmed right down and apologized, and told them that he'd just been a little cranky after waking up.

None of the kids had ever seen a live snowman before. It was awfully neat, the way he talked, like his mouth was full of soggy cereal. But he made them promise not to tell their parents, because then he'd have to go away and he wouldn't be able to tell them any of the fun stories he knew.

The children swore to die with a needle in their eye before they'd tell. Frosty (for that was what he said his name was) smiled a little at this and twinkled his bottlecap eyes.

Then he got them all to sit down, and he started to tell them one of his stories. It was about a man who had lived in town a long time ago, a man who did fun magic things. But the other people in town were mean and didn't like fun things, so they called him a lot of bad names, and then they took the man and burned him up because they thought he was a witch (the children were confused by this a little, because they thought witches were old ladies who flew through the air on sticks). Frosty stopped here and looked mad for a while, though he could have been sad. It was hard to tell with his face all made out of snow.

The boys liked hearing about the man getting burnt up, but one of the girls pouted because there hadn't been a happy ending. Frosty patted her on the head and told her that maybe there would be a happy ending, after all, but that would be another story.

It was getting late then, so Frosty told them to go home and come back tomorrow, but not to tell anybody about him, or he wouldn't talk to them anymore. The children crossed their hearts again before they left.

The next day Frosty was very happy. He popped off his head and put it back on, and rolled around on the ground until he was just a great big snowball, and showed them lots of other tricks. He told them how great it was being a snowman, because he could stay out all day and all night playing in the snow, and he never had to eat vegetables or pork chops. All the kids were jealous.

Then Frosty told them another story. It was a story about a little boy whose parents were the meanest in the world. They never let him stay up past his bedtime, and they made him eat all sorts of awful food, and when the boy showed them some of the magic tricks he had learned, they beat him with a stick.

But one day the boy snuck out of the house and ran into the forest. His parents chased after him, but the boy was friends with all the animals in the woods, and so when his parents came running into the forest they got eaten up by the wolves, and the boy lived happily ever after. All the kids cheered.

After the story, Frosty asked the children if they could bring him some things he needed. He said to get them from their parents without letting them find out. The kids promised they'd be careful, because even though Frosty wanted boring stuff like pencils and calendars and books and paper, it really was kind of fun to do things in secret, without their parents knowing.

They came back with the things the next day, though they brought crayons since they couldn't find any pencils. Frosty picked up a calendar and asked them what day it was, and then he looked at the calendar and frowned. The kids asked him what was wrong, but he smiled and said it was nothing. The children begged him for another story, and he eventually agreed, but first he said he was going to teach them some new words, some magic words.

Frosty wanted them to repeat the words after him, but

the words were hard like the ones they had to learn in school. The kids tried, but Frosty kept getting more and more frustrated. Finally he gave up and told them to sit down, and he'd tell them a story. That made the children happy again.

He told them about way back long ago, when all kids ever did was play and there were no such things as bedtimes. But then all the Moms and Dads in the world got together at a big meeting and decided that the children were having too much fun, and they had better do something about it. So they invented spankings and cough medicine and school, and forever after they made all the children go to bed by eight o'clock. This was a true story, Frosty whispered.

The story scared the children and made them sad. One little blonde girl was crying, she was so sad. She told Frosty she wished she could be a snowman too, so she wouldn't have to go to bed, and could have fun all the time. For just a second, Frosty looked like he was angry, terribly angry, but then he smiled, sort of, and told her that sometimes it wasn't fun being a snowman. He said sometimes it was like you had gotten snow inside your boots and your gloves and down your neck, except that you could never go inside and get warm again. The little girl snuffled back a tear and hugged Frosty, because she was sorry for him.

The next time the kids came back Frosty was playing with some dead rabbits and squirrels. He said it was a lot of fun. The kids thought that was neat, and persuaded him to let them play too, all except for a couple of girls who thought it was too gooshy since some of the animals' parts had come off. Frosty tried to show the children some games to play with the animals, but they were complicated, and too icky for even the boys to enjoy them very much.

Then he tried to teach magic words to the kids again, but pretty soon he had to give up and tell them stories instead. He told them about more kids who had mean parents, and all the stories had happy endings. The kids clapped and cheered.

Then Frosty became very serious and told them he wouldn't be around for very much longer. The kids were sad when they heard this, but Frosty said not to be, because he'd be back again some day—if they did him one special favor after he was gone. He wouldn't tell them what the special favor was, but he told them that when they did it, it would always be winter in the town, or that the town would go to where it was always winter, the kids couldn't quite figure it out, but Frosty made it sound like it would be great fun. When they had done that, then Frosty would be able to come back, and he'd send all the mean parents away for good, and he could even play with the children again. *I'll be able to play with you forever,* he said. *Forever, and ever, and ever.*

The very next day was the beginning of spring, and it was warm enough that the snow started to thaw. Suddenly scared, the children all rushed out to see Frosty, and they were almost too late, because, sure enough, he was melting too. Just about all the girls and even some of the boys started bawling then, since Frosty was dripping and getting slushy, and his bottlecap eyes fell off. With all the water rolling off his face it looked like he was crying too.

Then Frosty told all the kids to be quiet and listen to him carefully. First he told them to take care of his hat when he was gone, very good care. Then he gave them some pieces of paper with crayon-writing all over them, and said that it was a *rich-ool*. He said that when the calendar told them it was the right day they had to do the things the rich-ool told them to do. It was hard to understand what he was saying, because his mouth was getting all mushy. *You have to promise to do it and not tell your parents,* he said, *cross your heart and hope to die,* and he looked really awful now, with pieces of him falling off onto the ground all over, so the children managed to stop crying long enough to promise Frosty they'd do it, they'd do whatever he told them.

After everyone had done with all the promising, Frosty seemed to quiet down. He said a few more things, but since his mouth was almost melted right off, no one could understand him. It sounded a little like he was laughing. Finally he fell over and broke up into little pieces, and then the pieces shrank away, and then all that was left was his old silk hat.

The kids stood around and cried for a bit, but it was getting late and dinner would be ready soon. They passed the rich-ool around to see if anyone could understand it—but it turned out that nobody could read very well yet. They just hadn't had the heart to tell that to Frosty. All they could make out were some stars and triangles and some pictures of more gooshy animals. They would have asked their parents what it meant, but they had promised not to let them see it. Finally they gave the rich-ool to a boy who said that he would take it home, staple it together, put a nice title page on it, and take care of it as if it were one of the most important assignments his teacher had ever given him. It was soon lost and was never seen again.

The little blonde girl took Frosty's hat, and she really meant to take good care of it, but when she tried to put it on her dog's head, he grabbed it in his mouth and ran away. She found it again a few days later, but it was all torn up and covered in dog drool, so she had to throw it out.

But still, all the children remembered their snowman friend, though they sometimes forgot some of the stuff he'd done, and sometimes remembered other stuff that he actually hadn't done, and when they grew up and had children of their own, they told them all the wonderful story of Frosty the snowman, and how he came to life one day. •

CROSSROADS

Wesley Herbert

Scatter the highway.
The world all went to hell.

The sand grows over the black asphalt like spider webs. When I drive over it I crush the highway. Sand melts under the tires, gets kicked up in the air behind my tail fins. The skin on my left arm wants to shed, a snake on a rock in the summertime. I've left it hooked out the window too long.

Kat's asleep in the front seat, seen sideways out of the corner of my eye. The faded blue-jeans with too many holes. Yellow fingers of hair occasionally slip into a fast-forward twitch across one cheek. One strand looks for the pink tongue inside her mouth, which is half open, ready for the kiss a lover would give. Lips have no makeup but they're red. I want to kiss her, or laugh.

I smile and keep driving. It's a stretch but I reach over and take the cigarette case from the dash. It's hot from being in the window. I light one of Kat's herbal cigs with the tarnished Zippo lighter. My thumbnail follows the words on it: *Live to Ride, Ride to Live*. It and the case get left on the seat beside me. The landscape beyond the window bends away. One shadow by the side of the road gets bigger, grows into the rotting skull of a car: headlight sockets dull and empty, gap-toothed smile of a broken grille.

Over the baffle of the wind through the open windows, Jezzy's small voice tells half the words of the song she's mimicking. She'd taken my Walkman and Kat's card deck in the morning, trying to lay out the tarot and listen to my music alone in the big back seat. In her way, she wants to understand how both work. Jez is nineteen today. An imitation of me.

The derelict car slides by, an arrow in the passenger door, a long red scrawl of spray paint written on it.

"REPENT"

Goddamn Christian fundamentalist crazies.

You see everything on Route 66.
That's why we're here.

The interstate took most of the traffic from old 66. Somebody had left the gas station from the fifties. It had the lines of a Flash Gordon ray-gun emplacement. Pitted chrome and radiating fins in faded red paint would fit on the cover of an old *Amazing Stories* fanzine. The spaceman with his neutron pistol would be jet-packing over the building against the eerie backdrop of foreign stars. Unfamiliar planets with green and blue rings hover menacingly close. The '62 Mercury is a small starship drydocked to fill up its tank on Premium Leaded Hydrogen.

I get out, stretch every muscle. From my fingers down to my ankles. There's a middle-aged guy in greasy jeans near the giant ray-gun. I can smell the hot beans in the plate settled on his lap.

"Fill her up yourself. If you don't mind," he adds the last like an apology.

He's got the brittle. Crystal brittle. Not as bad as ones who went over the day the earth stood still, but if I hit him hard, he'd shatter. I ruffle at the smell of gasoline, put the nozzle in the tank's mouth anyway. Bits of sand give me eyelash kisses against the skin of my arms, my face. I buy a Coke with some change and lint from my pockets. The sun is getting real low, taking the New Moon with it; both burn in red frost. I pay for the gas.

Kat's in the driver's seat, fiddling with the radio. Slide guitars sing in and out over the speakers. Jez has her elbows spread on the front seat headrest. The headphones around her neck a fixture of junk jewelry.

"*¡Hola!* Kursey, can I have some?" Jez sticks a skinny arm out to take the can.

"Where are we now?" Kat looks back over her shoulder.

"'Bout an hour into Arizona. You drivin' now?"

She nods, experimentally holding her hair back in one hand.

"It's close now."

"It?" I sit down to eye level, my boots making gravel noises. "You gonna tell me before we get there?"

Jez gives me back the pop can, her white arm snakes back inside. She takes a red elastic spread around three fingers like a cat's cradle to tie up Kat's hair. Huh, Kat's cradle. I wait for an answer.

Kat looks out the windscreen, at the sun.

"You should get in the car," she says, "Don't worry, we won't be there tonight."

I have heard this before, Kat evading questions, I know I'll get no answers. I get in the car. Have a drink. Kat is watching the long muscles in my throat work. Gulp, gulp. Maybe she doesn't know how much I see and hear. I reconsider. She knows.

"How long does this desert go on?" I settle into the same corner Kat had slept in.

"You've seen the map, you know." Kat shrugs.

"No deserts in Panama," I smile, a row of even teeth. I am missing only one.

My time is coming.
Panama was a while ago.

My eyes pop open. Jim Morrison. The luminescent dash leaves glow trails burned across my vision till I adjust. I push out from the shirt I'm sleeping under. Lots of big noise. Kat bobs her head, green light catching on her chin, her lashes, her ears that are a bit too long, a bit too sharp towards the end. Outside it's black, only I can see the Old Moon putting a gilt edge on the highway. I yawn from my jaws to my toes. The radio.

"Katja, what the hell is this?" Jezzy complains. She was sleeping too.

"Hey, it's the Doors," Kat grins, "You don't get music like this anymore."

The elaborate prophecies of Morrison keep me awake

until my eyes get heavy. My chin hits my chest and I close them.

I go back to sleep.
In the morning we'll be at the crossroads.

I wake up in a different landscape, my eyes lidded down with sleep. The car rests on an angle, on the soft shoulder of the gravel road. Jez and Kat are gone, the yellow light bulb of the rising sun has woken me. I get dressed in the front seat, jeans and my leather jacket, open the doors and rest my toes on cold, prickly gravel. I stomp my feet into my cowboy boots. The boots are more worn and scarred than the jacket, but younger. The creases around the ankles are the deep lines of an old man's face.

We aren't in the sun-bleached land of the cold desert; we drove all night. There are shaggy heads of trees and gently lapping waves of long-stalked grain. Farmers' country. Farmers have the earth in their veins like chocolate syrup. When the Goddess came back, farmers just met an old friend. I think. Think twice. I open the glove compartment, scatter a lot of odds and ends. The plastic gun is near the back. I pull it out, a cool heaviness under my fingers. A leather thong has been wrapped around the trigger guard, at the end is a small ebony cat. I remember it now, bought from a half-Indian jewelry maker in Utah. I hold it up to the sun and squint with one eye to make out black on black nose and ears. Its lines are unintentionally Egyptian. Bast. The goddess of cats. I smile; it creeps up on one corner of my mouth, breaks my whole face into a grin. I unwind the thong and put it around my neck. The automatic I leave sticking out of the belt of my jeans at the spine. Clint Eastwood. Bang, bang!

I have never fired this gun.
Kat and Jezzy came back.

We walk up the road. The dust seems cleaner in the new morning light. I maneuver a thick slice of fresh bread, warm butter and honey running between my knuckles.

The bread is good enough just to smell. I wish I had a small room to set the bread down where I could digest my breakfast nasally. I have apples in my pockets, a glass bottle of milk tucked cold and smooth under one arm.

"This farmer was generous," I say.

"*Si*, generous," Kat mimics me, "He did not even have a gun." She gives me a harsh sideways look, a disappointed mother.

I give my best disarming smile.

"Not everyone respects your talents. I like to be careful." I am remembering the Christian graffiti of yesterday. "What happened anyway?"

"He had bad *sidhe* in his garden patch."

I consider. "It couldn't be rabbits?"

"No, it's *sidhe*," she says.

Jezzy is licking a thumb. "What's *sidhe?*"

"Pixies," Kat explains, "Manitou, Brownies, Tengu, Faeries, Elves. Mischievous spirits. I made a stone altar and left bread and cider to the Goddess—"

"You said Brigid and Demeter before," Jezzy interrupts again.

"They're all Mother Earth," Kat says, maybe annoyed. "I marked the soil so the spirits would play somewhere else."

Jez is younger today, her mid-teens. Perched on the end of her nose, the matte-black sunglasses are too big around her eyes. Her clothes all fit like a girl in her mother's old dress. She is blonde with a smooth round face. Different from yesterday's long black hair. She smears honey out of the corner of her mouth with one hand. I wonder what her real age is. At times, like now, she is almost a child. I imagine her as one of the cherubs from an old fabric softener commercial. I can't make it last long. Perhaps Kat sees her true nature, as she does all others. Old enough for Kat to love, anyway.

I see where we are walking. Nothing in the sky moves. Hot wind pulls up orange soil and sings it past us. It's at my back, around the gun, in the fine hairs at the nape of my neck. It kicks up its heels, dust-devils waltz into the middle of the road. Katja kneels to open her bag in a movement so gentle I don't notice until she is standing again.

She's in the center of the two dirt roads, they rise to meet each other. A square post leans outwards in age. I guess it used to have some sign. I feel a reluctance to follow Kat, a fear of being run down by traffic that is hidden behind the next bush. It is the crossroads speaking. Someone with no ears could hear it.

Kat stops and holds out her arms palms up, tan with white on the insides. I reach to my neck, trickle the wood cat into her left hand. In her right, Jezzy puts a green braid of three side road daisies. Kat draws a circle around herself with one bare foot. Inside her protection, she dangles a small iron arrow formerly of a weather vane. It's held by the center, a line of frayed leather and colored string. Wound up in her fist with the narrow line are the cat and flowers. A true fey couldn't hold so much iron, but Kat wasn't born in Eire of a *sidhe* princess. She was suckled on LSD and the Sex Pistols; television and the greenhouse effect; Starhawk and LeGuin. Magic doesn't work the same way now as it did for Taliesin.

Kat stands alone, says the words. The arrow spins on its tether. At places, iron finds magic like true north. It points at right angles to the wind. It's an arrow pointing down the road.

We follow the arrow.
It is not the last crossroads.

Seven kids squat around dice and a circle gouged in the concrete. My eyes swing over once, count. Seven. They are like children in the feria, in rags of denim and cotton T-shirts. More and more of those kids in Wondrous America than ever used to be; not so much the difference between rich and poor, but between lost souls and survivors. The Chicago slum smell of boiling laundry, roast chicken from a nearby restaurant, rotten garbage. I sit on the corner of the car fender, one tone darker in the shade. One leg swings, the heel of my boot spurring the steel flank. The kids pick up the idle movement, one cat watching another cat twitching tail. My hands move over the pistol I have. Gunmetal green plastic a quick toy in my fingers. I look at

it. Smile. I rub it with a red bandanna. It has *Glock-17*
stamped in the side. A brand name. A dead Columbian had
it when it came to me. One hand had been sawed off, something I hadn't seen before. With the guerrillas in El Salva-
dor, I found out. He'd had a briefcase manacled to his arm.
What was in it was much more expensive than the gun. I
eject each bullet by hand, heavy lead pills drop into my
palm. It can hold seventeen. I count. Only eleven. There
are always eleven.

One of the kids is watching the gun. I reload it. They bob
and cluck over the dice. Jezzy sits beside them, younger
again today. Her bare knees are up almost to her shoulders. The dice scatter and kick. Nobody has touched them.
Manna Ferals, the first to be born fey, grew up with it. I
hear the *chick chock* of big plastic dice and Jezzy betting
odds. Something hot presses between my shoulders, like
someone staring at me. This city stabs at me. The bricks
and steel trees supporting floor upon floor are all glass
inside. The brittle. The cities went bad, science atrophied,
technology became a shriveled apple. I hate the city. I can
feel the casket closing.

Kat has a brown paper bag open on the hood. The bag is
so crumpled it's soft. One of the kids, pre-pubescently
scrawny, is rolling a peyote bud across the palm of his
chalky hand. Kat is selling to keep us rolling. The air is
cool under the shelf of the parking garage. The blacks of
my eyes sink and widen quicker than most. Quick as the
old man.

He comes in with a gun waving. In my eye he's pushing
through amber. His arm is still frames of a movie; advance, click, advance one more. Slow. Spit rolls out of his
scraggly mouth, slow. Kat is speaking, words she hasn't
taught me before. His hands flare up like matchheads. His
feet stop running under him. The skid of steel when his
gun hits the ground. The hoots of the kids bouncing off the
ceiling, out into the heat, and they're all over him. They
pin his old, but whole, hands to the ground. White magic.
Kat's illusion.

"Bastard children," he screams out of syphillated lips.
"Satan's spawn risen again from hell! The end is near,

abominations. God shall not permit your presence in heaven or earth. You are doubly damned, you who worship not the one True God!" He is sweating in fanaticism, or fever. Eyes rove in his head, searching for the bolt of lightning to strike us down. "The end of the world is nigh," his voice scrawls out.

"No, old man." Jezzy is almost kneeling on his chest, a sea of laughing Ferals around her, "It's only just begun."

Relic of the old world.
They told us about the movie.

I watch. The movie is old, a midnight show, but the lot is full. A tent and RV city around the big screen. It's funny, the things that came back. When their brave new world died, people turned to the icons of the past. Drive-ins, for instance. I pick at a hot dog Jez left on the dash and watch the film. It is a story of humanity and God and destiny. Where did we come from? Where are we going? How long have we got? The questions of the crossroads.

From where I sit on the dash, I have a perfect view of the movie. My eyes slit open wide. I take it all in. Jez is straddled on Katja in the back seat, both hands cupped around the small, perfect breasts of her lover. Jez's features do a slow photo-dissolve. For a moment she is all races and none. She changes. Her nose is shorter, broader, her cheek bones delicate and sculpted, hair fuller and more yellow; the morph extends along to the tips of her ears, longer, more angular, pointed. Change ripples down from her shoulders. The rest of her body becomes longer and curved, her breasts the same roundness as Kat's.

Katja opens her eyes and looks into a mirror of herself. Jez feels for the first time how far she's given over to her lovemaking. She grins sheepishly.

"Sorry, I wasn't concentrating."

Katja, the true Kat, laughs. Slow at first, but she lets herself into it until tears are rolling down her cheeks. Jezzy starts too, in the same voice. That last is too much for me. I jump to the car seat and out the open window. Outside, nobody notices me, a dark-haired cat on darker ground. I wait under a nearby car, cool asphalt under padded feet. My ears reel back and I can hear Jezzy's voice.

"Hey, watch this!"

Both girls howl in laughter that even humans could hear this far away.

It's late. The movie is almost over and I can hear the rain coming. I have roamed too far, to the concessions stand. I make the trip back fast. In the day I can see from the height of a six-foot tower. By night the movie lot is an endless range of hills. I wear no talismans and have no voice to petition the wind. Hold a little longer, I say.

The rain is streaming down. I think the Trickster is sitting on the clouds with a garden hose, pissing on my head. I take pride in my cat-ness. I cut a nice figure, even among cats, but my fur has turned on me. I walk the rest of the way to the car. Even whiskers droop with water. The windows traditionally steamed up, I can find no way in. I parade along the trunk of the car with my pitiful routine. One step, raise a paw and shake it. Two steps, then shiver. I check with the corner of my ear. They talk softly to each other inside; they haven't noticed. The hell with this.

I howl. I howl a song learned from every city tom and alley cat opera star in twenty states and six countries. I have learned, also, that it's fun. I pour my soul, my heart into a symphony of despair and longing. Should a cat someday understand it, he would love Beethoven, and the Blues.

A rear window squeals downwards. "Kursey, c'mon boy!" I jump in the back window, landing in Jezzy's lap. I shake a layer of mud and wetness around me. Kat and Jez jump back like I'd brought a dead groundhog with me. Hey, I've learned since then.

Kat smiles, "Sonofabitch, I bet you planned that."

I force a smile onto carnivore jaws reserved for bird-ripping and crunch-mousing. So maybe I did.

Blade Runner was a good movie.

Kat does love us both.

•

At the border there isn't even a guard anymore. No gates, not a fence. Like there never was one. They used to burn a hundred-foot path along the 49th parallel with Agent Orange. Used to. There's nothing but the trees and the road now, always the road. The forest takes back its own but leaves the frozen tar slick. The front doors of the car are open like a beetle's shell pinned inside a glass case. The ground is cold through my jeans, my elbows rest on crossed legs. Eyes closed. I feel the cold mist out of the ground, the wet combed trees, the sun cutting its space in the sky from the clouds. It reminds me of the jungle. Except the cold. This day is good, it's like the dark. The sun is too hard, it cuts the line too clean; at night there's a softer edge, everything is gray again.

There is a knife in my boot strapped around my leg. I open my eyes, reach and pull the knife out; a rubber grip and 8-inch blade for diving. Softgrind out of the sheath. The box is dirty but sort of new. Peeled leather still mostly on. It's what the Columbian had been missing, a briefcase. I compare the blade to the lock's mouth. Serrated steel edge like a shark's smile before his eyes roll back. I put it away, find the complicated smallness of the Swiss Army knife instead.

I play with the combination lock a few times but one number is frozen up. Each adapter on the knife takes its turn to pry it open. Jez comes from the car, older than me today, and different. She wears a skirt long enough to reach her ankles, almost, and her boots and my jean jacket. Nothing else. She stops across from me and sits. Her boots drag dirt. I continue with each blade. Nothing works. Jez is still waiting but bored. There is a chubby fullness to her hands, her face, the curve of her breasts down the open front of the jacket. The tightest long ringlets of hair collect around her shoulders, the color of red wine.

"You could spell it open." Her voice, at least, is the same as yesterday's.

I don't look up, "That's not the point."

"You could open it but you won't?" She knits pale eyebrows.

"Kursey's sleeping, Jezzy." Kat's voice. She sits on the

car seat, turns over yellow hair with her hand.

"He sleeps with his eyes open then," Jezzy shrugs.

"He's the Sleeping Giant, Jez. He could've opened it when you found it, but he only works as hard as he has to." Katja's voice is smiling. A professional joke. There is a crooked curve to the side of her mouth.

I collapse my army knife. "Patience is a virtue of the crossroads, Kat. You should know that as well as I do." I take the leg knife and put it between the lids of the case. When my hand comes down, the blade goes through the weak point and it opens.

Satisfied, the knife goes away happily. Jez is already inside the box. She pulls out what she wants. I watch. Each treasure has less to do with the items before it. A pen, gloves, a diaphragm, garden shears, a coffee mug, men's underwear, a glass eye, some dominoes, a dog collar, a crab fork, a faucet, postcards, a bow tie, a bicycle pump, gauze, T-pins, a light bulb. She spreads a semicircle of them around herself. It's like a puzzle. She waits, switches the places of two. Squints to see. She turns one sideways and watches again. Funny. How she learns. Benefits of a crossroads education.

It's got no sense to it until I see the last thing rolling at the bottom of the case. I pick it up with a thumb and forefinger, roll it back and forth. I blow on it like a birthday candle and the dust comes away. The imprint reads in a circle, *9 mm*.

"Watcha got, Kursey?" Jez watches my hand.

I reach into my pocket, take out the red bandanna and the gun. I polish the bullet; when it goes into the clip, it's like it always belonged. Waiting for me to find it. Twelve. I count. There's always twelve. One day there'll be all seventeen. That'll be the last day. Count Zero, Ragnarok. Kat is singing to herself. Janis Joplin or Patsy Cline, I can't tell which. There's a red apple in her hands; she cuts it in half through the width.

"Jezzy," she says, now only humming the tune. Jez switches attention, looks to her. "When Lilith came to Adam, she knew the apple, she knew its magic and knew the woman's spirit inside her. Because of this, Adam and the sky god, Yahweh, wouldn't have her. Yahweh made another first woman and told her the magic was bad, but the Goddess was smarter than he was and made sure even Eve found the magic in the apple. Long before, she'd taught Shaytan, the serpent, the wisdom of the moon's blood and set him to guard the knowledge and always test the judgment of his father, Yahweh. Shaytan told Eve what Yahweh didn't want her to know was in the apple." Kat opens the halves, shows the star on the wet background. Magic symbol long before the Christians were born. "And that's part of the reason Christians followed Yahweh's war against the Goddess, that's how they almost won by burning out Mother Earth." Kat puts her eyes on me. "That's why Kursey wears so much leather; he thinks that in the back of everyone's head is a fear that he'll shed his skin like a big snake."

"That's Carl Sagan and Thunder Lizards," I shake my head, "not the Midgard Serpent."

Kat gives half the apple to Jezzy, goes back to singing. Lesson over. If I asked, Jezzy could tell me the whole thing, word for word. She's fast, Kat's apprentice. Kat hums again while she chews.

Jez holds the apple in her teeth, sits over her pathway spread of debris. Her eyes get funny and half closed. A patchwork of light bounced off shiny bits hits her face. It's calm but I can smell her magic working. Her head turns sideways, considering. Listening. A wind is coming at our backs; it's how they speak to us, the wind spirits, it's how we know. Change is coming.

"It was a man," Jezzy tells me. "This was his." She licks her lip, head turns even steeper, "He had two children and he talked to them on a wire from far away—"

"Telephone, Jez," Kat corrects softly, but the seer has no hearing. She talks like no one's there.

"He was small and he had no world but his work. He talked with computers more than he talked to people." She rubs her hands on the grass, to get them clean.

"That's how things used to be," Kat says.

"You'd like to think those days gone, Kat. It's still a long way off." I lift the gloves from the pile of odds and try them on.

"What?" Jezzy looks up.

"You see, Kursey, you've scared her now." Kat sits next to her and sweeps the junk into a pile with her hands, "Don't sweat it, Jez, things are different now."

I've seen the things done with computers, some good, some bad. Not so much the problem with the machines as the times they got used in.

The wind has arrived. Mist and grit push us on. Jezzy and Kat wait in the front seat, engine running. The last fingertips come off the thin leather gloves. I reach back and toss the ends at the sky. Wind dogs pick them up and chase them through the air. Gloves on, I pitch the garden shears. Underhand throw lets them bounce and roll like a pinwheel. Kicking up dirt and flecks of peeling brown paint to blow away. I don't wait to see them stop and close the door behind me. The car pulls away.

The briefcase was waiting for us.
We have come the right way.

Time. Time enough. I am young: my life measured in cat-naps. Kat is older. She has always been Kat, always will be; even I can only guess at when she truly comes from; after all, she and I are only the most glorified kind of hitch-hiker and traveler. And Jezzy, she is what she feels. There are leftover mountains in Ontario. Not the big mountains of the west, but the oldest rock in the land, so old they've been worn down to hills. Clean cuts of valley and stands of slope hills. Even some trees. I remember some of the fey that roost hereabouts, piecing together what the Old World left of clear-cut deserts. I could never do it, stay put and heal the land, but I respect the ones who do. Selfish maybe, to want answers instead, but I do.

The road runs ahead. Heat spirits sway off the blacktop. There are miles before I can meet sleep again, but the gloves make me feel like a racer. One eye on the road, I give the radio tuner a random twist. Sure must be something better than so-called CBC. I can't see the dial for all the talismans on the dash. More hanging from the rear view mirror. Empty brass shells click with a gold pocket watch. Strings of copper pennies with holes knocked through. Caribou and gecko bones with bleached drift-wood. Mistletoe and garlic. Tiny Chinese lanterns with silky tassels and string ties with steer skulls in pewter. A plastic Buddha is glued squarely in the middle of the dash. I smile back at him. Kat slaps my hand, turns off the radio.

"We can stop here."

The arrow pointed the way.
It was close enough to walk.

The trees around the crossed roads have a heavy green leafiness. Kat walks first, dappled in blue shadows of leaves. We hear our footsteps on gravel, the end of the road is only a spill of stones into long grass. But there is the church. Kat bends her back to see the spire above the trees. Funny how it's not there from the road. It's old and stone, ivy digging its long fingers into the walls. Wooden door broken or gone with just an arch of pitted stonework.

Jezzy whispers, "It's so old."

"No," says Kat. "Acid rain."

Our legs take us to the low steps. Light falls through the spread of trees to make a drapery of pale yellow around us. It's a small country church, not like the burned-out cathedrals I walked in Central America. Broken-out and falling-apart pieces of stained glass litter the front step. Kat walks in first. I forget, until glass snaps under my boots, that Kat has no shoes. My mouth pops half open to warn her but she's fine. She looks above and around. Steps make no noise. I close my mouth. Shrug. The Christian god of love could walk on water, couldn't he?

The air is thick and hot; only a cool whisper dips from the broken windows above. Pale half-light shows the in-side. The floor is swept clean. Only drifts of dirt and leaves pile in the corners. My eyes click around the room; top to bottom, side to side. No crosses. No censers. No holy rega-lia. Only the stubs of beeswax candles, ashes of charcoal incense and sprigs of oak.

"This isn't a holy place of Christians," I say.

Kat almost shakes her head. "But it is holy to someone."

Kat blinks. I listen and hear it outside. Sniff. Whoever she is, she is good to get so close before I can tell she is there.

"You guess right, do you want to know what you've won?" the woman says.

Kat smiles but keeps studying the altar. Only Jezzy turns to see her right away. I speak without looking.

"You should clean up the glass on the front step. If this is your place."

"I've been thinking of it." Her voice is kind. A polite pause. "My name is Karen. If I knew yours, we could have some tea."

Sometimes we find what we look for.
The best gifts are ones we don't expect.

The light is low in the trees. More orange than yellow. Inside I feel the contented ticking of my fey; it will be the time of cats soon. The tea is good; some herbal relaxer culled from the wild, and Karen dishes out rice and beans onto plates. There's ham for those of us who eat meat. Mainly me. Karen is a truer version of Jez's redhead. Pale and earthy and in her thirties with a delicate headful of long redbrown hair. She's a curandera. A witch, like us. Drowsy insects hang in the air around the courtyard, swim by me in the hazy air. I eat, but the sleepiness creeps up on me.

"Tell me about your crossroads," Karen says. The bells at the hem of her Indian cotton dress make little noises.

"The destinations aren't important," Jezzy pipes.

Karen folds her hands in her lap. "Yes. But why?"

Jez shifts and tucks her legs under her skirt. A moment of silence before Katja speaks up.

"There are places," Kat begins, and that silence falls heavy, "and times where the roads come together. I've heard him called Maître Carrefour, the Lord of the Cross-roads. Everyone with a little piece of the crossroads in them feels it. It's a need to move on, and find where the road ends. All roads lead somewhere."

"Rome, maybe?" Karen laughs.

Kat sniffs. "I thought of that. It doesn't fit."

We all eat for a while, and Jezzy keeps looking to Kat for an answer. I know Jez and I know Kat; one is worried there is no answer to Karen's question.

"They used to bury vampires at crossroads," Karen says, "and it used to be the spot to meet the devil, make a deal."

"The death card doesn't mean death," Kat counters, "it means change. The crossroads are sacred to Hecate too, the magic of different paths, some taken, some not. Crossroads are change, are chances."

Karen smiles, a genuine smile. "I thought you knew about the real magic. I had to be sure."

Kat blinks, then laughs with her. A teasing at the corners of her mouth. Jezzy's the only one who seems upset; she's learned to trust more than I have, but she doesn't read intentions so well yet.

The sun is on the edge of the world. In the dusk, the devas and hobs slip out from shadow to shadow. I spot two twig men and a pixie with a paper cup hat moonwalking. No sense of style, those little people.

"I'll tell you something," Karen pours cups of hard cider, "because I think it's what you need to hear. Mother Earth channels powers across the lands. Those ley lines are a good way to find answers, but the important part is, they don't always follow asphalt."

Karen's eyes rest on me. I stare back and she blinks first.

"And what about you, Sleeping Giant Kursey. What do you think?"

I consider. " 'There are more things in heaven and earth, Horatio, than are dreamt of in your philosophy.' "

"Now why," Karen laughs again, "do I think you might just be lazy? You'll have a chance soon, I bet, to prove me wrong."

We moved on a long way.
Only the ocean stopped our tires.

After it all, I wondered if the answers wouldn't be out

there. One afternoon one long day ago the '62 Mercury found me and I drove out of Panama for the road, and to find something. Find someone. I thought it was Katja when I met her; the way she dropped down in the front seat with nothing but her ripped-open jeans and bag full of medicine. "Just drive," she said. And later, after our first night together, I made the change back to human and she kissed me and said, "Let me tell you about the crossroads." But it wasn't Kat, and it wasn't Jez when we picked her out of a den shooting tarantula venom.

Only one person has the answers. It's the journey that's important, not where you go.

The waves crash up on the big beach, split on rocks and jump for the sky. Gull sound away overhead and the slow tick of the car engine while it cools. The sand gives and spreads under my heels. Kat is crouched over the wet sand, water runs up the beach and over her bare feet and ankles, then slides away. It brings the turtles up with it, to crawl up the beach. Even the wind has a cold wet feel, deep with salt smell.

"So, genius," Jezzy sits on the hood of the car and keeps a sand crab from slip walking off the edge of the car. Short kid today: teenage, brown hair, vitiligo spot on the side of her neck. On days she's bored, this is the shape she takes, and I wonder if maybe it isn't her true shape. "Now that we're here, how you gonna get us across?" she puffs. "Rainbow bridge? You gonna part water, Sleeping Giant?"

Kat walks back up the beach, curved wet footprints in the sand behind her, careful to walk around the she-turtles and mounds of dirt over fresh eggs.

"Let me tell you something," I say, "about spawning season."

Jez rolls her eyes, but Kat smiles a sympathy smile.

"Get in the car, we've got to drive over to that peninsula, there," I point. It's a mound of rocks on the edge of the shore; barely a finger of land connecting it to the mainland and covered in green trees and brush and birds.

I manage the car up to the crest of the rocky outreach and we get out again. Now with the view of the shore spread out behind, a sandy beach with rocky mounds studded into the sand and nearby islands of rocks. I pocket my sunglasses.

"Just watch," I nod.

For a moment, nothing, then one of the islands moves. Up, onto the beach. I send out my fey to touch the ground under our feet, and she talks back to me. Old, so much older than any of us. The land tilts slightly, water brushes off her shores, and slowly the whole grassy rock drifts out to sea. Just below the water, the shadow lines of barnacle-crusted green fins sweep through the shallows, and somewhere far ahead, the gleam of an eye.

Jez breaks into a smile and she melts down from the top of her head, changes into someone who could be my sister. "Way cool, Kursey!"

Kat puts an arm around me and slides her hand into my pocket. "The giant woke up today," she whispers.

"Well," I say, "we're all just adrift on Turtle Island, anyway. I figure, why don't I hitch a ride for a change, with one of her grandchildren."

The island rocks gently and a flight of birds wheels overhead, to land back in their nests. A couple of goats poke out of the brush to take a look, then go back to grazing.

"Where to?" Jez asks.

"She knows better than you or I," I say.   •

WHAT HAPPENED TO THE GIRL?
Wade Bell

I said, 2:12 p.m., March 15, 2012. That's all I said. She asked me the time and I told her. I threw in the date for the hell of it, because it was there on the face of my watch. There's no law against that, is there?

I didn't think so, though you have to admit it's hard to keep up.

Other than that? No, not a word.

No, I did not see her go in. No, I did not see her come out. No, I had nothing to do with it. No, I tell you. I'm hungry and I want to go home.

No, I had no particular business here. No, I was going to meet no one. No, I do not usually find myself in this neighborhood. No. I was with no one.

That's right, I had no business here.

No, I did not know the girl in question. Yes, I would say she was a stranger to me, yes, an absolute stranger.

No, not a pretty girl. Common looking would be more like it.

Of course I was aware that she was beside me on the bench. What do you think, I have no eyes to see, or ears to hear or nose to smell?

Her perfume.

Yes, she was wearing perfume.

Well, if you like, yes, I did find it odd. But I am of another generation, girls of that age now, who knows?

A good perfume, an expensive cologne.

Not eau de cologne, no.

No.

Because you didn't ask me before. It was a sensation that was there and then gone. Do you think I wanted to make a memory of it, to hold on to it and then take it out and use it later on?

I mean take it out and use it for my own purposes. Private purposes.

No, her legs were covered by loose trousers.

I didn't look at her.

I didn't look at her that way.

She was a form. A young female form on the bench beside me in the park in the sun on a warm Friday morning in March. What do you think, that she was dressed for the beach? It is March, after all.

A sweater. A heavy sweater. Brown.

She was too young.

I don't know. I didn't notice.

Hardly developed at all, then, if that's what you want to hear.

A glance. One glance. Two. She carried a paper bag. A small paper bag. It could have been her lunch. It could have been popcorn or something else to feed the pigeons.

I don't know what else. What sort of stupid question is that? Whatever else pigeons might like.

No, I don't feed pigeons. No. I have other things to do with my money than buy food for pigeons. Would I get points if I did?

A pension.

Yes, that's all. And a small one at that.

I have no criminal record.

I have no criminal record.

No, I am not in the habit of loitering. I have things to do with my time. Some of them even you might consider worthwhile.

I was not loitering.

No. I do not loiter.

Even the word is ugly and offensive. I do not do ugly and offensive things.

I find that question offensive. You have no right to be offensive with me.

I would not say she was pretty, no. I would say she was plain.

A bag in her hands, yes.

No, she did not feed the pigeons. No. She did not open

the bag.

I would have heard the paper rustle.

No, I did not hear her clothes rustle. What sort of question is that?

Well, maybe I did. Do you hear my clothes rustle if I shift my body? Do you hear me move? And if you do, will you remember that you did five minutes from now? I think you are being very stupid, you know. You're wasting your time and mine.

No, I would not say I lack respect for authority.

No, I would not say I lack feeling. Perhaps I am more upset than you think by what happened to the girl.

I did not see her come out of the alley, I tell you.

I know, because I can imagine that something dreadful must have happened to her. Why else would you be interrogating me?

A yellow sweater.

Brownish yellow.

Only slacks. Shapeless. Plain. Ordinary. What else can I tell you?

One glance. Two. Maybe three.

Blonde.

I have no sexual habits.

Prove it? How can one prove one has no sexual habits? If you found photographs in my apartment, certain books, you might prove otherwise, but how can you prove I'm celibate? And I mean celibate in both mind and body.

Once, yes. Long ago.

No, no children.

Children are fine. I have no thoughts about them one way or another.

Could it not be a coincidence that we shared a bench?

Blood? Are you joking? Of course they would find no blood on my clothing. Was there blood?

I'm not thinking anything. I'm just being silent for a moment. After all, if you say there was blood...

Well, you indicated there was blood. You brought up the subject of blood.

Then there was no blood.

No, I know I have no right to be told. I am neither a

relative or a friend of hers.

I said I was not a friend.

Oh, shit, here we go again!

No, I am not in the habit of using foul language. Sometimes I do, of course. Who doesn't?

No, it indicates nothing about my character. You are being stupid.

Age gives me the right to call you stupid.

No, age does not give me the right to be uncivil. I apologize.

No, I do not have a violent temper.

She said nothing to me.

Nothing. Nothing.

No.

I told you. I was not acquainted with her.

No, I did not see her on the street. I did not follow her to the park. I was sitting on the bench before she arrived.

I did not lure her. I did not even see her until she sat down.

Fourteen, thirteen. The way they dress these days...

She was dressed plainly. I meant others, other young girls. They all look older than they are.

Of course I notice young girls. It would be impossible to be alive and not notice young girls.

Fifty-eight. Soon to be sixty. Soon to lose more points just because I've grown old.

August fourteenth nineteen fifty-two. It's right there on my driver's license.

Yes, I got up and left shortly after she did.

A minute, maybe two.

Yes, maybe less. Maybe half a minute. Do you think I looked at my watch?

Because I wanted to leave. The sky was clouding over. It was obviously going to rain.

Perhaps we both noticed the clouds at the same time.

No, no comment at all, no remarks, not one word.

If I followed her, it was unwittingly.

I clearly couldn't make it home before the rain started. I thought I would spend some time in the department store there.

I didn't know I was following her.

I did not catch up with her.

To the department store.

Underwear, socks. I needed some things. I hadn't planned to shop, but if a rain shower was going to delay my walk home, I thought I could put the time to use by buying a few things I needed.

No, I did not go into the store immediately.

No, I ducked into the alley.

Perhaps I saw something there. I don't know. I don't think so.

No, I can't explain what I saw. Movement, perhaps. Perhaps nothing.

Boxes, garbage bins, a couple of parked cars. Maybe a van. I'm not sure.

Yes, I had a moment to look.

No, no people.

Well, if there was movement, then it must have been people because the vehicles and the garbage bins didn't move.

White. Dirty. A dirty white delivery van, some years old.

No, don't ask me why.

Because I had to go to the bathroom.

It happens sometimes.

Because I couldn't recall where the bathrooms were located in the department store, I didn't know how long it might take me to find them...

Yes, it was sudden. My bladder works that way now.

How could I have known she went into the alley ahead of me? I didn't see her. How can you say I followed her if I didn't see her go in?

Then I went into the department store.

Ten minutes, twenty.

I didn't like the price.

Seventy-nine dollars for a pair of cheap socks. If you want to talk about a crime, talk about inflation.

No, I am not being flippant.

But I don't know what happened to her. If you say it was serious, then it was serious. I have to believe you, don't I?

Yes, I came back out. Of course I came back out. I didn't

buy anything so I came back out.

I walked across the street.

Yes, to the park again.

I suppose I passed the alley. Yes, I must have.

No, I didn't go into it again. I had no reason to.

The same bench, the same bench as before, yes.

The storm clouds seemed to be passing. I wanted to consider whether I should walk home or take the bus.

Yes, I was sitting there when the police vehicle arrived. Yes.

Why should I have run?

If there are witnesses who saw me go into and out of the alley, that is because I went into and came out of the alley.

No, I saw no one in the alley.

I don't care what you think. You have no right to assume anything at all about me.

I even have the right to lie to you. Do you know that?

The human right. The human right to lie.

Uncooperative, yes.

Antisocial, no. Asocial, yes. I've never really thought about it.

Ask what you like. I won't guarantee the truth of my answers anymore.

Not a word.

No, not one word.

I have no idea.

Never.

No. Never.

That's right. Two hundred and fourteen points. Do you know yet how many the girl had?

Why not? Are the computers down? I thought information like that was at your fingertips.

Because in the end that's what it will come down to, won't it? The weight of the law will rest most easily on whoever has the most points, isn't that right?

Everybody knows that's the way it works. Have you ever known a man with a thousand points or more to even be tried for a crime, let alone punished for one?

Of course I agree with the new system. How could any sane person not?

Two hundred and fourteen, I said. The computers will confirm it. An average count.

Barely average, then. Only fourteen points above the shadow category but still officially above it.

I lost points for the divorce, for one thing. That's automatic.

A few points for causing rows when my wife and I were in the fighting stage. The apartment block warden was very alert to our troubles. Neighbors complained about us.

Five or six points. We weren't that bad.

The quality of my education. They say it doesn't matter but it does. A dentist or a doctor or an engineer has to do a lot to lose points, a college dropout, well...

Of course I'm speculating. In the absence of public information about the administration of the system, everyone speculates.

They only tell us what they want to. One year you've got X number of points, the next year X minus so many. Sometimes they add points, but again, rarely for the average person like me.

Average, I said. As far as I know I'm still in the average category.

Last year? Three hundred and fourteen.

Drunk driving. A hundred frigging points off right there.

I thought you meant arrested for other things. I paid for that one, a hundred points off.

Because I hit another vehicle and injured a man who had more points—a lot more points—than I had. If it had been the other way around, if he'd been the one to hit me, he would have lost only five or six points.

For not finishing my university program. That hurt. That set me back right at the start.

No, I'm not bitter. Of course I'm not bitter. I'm not complaining. It's a good system. Everybody knows that. It's solved a lot of society's problems. I voted to put the system in place. Baseness is part of human nature. We are all not perfectible. Some people are better than others. The truth of that has always been known; acknowledging that truth in our legal system was a huge leap forward.

Of course I'm not saying that to get on the good side of

you. I probably know the system better than you do because I was around at the very beginning of the debate
about it. I heard all the arguments not only for it but
against it as well. You were scarcely born then.

Well, you were pretty young.

The rating system? Yes, sometimes the simplest ideas
are the most effective. And the idea of keeping an individual's rating strictly confidential, the idea of giving it out
to us each year along with the verification of our income
tax return, now that was brilliant. The man who thought
that up was given an Order of the Nation, you can be sure
of that. Two thousand points. An untouchable. Do you
know you can't even sue somebody with an Order of the
Nation. They're gods.

Don't worry. I'm not blaspheming. I'm just envious of
those types. Who wouldn't be? Two thousand points and
they get more each year just for being alive! They say it's
for service to the country, but I'm sure it's just for being
alive, for being such good people. I'm sure it is. Bloody
right, they're untouchable. Untouchable by the likes of you
and me! But maybe you're a hero or something. Maybe you
saved the lives of a gaggle of school kids.

I know I'm not supposed to know the girl's number, but
when it comes over the radio I'll hear it, won't I?

Don't worry.

You know as well as I do that the ratings are not as secret as they're supposed to be. People have ways of finding
out their neighbor's number. Everyone is corruptible. Otherwise we wouldn't need our system, would we?

No, I wouldn't say I was a cynic. A realist, perhaps, but
I don't think a cynic.

For fighting with my boss and quitting my job.

All right, for getting fired.

And a few points off before that because the workplace
warden decided I wasn't getting along well with my fellow
employees.

Asocial, yes. I must be asocial.

That's all I can think of. The divorce was the worst.

No, there was nothing else.

No. I've told you everything.

The divorce, the divorce. That took off a lot of points. How many times do I have to tell you?

Why are you pushing me? Why can't you leave me alone until we hear what the girl's point count is?

Is it any of your business? Is it really relevant to the fact that by accident I shared a park bench with a girl, a child, who later got into trouble, the nature of which you will not tell me?

No, my wife never had an abortion. At least not while she was married to me.

No, I have never molested children.

No, I have never knowingly put another's life in danger or run away from the opportunity to save someone from harm.

Drugs? Good God, no!

If I go to court. And that's a big if! You don't go to court for sitting on a park bench! Or for pissing in an alley! And if I don't go to court my record remains private even from you.

Look, it's not illegal to swear. You may not like it but it isn't illegal.

For collecting charity from the government while I was unemployed. All right? It takes a long time to regain those lost points. You have to work at your new job for years and get into no job related trouble before they hand those points back to you. I got ill and had to take my pension early, before I'd had the chance to earn those points back. What could I...?

Listen!

Don't worry, I'm waiting, I'll shut up.

See? Two hundred and fourteen points! Just as I told you!

What? Eighty-nine points? Did I hear right? Only eighty-nine points for the girl? Is that what they said? Unbelievable!

Amazing, yes! An undesirable! An authentic, official undesirable!

What could the poor kid have done in her short life to have lost so many points?

Yes, I know, it is sad. It's truly sad.

I wasn't laughing. Really, I wasn't laughing.

I know that does it. I know I'm free to go.

I will, I'll go. I was just thinking about that poor girl. I'm stunned. Really, I'm stunned. At her age, already less than a hundred points. What could she possibly have done?

Yes. I'm going.

Goodbye, then. And remember, most of the time I cooperated with you fully. Right? No points off for bad behavior.

Right?

Don't worry, I'm going.

No, you're wrong. I'm not lucky. I was telling you the truth. Whatever was done to her, I didn't do it. Even if she'd been the daughter of an Order of the Nation you couldn't have proved I did anything to her.

No, I promise. You won't catch me around this part of town again. Really, I promise.

Goodbye, then.

Yes, goodbye.

You stupid moron. It was popcorn in the bag. We did feed the pigeons. •

CIRCLE DANCE
Eileen Kernaghan

THE FIRST FIGURE:

A circle is a zone of magnified power. By concentrating energy within a confined space, the circle generates metaphysical resonances which manifest themselves in occult phenomena.

•

> *In order to begin any ritual circumstance a Circle must be cast. The Circle is generally nine feet in diameter. If possible, a permanent Circle should be painted or drawn on the floor. When this cannot be done, the Circle can be laid out with rope or string...*
>
> (A Book of Pagan Rituals)

Within the Magic Circle, which is green, are inscribed in flaming vermilion the infinitely various names of God. Outside the circle are nine pentagrams, equidistant. In the center of each one a small lamp burns; these are the fortresses upon the frontiers of the abyss.

•

Through the Circle the magician affirms her identity with the infinite. At the same time she affirms the limitation imposed by her devotion to the Great Work. No more does she wander aimlessly through the world.

•

THE SECOND FIGURE:

A circle is a one-dimensional shape perceived in two dimensions. Add a third and it becomes a tube, a cylinder, an orifice. Annular or probosciform, it takes on sexual connotations. The purity of the design is lost. Collapsed to a singularity, the circle sucks us through the event horizon into the regions of infinite density at the end of time.

•

Time is not linear, but circumambient. We are bathed in entropy as in amniotic fluid.

•

Time measures itself in rings of stone, in the moon's discarded shadow, in your face, your eyes.

•

Through the green circles of their years trees grow into time.

THE THIRD FIGURE:

Five ways to think about the universe:
as a silver egg,
as a finite yet unbounded sphere,
as the Great Serpent that devours its tail,
as an ever-widening loop of string,
as a mandala circumscribed by fire.

•

A circle is that which remains when anything is subtracted from itself. Signifying nothing, it implies all possibilities. It is the starting point from which all measurements are reckoned.

•

The nature of God is a circle
of which the center is everywhere
and the circumference is nowhere.
(attributed, variously, to Pascal; to *The Book of the Twenty-Four Philosophers,* an early medieval text; and to anon.)

•

In Her name praise all things circling, spiraling, whorled and cyclic. Praise orbs, spheres, helices, ellipses. Praise what spins, turns, revolves and gyrates. Praise moon and labyrinth and mirror. Praise pear. Praise pomegranate.

THE FOURTH FIGURE:

Love may be compared to the Circle of Perpetual Apparition: the boundary of that space around the elevated celestial pole within which the stars never set.

•

Awaken the coiled white serpent that sleeps below the belly. Enter the region of white light, the place of no sound in which all sound is imminent.

•

The language love speaks is circumspect, circuitous and circumlocutory.

•

Tonight your mouth is the circle
that defines my universe,
and I am the boundless circle
that surrounds you. •

THREE MORAL TALES

Dirk L. Schaeffer

ONE: THE SEA OF LIFE

> *Vampires do not experience emotion; they have*
> *developed an alternative mode of interaction instead.*
> *Forming close couples, over centuries together their*
> *personalities merge to the point where each is*
> *distinguishable from the other only in physical form.*
> (Frederik Falsch: *Psychodynamics*
> *of the Occult,* p. 183.)

—It's dark.

—Yes.

—Are we ready?

—Almost. How am I?

—Turn; ...a little too much color. Here.

—Umh. Sometimes I wish...

—Wish?

—We could see ourselves. It's such a—convenience. What would I do without you?

—Be a mess. But a beautiful mess.

—Not like you.

—Come on.

—Where are we going?

—That party, remember? At the gallery, some new artist.

—Oh. Am I all right now?

—Yes. Come on.

—In a hurry? Hungry?

—Yes. You aren't?

—Only a little. Maybe just a snack.

—I need more.

—Will you need help?

—Not if I'm in luck. If there are enough people, the time should be right for one.

—And you'll find her.

—Of course. Come on.

> *Vampires need not kill their feed. Like all crea-*
> *tures, they seek the warmth and flow of life. While*
> *blood is best, any fresh fluid—tears, sweat, urine,*
> *the secretions of sex—may sate them as well.*
>
> (ibid., p. 197.)

I found her, of course. Young, a little plump, and very ripe. I said the usual things: *Don't you think...? That's very perceptive... No, really, I never looked at it that way before...*

She was attracted, of course, but understandably hesi-tant: ripe. I offered interest, almost without lust, and the attraction won. We went to her place, for just a drink. Her roommate was out.

It was an apartment, no more, high enough for a view, interchangeable with thousands of others. I looked for the usual clues, books, music, pictures. There was little save fashion magazines: I complimented her on her clothes. Really? She made this one herself. We talked, we smiled, she drank.

It's much easier when you're not too hungry. I took my time to find the one. Lean, bearded, almost intelligent, something in media. I was fascinated and we went to his place. Brimming with lust, though I had other things in mind.

She was beginning to weave a little with the wine. She had opinions, it turned out. She looked me forthrightly in the eye, but shied away when I met her gaze. When my eyes found other places, she'd move or shift. Her breasts were soft, and her opinions could have been worse. As hesitation faded, anxiety grew; over her ripeness, a gentle sheen of perspiration appeared. Patience.

"You're not drinking," she noticed again.

"I don't drink—wine." Inevitably.

"That's not fair."

"Is grass fairer?"

"Oh. No, I don't...but you go ahead if you want."

I lit up and waited.

"Is it...?"

"Columbian... You're sure?"

"I know I shouldn't..."

"Why?"

"Well..." We smiled conspiratorially; I touched her hand; she blushed. Really. We smoked, we talked, she drank, we talked. Patience, patience.

There had only been wine at the gallery, which is best: other things change the taste. It had been easy, there, to fake a sip now and then, but it was harder here. And I had to ask for some, to keep him from switching. But that was the only problem; he did everything else for me. Soft lights, soft music, dance. A lovely clean smell, close: the arousal, working its way through the bland antiperspirant. And that lean body, flat in front, just rightly rounded behind. I couldn't resist his ass and it turned him on. He moved against me, rising.

"Let's do some coke." I put the wine glass down.

"Oh, yeah. Do you...?"

"Umh-hmm." I spread it on the coffee table.

"I—" The other pressure grew. "Excuse me, I'll be right back."

"No, wait." I took his hand. "Help me fix this."

He was torn, but my fingers brushed the front of his fly. He sat down and we sniffed, then leaned back to let it take.

He started to get up. " 'Scuse..."

"Wait. It's better if you wait."

"I really have to..."

"Shhh." We kissed, my hand rubbed on his fly.

In my ear, whispering, "You're cold, your mouth is dry."

"It's the coke."

He was fuzzy. "It was before."

We kissed some more, my mouth growing moist.

"You smell so good. Here," below her ear, and I nibbled.
"And here," between above her breasts.

"What? No, don't, please..." she started, too late to resist.
"Your tongue is dry."

"Wet it for me." She was lazy with the dope, mouth open
to wiggle her tongue. We giggled, kissing.

"It is, it's really dry." Those sips, those little sips. And
she so warm and wet and ripe. I pushed her shirt away,
unbuttoning.

"Don't." I pushed and nibbled. "Please." I worked her
skirt. "Please, you'll get me..." Button, zipper, her skirt
opened down. The ripeness, rich, rose from her flesh, my
head descending.

"No." I paused. "I mean, it's...it's the wrong time, you
know?"

"I know. It's all right."

"No. Please."

"It's all right. Really." Her bra came off. She lay back on
the couch as I nibbled on the rich ripe, the touch of sweat
beneath her nipple, the armpit's edge, the soft warm stomach.

"Oh, please." I carried her to bed.

"I need to—excuse me, I really have to go... It's all that
wine."

I held him back. "Wait. Can you do it," I smiled, "could
you do it when you're aroused? I mean, which do you think
is stronger, for most guys?"

"Huh? I don't know, I guess..."

"What?"

"Well, yeah, if they're really, I guess they can't. I don't
know, I never tried. If they're only, like halfway, I don't
know."

"Think you can?"

"What? You mean..." He was hooked.

"I'll make a bet." He was curious. "You need to, bad?"

"Yeah. Pretty bad."

"I'll bet...I can keep you so you can't."

"Huh?"

"If you go first, you win. If you come first, I win."

"Holy... You really want to...?"

"Uhm-hmm."

"Yeah. Sure." He leaned back. Belt, buttons, zipper, and my head went down. "Wait a minute. What are we betting for?" he remembered.

"We'll think of something."

The first of it was dark, a little stale. She was dry from the tampon and I couldn't help. I moved my tongue around the outside and her hips responded. I concentrated on the soft ripe warmth, rocking with her hips, gentling, teasing with my tongue. It wasn't long. Her body tensed, her breath came hard. She gasped, thighs clenched, back arched. My tongue slid in, moist there now, the last of the dark. She carried higher, hips clenching. Sweet clear fluid and now the fresh bright red. I dug in deep, sucking, drinking full. She came, warm and wet. I pulled back a little, my mouth still holding. Her hands tangled my hair, upper body twisting to look down. My tongue came out and she sank back. Sweet, clear, hips rocking, and more rich red. I drank, she came, I drank, I drank.

The wine was clear and warm, anxious puzzled spurts at first and then the rich hot flow. Over the coke the tingle spread from my stomach out, out to my fingertips, my toes. I drained it and it was almost enough. So much warmth, so wet, so sweet. My mouth stayed still when he was done, then moved again as he revived, sucking, sipping, tonguing for dessert.

When hunger stills, the rest remains. I curled into the soft lean body close— "you're still so cold" —and warmed and warmed throughout the night.

I flew back to the nest at dawn and paused, again, beneath the door. The old horseshoe, engraved, above the sill looked down. NON TIMENT it said up one leg, the rest worn flat, obscured.

"Those who do not fear," I wondered, again, what is it they do, what message I should learn? Then I flew back to the nest too.

—*Feed well?* I asked.

—*Oh yes,* I said. *And you?*

—*Mine was soft,* I said, *her second day, and very ripe.*

—*I know,* I said, *I smelled it too. Mine was lean and very full.*

—*And very warm.*

—*Yes, always warm.* I came to bed and we made love. Slow with care at first, against the dry, but stronger then and for a long long time.

> *Vampires feed on the warmth of living flesh and its fluids. Cold and dry themselves, they lack the liquids that would allow true orgasm.*
>
> (ibid., p. 204.)

TWO: THE HEAT OF LOVE

> *Like the conversion hysterias (anesthesias, paralyses), the dissociative reactions (amnesiac fugues, multiple personalities) are characterized by a primary repressive component, which bars unacceptable behaviors and thoughts from awareness, and a secondary gain component, which allows their victims to engage in thoughts and behaviors otherwise too repugnant to be imagined. Although rare, lycanthropy too represents a dissociative disorder.*
>
> (Frederik Falsch: *Psychodynamics of the Occult,* p. 79.)

: Sometimes I don't always know what I'm doing. No, that's not right. I do know what I'm doing; only I don't remember. Fugues, *the shrink said. Sometimes I'll wake up and just not know, but it will feel wrong. Other times, there'll be things to notice—I'll be naked when I remember putting my*

pyjamas on the night before, or there'll be scratches or
bruises, sometimes blood, on my arms or legs or face :

He was lying on the beach, just above the high water level,
almost under a pier. His pants were torn, salt-dried, the
rest of him naked. There was no hair on his chest or arms,
nor any beard despite the dawn. His eyes opened when she
shook his shoulder. "Are you all right?"

"Uh." He pushed himself to one elbow. His body was
lean, young, almost soft. There was a trickle of dried blood,
starting at the corner of his mouth and down his chin, and
his lower lip was puffy on that side. "Morning." He came
to a sitting position, wincing, and looked at his ribs. "Stiff.
Shouldn't sleep on sand. Hi," he looked up smiling.

"You've been here all night? You must be frozen."

"Uh, yeah." He rubbed his arms, sides. "Well, I guess you
get used..."

"Put this on." She peeled off the top of her running suit.
Underneath, the red elasticized bandeau pushed her
breasts forward and in, as much as their weight would allow. "Come on, you need some coffee."

He hung the sweatshirt from his shoulders and got up,
creaking. They went back under the pier, close to the
water's edge, and up along the beach. He detoured to find
his shirt and sneakers, then looked up, watching her body
again.

"You do this often?" she asked, slowing to let him catch
up.

"Uh, no. I—um, it's hard to remember. I guess I had too
much to drink. I remember a bunch of us driving out here
and then, I don't know, I decided to go wading or something. The others didn't want to, I guess they left."

"Neat friends." This far out, there were no more houses
and the pier under which he'd slept had mostly collapsed.
After a while, the cottage appeared. She walked briskly,
and his muscles first protested, then unwound.

He paused at the door with the horseshoe above, engraved once, but worn with age so only part of it was leg-
ible: arced across the top, AMARE. "*Amo, amas, amat.* To
love?" he asked.

"It's always been there," she said.

Inside, the hearth had taken the chill off the morning. "I'll make coffee," she said, going to the kitchen. He stood just inside the door, looking around, then moved closer to the fire.

The natural habitat of wolves is tundra and steppe. Their pelts thicken against the permanent cold, but it never leaves their thoughts. Werewolves, too, hunting or at rest, cannot forget the cold.

(ibid., p. 76.)

When she came back he had the shivers, slow waves seeping up and down his body, teeth chattering. "I told you you'd freeze," she said. "Come on, you need a shower." She took his hand and led him to the bathroom, turning the taps to let the water run hot. "Inside." He let the shirt slide off his shoulders and unbuckled his belt: pale to almost white save at the patch above his sex shrunken, shriveled with the cold. Her sweatpants and bikini came off in one motion; the bandeau rolled up over her head. The mirror caught her body: perfectly hairless; legs, pelvis, underarms; smooth skin and stomach flat down to the pristine rise of pubic mound curving to where the slight lips vanished between her thighs. The breasts were very round, pink nipples almost flat against the small pale aureolae; the waistline tucked.

She stepped into the tub, pulling him behind, and switched the stream to shower. She bent to rinse some sand from her ankles, then moved to let him under. It hit hot, but the shivers went away. She soaped herself and they changed places to let her rinse. Then she soaped him, turning his smooth body slick with suds to do his back and again for the front, then he did hers. Each time they changed places she brushed with breast or hip. They stood close, both under the stream, and she slowly turned the water hotter. "I like it when it steams," she said, shivering a little, close, her nipples on his chest, stomach against his pelvis. An erection grew; she rose on tiptoes as he bent his knees to get her above and let the moist insides embrace.

: *Alone, cold air, cold snow beneath the pads. And moonlight silver on the trees, and snow. Filter air, checking; crisp scent of pine, leaves scraped free of snow, a rabbit once but gone, lost in the crisp. Sounds? Filter, check. Hunger? No, just running, free, and checking, cold air, cold snow* :

Standing, it was quick and urgent. They dried, moving out of the steamed bathroom. "You're still not warm," she said. "Get in bed, I'll bring coffee."

Under the covers, he watched her when she came back in. His eyes seemed to grow to enfold her nakedness; then narrow tracing the clean smooth hips to find her lower lips again, thin and unruffled despite the strain. She got into bed, watching his eyes watching her lips, and snuggled beside him, head on his ripply hairless chest, as he sipped the coffee. When he set the cup down she moved her head up to tongue his earlobe, then hunched closer to let him find the lips again.

: *Running, free. Cold snow, crisp air, almost scentless, dry. Push with the hindlegs, roll with the front. Running loose against the crisp. Brace with the hindlegs, roll with the front. Find the pace...now...hold it, push it, roll it, push it roll, running, dancing, free* :

Lying, urgency gone, it took its time. He pushed the blanket away, sweating. She pulled it back. "I like it warm." She may have slept.

He found some bread in the kitchen and made toast. She sipped coffee while he ate. There was no food in the house: "I hate to cook," she explained. He didn't though, he said, and talked of going to town before the stores were closed. They went back to bed first, snuggling under the blankets

: *running, free, under the sun, trees, shadows, hiding, scenting, spoor? Not yet, just running push roll free* :

then took her car to town for food. And talked, driving there and back. He was in computers, he said, programming, and did what one does in town when not at work. She had worked in bookstores and galleries until the summer, she said, then come back to the beach where her parents had left her the cottage and a fund. When summer ended, she stayed on. Not finding herself, she said, just nothing else to do.

They went to bed again

: *running, free, sun, shadow, chill, running, heat, running, running, free* :

and loafed about the house. Outside, clouds held the beach to nighttime cool. Inside, "you do this often?" he asked.

"What?"

"Pick up guys and screw them limp," grinning satedly.

"Oh." Pause.

"Well?"

"No, of course not."

"Then...?"

"I don't know. The first time was because I liked you. And after that, it just seemed nice. Didn't it?"

"Oh yeah. Yeah, sure. Very nice, in fact."

"We could do it again..."

"No. Tell me."

"What?"

"You know, other guys..."

"What?"

"I mean, is there anyone now? Or when you lived in town? How many?"

"No; of course; enough."

"Look, I'm not trying to pry. It's just, I think I like you. Maybe I even love you. I want to know you more."

"I know. I like you too.."

He nuzzled in her stomach, tonguing, kissing, nipping. "You're so smooth." Lower. "How do you get it so smooth?"

"Uhm, don't stop. Wax."

"What?"

"You cover it with wax, then yank it off. It comes out by the roots."

"Doesn't it hurt?"

"Yes. Do it some more. But I don't like...hair. That's what I first liked about you."

"Thanks. Makes me feel like a real man."

"Silly. Uhm, you do that so good... Don't you sometimes wish, you could do it to yourself?"

"I can."

"No."

"Watch." He rolled on his back and moved to prop himself against the head of the bed. Bending forward he lifted his legs, hooking his hands behind his knees to curl up tight. His tongue went forward to touch the tip.

"Ohhh. I wish I could do that..."

"There're nicer ways." He slid back down and rolled to enter smooth

: Running, brace and rolling, running, free :

Making dinner, he turned the radio on. After music there was news. Locally, farmers were worried about wolves on the loose: a third goat had been killed the night before, mangled and eaten. Wolves hadn't come this close in twenty years, but farmers now were armed and talking about a search.

"Doesn't that worry you, out here all alone?"

"Wolves? They don't hurt people, do they?"

"Sure. Don't you remember all those stories, the Russian steppes?"

"But that's only when there's nothing else to eat."

> *Wolves mate for life; their packs are family groups.*
> *They claim their territory, respecting that of oth-*
> *ers. An occasional isolate can hunt at will, but*
> *runs the risk of offending territories already*
> *claimed. Their needs are simple: fresh kill each*
> *day or two, shelter, and sex.*

(ibid., p. 77.)

The steaks were very rare and the salad crisp. "Are they too rare?" he observed.

"No, it's fine. I'm not too hungry, I guess."

"After all that workout? You've got to be kidding."

"It's not really work, you know."

"That wasn't the way I meant. Come on, eat." She took some meat.

They did the dishes and went to bed, tonguing, nipping

: running warm and free :

loving.

"Come live with me," he said.

"What?"

"Winter's coming, you can't stay here. Come back to town, live with me."

He watched again as she got up, her lips now loose and pink, hanging below the smooth curve of the mound, her nipples paler pink but out beyond the breasts. She went to the window, cloudless now but dark before the moon.

"I'm serious, live with me."

"I know. But you don't even know me..."

"I know enough. I think I love you. If I know you more, I'll only love you more."

"No you won't."

"What is it?"

"Nothing. I'm just not a...very lovable person."

"Come on."

"Please. Maybe you should go."

"Now? There won't be any trains. Besides, we still have all day Sunday."

"Look, I like you, really. You're a very nice person and we do crazy things in bed. But I'm not ready for ... permanence, attachments, you know?"

"No. I mean, I didn't ask you to marry me, yet. Just live with me a while, until we get to know."

"I can't, really."

"Oh. Well, is it all right to spend the night?"

"I don't know," she said, dropping back to bed, her head down on his chest. "It's full moon and I don't know. Maybe I love you too. I don't want you to go but I'm not ready for you to stay."

"Well, maybe I should. Is there still a train? Or we could go in together, spend tomorrow at my place."

"No, not now. It's all right, you can stay."

He pulled her up and nuzzled her nipple. "That's nice," he said.

They were still making love

: running, scenting, crisp and warm and free :

when the moon entered the room and crossed to the bed,

silvering her body where he had pulled the covers off. They lay side by side, her thighs embracing his as he rocked gently. The moonlight touched the smoothness of her body, shimmering and silvering until it took on a glow, wavering before his eyes. He closed them against the glare, continuing the gentle rock, feeling the smooth moist muscles' grasp, the soft thighs about him, silken, brushing.

When he opened his eyes, the moonlight had turned her gray pelt to startling silver. She moved her muzzle to his shoulder and gently lapped his ear. He started to pull back, but by then it felt too good to stop.

> *The mating bond that werewolves form is an illusion, a matter of sexual convenience only. They lust; and then seek sex at any price.*
>
> (ibid., p. 78.)

THREE:
THE CRIES OF EARTH, THE STILL ABOVE

> *Ghosts, ghouls, and zombies have unfinished business on earth. Commonly, ghosts abide until an injustice has been set right, while zombies are re-awakened by desecration or other affront.*
> (Frederik Falsch: *Psychodynamics of the Occult*, p. 246.)

When we moved back into our old house, Mother and Father gave us separate rooms but we found a passage that connected and cuddled in one bed. Head to toes at first with tongues and lips and fingers. Then straight, in front, behind, we'd come and go right on. We had to do it lots since it was our first night back.

In the morning we went back to our own beds and came down to breakfast one at a time. Father and Mother did not look too well.

"Well," Father tried to be hearty; he wasn't our real father anyway. "Did you children sleep well?"

"Oh yes, and you?" we asked politely.

"There were some noises in the night. They didn't disturb you?"

"Noises, Father?"

"Just the wind, I think, in the attic. These old houses have strange drafts. It kept your mother awake."

She wasn't our real mother either. She used to be our governess, when we were very small. One day she was out walking with Mummy along the cliff and Mummy fell and had to die. Then she married Daddy, only the brakes failed on his car and crashed. So she married Father, who knew as much about cars as she did about cliffs, and never had an accident. The police asked a lot of questions but we were much too young and besides, they had no evidence. So now we live with Mother and Father.

"Well, go out and play, children," Father said when breakfast was done.

"But not in the cemetery," Mother said.

"Why not?"

"Oh, it's all overgrown, and brambly. You'll tear your clothes." Mother was very neat.

"All right," we said and went to the cemetery. It was on a little hill behind the house with trees around. Mummy and Daddy were there and Daddy's parents and aunts and uncles and Greatgrandad, who had built the house. Mother and Father didn't like it much, but we had to come back when Daddy's money all ran out.

We played there for a while and did it once on Mummy's grave cause that seemed right. But it was pretty brambly and overgrown so we went back to the house and explored some more. It was full of secret passages and hidden doors and peepholes so it took us a long time to get it all straight.

That night Mummy and Daddy came back when we were in bed again. They just sort of drifted through the door and stood there watching us fool around like they used to. They didn't look too good, all white and shimmery like you could look right through them. We didn't say anything and they didn't either. After a while Mummy came to the bed and reached down to stroke our hair like she liked. Her hand felt cold and clammy and it didn't really

stroke us at all, like it almost went through us instead of
on us. We each reached for a titty but we couldn't get her
buttons open. When she undid them for us it didn't feel
right at all and then she started to cry, just tears rolling,
not making a sound, and ran to Daddy. He had his thing
out and got into her, lifting her skirt and pushing. But we
could tell that wasn't working either and after a while they
stopped. We did too and everybody just looked sad, and
then they went away. We lay in bed just holding each
other, without fooling around or anything, for a long time.

But then the old house really got noisy, moaning and
creaking and wailing all over. When we heard Father come
out of his room to see what was happening we jumped into
our pyjamas in case he came to check on us. Sure enough,
he did.

"What are you doing here?" he said angrily.

"Oh, I was just in the bathroom, and then I heard all
that noise so I ran in here..."

"Well, you should have run to your own room. I'll see to
the noises; it's probably just a loose window in the attic.
You get back to your room."

"Yes, sir."

So we spent the night alone. The noises went on for a
long while, even after Father checked.

Next day, Father and Mother looked even worse. After
we went out to play we remembered we hadn't done it on
Daddy's grave and that didn't seem fair. So we went back
to the cemetery and did and then we fooled around, looking at the other graves and trying to read the old head-
stones. All they said was names and dates, except
Greatgrandad's which had writing curled around. It was
so old now we couldn't read it except some of the letters: NON, it looked like at the beginning, down near the
ground; and NON TIMENT on the other side. There were
some other letters going around the top, M's and T's and
E's.

"What's it say?"

"I don't know. *Non* is not, and *non timent* is like they're
not afraid, but I can't tell the rest. Nobody something
something are not afraid. Nobody who something, I guess."

"Maybe, it looks like it's the same on both sides."

"That's silly. If you're not afraid of course you're not afraid."

"Well can you think of anything better?"

"Not me." We had to pee then so we made up a contest. We lay on our backs and tried to squirt the letters one at a time. And that got us started again.

Then we went inside and explored some more. There was a passage that went on top of the front parlor where Mother and Father were sitting talking.

"We must do something about those children, Howard," Mother said. "I don't want to think what they were doing together last night."

"They're only children, Alicia."

"Yes, but you have no idea what their father was like. I'm sure they inherited his tastes. He was vile, Howard, simply vile."

"You spent a lot of time finding out, as I recall, my dear."

"You know how I hated every moment, Howard. We had no choice. I tried to think better of him but I know he only married me to appease his lust. What else could I do?"

"Enjoyed it, perhaps, my dear."

"With that animal? On me at all hours of the day, pawing, poking with that vile thing? How could you expect me to enjoy that?"

"Yes, dear, I know."

"Well, do something about the children then, they're monsters just like their parents were."

"What would you have me do? We can't send them to a school, there's no telling what they'd tell people. And you won't have another governess. We can't watch them night and day."

"Couldn't they...well, you know, some kind of accident, playing? On the roof maybe, or the cliff."

"Alicia, Alicia, didn't we have enough questions from the police the last time? Do you want to go through all that again?"

"Well, I know. But we can't let them grow up so perverted and vile."

"I'm sure you're just imagining things, dear. They're

only children after all, leave them be."

So we went back to our room and fucked some more.

That night we found another passage and watched Mother and Father going to bed. She sure had a neat pair. Not soft and juicy like Mummy's, but they sure were big. Father came up behind her when she was brushing her hair and started to play with them but she just pushed him away. Then he went to his bed and she went into hers and that was all they did. It was pretty strange. So we went back to bed.

Mummy and Daddy came in later and just stood watching us again. We watched them too and we all got so sad we couldn't even mess around any more. That night the noise and banging went on outside the house too, instead of just upstairs.

> *Ghosts are exempt from physical law but in exchange may have no real effects: they cannot move objects nor block the light. Zombies, on the other hand, are bound by space to do what harm they can. Often this takes bizarre form, as if they were unsure of their powers.*

(ibid., p. 247.)

Next day we went back to the cemetery first, because it was getting to be like our private place. It looked different. One of the graves, Greatgrandad's in fact, was all messed up. The ground was torn and all lying around in clumps and even the coffin was showing, old and sort of rotten looking. We wondered what could have done that. Then we decided to pee on all the other graves too, just for fun. And then we noticed some writing way down at the bottom of one of the gravestones where it had come loose of the ground. It said

> *Vampires suck*
> *Werewolves fuck*
> *Ghosts and ghoulies*
> *Out of luck*

"Did you put that there?"

"No, I didn't. Did you?"

"No, I never. Besides, we've been together all the time."

"Well, who did then?"

"I don't know. Didn't you?"

"I told you."

"Well, do you think it's true?"

"I don't know. I sure hope so."

"Me too. Only what about Mummy and Daddy?"

"Gee. Oh, that's so sad."

So we messed around a lot until we felt better.

That night things really got noisy. All the zombies broke loose and headed for the house, probably looking for whoever it could have been who peed on their graves. They came up to our room pretty quick and just charged right in the door. They sure were ugly. Their teeth were too long and like they didn't have any lips and their fingernails and hair seemed to go on all over the place. Their clothes were all raggedy and it looked like their flesh was too, sort of rotting and falling off. They saw us in the bed and came right for us, all stiff and slow. We tried to hide at the top end of the bed but it didn't look like they wanted to let us get away.

Then Mummy and Daddy sort of slid through the wall right by the bed and got between them and us. They held up their hands and the zombies all stopped. Daddy pointed outside toward Mother and Father's room and they just turned and started shuffling out the door again. We sure felt better.

But they were doing so much rattling and clanking that Father came out again to see. We heard his door open and then he screamed "Alicia" and we heard the door slam. So we went out in the hall to watch. It didn't take those zombies long to break the door down. Father must have got his gun because there were a lot of shots then, but they didn't stop the zombies. They just shuffled right in.

Then there was a pause while Mother screamed a lot and Father reloaded the gun and fired some more. We heard the door slam to their bathroom and then they came through there and out the hall door. All the zombies were still in the bedroom.

Father yelled, "For God's sake, hide," without even asking why we were together again and then he and Mother ran upstairs. The zombies came out through the bathroom door and Daddy pointed up the stairs. Some of them went up that way after Father and Mother but the others stayed in case they came back down. Sure enough they did, down the back stairs and when they saw the zombies they just kept right on going.

So the zombies followed them downstairs and then down to the basement and all the way to the back where there was a tiny winecellar with a heavy old door. They barricaded themselves behind that and the zombies couldn't break it down. So they locked it on the outside and took the key and went away.

And we went back to bed.

Next day we could hear Mother and Father in there, shouting and banging, but there wasn't much we could do without the key. So we went out and looked at the cemetery and it sure was a mess. We didn't even feel like fooling around there so we went to Mother and Father's room and did it there. First on her bed, then on his. Then on ours.

Things were pretty quiet that night for a change, except when the zombies came to check the basement. Mother and Father still wouldn't let them in and they went away.

A couple of days later we heard a shot in the basement. Probably they'd gotten tired of starving to death and killed themselves instead. Then later the police came, because nobody had seen or heard from Mother and Father in a long time. It didn't take them long to find the mess all over and follow it back to the winecellar. They broke the door down and found the bodies. That made them get really sick. What they said was it looked like Father had killed Mother first to put her out of her misery. And then he had something to eat so she didn't have such nice tits or much ass or legs anymore. But what really got them was his come, it was all over. Not just in her puss or mouth or ass like you'd expect, but in her ears and nose; he'd even gouged one eye and done a socket job. We couldn't figure

where he got the energy to come like that, starving and all.
Probably he'd just had to save it up a long while before. It
sure bothered the cops though. We could hear them talking all over the house and then looking for us, but they
never found where we hid.

So now we live here all alone with nobody to tell us what
to do or not. In the daytime we mostly just mess around.
At night when there's a moon we go out flying with the
bats or running with the wolves, just being free. But we
still feel sad about Mummy and Daddy sometimes.

> *The disposition to assume non-human form is, of
> course, hereditary, although the mechanisms are far
> from clear. It is still uncertain, for example, whether
> such transmogrification is triggered by the height-
> ened sexual drives invariably found in these cases, or
> whether these represent merely a secondary phenom-
> enon of the condition.*
>
> (ibid., p. 283.)

But one thing was sort of funny. After the first time the
zombies came we went out in the cemetery and all the
graves were open and coffins lying around, stones all
knocked over and everything. But later when things got
quiet again and we went back it was all straightened out
and neat, the brambles gone and the coffins all back in the
ground. Except Greatgrandad's grave was still open with
all the dirt piled at the top so we filled it in for him. And
then we noticed that the old carving on his stone had been
fixed up too so that you could read it all. NON TIMENT it
said up the left arm, and AMARE, across the top, and then
NON TIMENT down the right. We thought that was
strange, like why would you have to tell anybody that? •

BETRAYAL OF THE SUN

Richard deMeulles

Dead. All of my friends. Most of my family. Dead. We are in the valley of the dead, betrayed by death. I am death itself. I sit alone in the heat waiting for my wife to come home. When she returns I will kill her. I have no choice.

The gun is on my lap.

I watch the morning heat rise from the desolate street. Abandoned cars wait in vain for their dead owners to rescue them. Gutted store fronts shimmer before my eyes. It might be just the heat waves distorting my vision. Or it could be reality itself dissolving, incipient dementia. I may be starting to rave...just like the rest.

Soon the burning season will be upon us, when unbearable heat will twist even the plastic furniture into a distorted image of its true self. I stay indoors, except for essential trips to the Rescue Station in Sector R to exchange ration stamps for food and the bottles of the liquid that's supposed to ease our horror. Beneath my burnoose that protects me from the sun, I carry my target pistol in defense against the Marauders. When the auto-trains are running I risk the Underground. Otherwise, I walk the hollow concrete vistas. Each year the burning season comes sooner, but I remember when it did not come at all.

Francine and I are on a tropical beach and she is twenty-five again. Her legs are smooth and lightly browned, and her black hair falls on her shoulders. She stands in the water with the afternoon sun behind her.

"Don't get too much sun," I warn.

"But it feels so good. I can never get too much. I want to be warm forever."

From the shore I promise her there will be no more seasons, only continuous summer and a thousand years of peace. When she is finished her swim, we return to the hotel room and make love. Our body potions mix. In a moment of time too small to measure, our daughter Pigeon becomes a person. Two years later Luc is conceived.

We invent our children, and they invent us. It's the process of love. We are the creators—and destroyers—of each other.

The shattering of glass shakes me from my dream. I look at the mute television, but remember that there have been no transmissions this week. The noise has come from outside. A Marauder, in the last phase of raving, has crawled from his dark hole in the guts of a burned out building and broken an empty bottle of Compose against the pavement. His blue-veined face is exposed to the sun. His chuckles sound like drowning noises.

I shoot at the pavement and he scurries back into the shadows. I should have given the gun to Pigeon before she left. She always has been the strongest one in the family, and she could kill if she had to.

I see Pigeon holding Luc's hand as they dance around the wading pool. A hornet lands on his face. She gently plucks the insect from his delicate skin without alarming him. Then she grinds the hornet into paste in her hand. She is five years old.

Luc began to rave last year. Every day Pigeon took him for a walk. She combed his hair and led him by the hand. Her calm words soothed his loud and fearful voice, so the roving Mental Health Consultants wouldn't notice him.

The armored cruiser must have spotted his stumbling gait and followed them home. They kicked the door in when I answered it, and they clubbed me unconscious with their truncheons. Pigeon fought them but they broke her jaw and dragged Luc away to the Mental Health Center. There, the patients are immobilized with tranquilizers and languish in crowded dormitories where they eat and sleep together. Attendants hose down the floors with disinfectant. There is no care or comfort, and no one is ever released.

I pray Luc has died quickly at the Center. It drains my humanity to think of him so far from his family. Pigeon tells me she should have killed him, to save him from this. She says she will not let it happen again. I believe her.

The same old announcement on the radio says it is only going to be 100 degrees today. It is a lie. Just like the propaganda of going north. Before the inter-city raids the Controlling Coalition tried to herd us north in trains, across the fire-charred forests. Some believed these lies and went, and we never heard from them again.

When the television service works, I watch old film slips of news stories showing the same scene: smiling people in shady northern valleys, living the good life. But the trains don't even run north anymore; there's nothing up there but a stagnant inland sea. I wonder why they keep showing the same news story—perhaps the person responsible for stopping them has died.

Pigeon is almost twenty. It is the hopeful years before the first burning season. She and Luc are getting ready to break away from us and live their own lives. Francine lies in my arms while the children make plans downstairs.

"Wouldn't it be nice to start over again? Just keep making babies, watch them grow, watch the world go round and round, with everything growing!"

I know what she means, but I answer, "Our job now is not to create new life, but to watch and grow old."

"I don't want that." Her tears fall on my forearm and mix with the dust of the day. "I don't want to think of getting old and helpless. Promise me we will not go to one of those places where you sit and watch each other die."

"No," I promise, a comforting lie. But this lie grows into a truth as solemn as a wedding vow.

I wish this nightmare would end.

They say it is the algae in the reservoir that causes the cancer and fever that makes us mad. I think it is the thought of the world slowly dying that drives us insane. I know I am slipping away, too. I can't trust my thoughts. In a crazy world how much paranoia is justified? How do you know just when the true craziness sets in? All I know for certain is I die a little more as my family is diminished.

The inter-city raids have begun, and food is scarce because the inland sea is flooding what's left of the farmland.

The children come home. We all agree it is just temporary, just until the worst is over. We act as if it's just a family reunion. We create this lie to give us hope.

After the others have all gone to bed, Pigeon comes to my reading chair and sits on the arm.

"It is the end, isn't it, Daddy?"

I have no response. I ramble about how our family will keep strong for each other. But it's just words. I give her a hug and tell her to get ready for bed.

"It's okay," she replies, "I'll take care of us." I know she sees the coming nightmare. In my silence I allow her to accept a responsibility that should not be hers. I repeat one of the bedtime stories I used to tell her when she was a little girl. I pretend everything is all right, and she pretends to believe me.

The sun is low on the horizon. I look directly into the sun and see solar flares, sunspots, evil portent.

Francine raved last night. I sponged her head with a damp cloth dipped in our water ration. She spoke about Luc and Pigeon as if they were still children and then about us having grandchildren. I comforted her and agreed. This calmed her and helped to soothe my nerves, too. This morning she remembered nothing of the raving, but spoke about going to see Luc at his home. She looked weirdly energetic. When Pigeon got up she asked: "Was there a problem with Mom last night?"

"Just too much heat," I replied.

"Are you sure?"

"Of course."

Francine was disheveled when she came out of the bedroom. Her beautiful hair was uncombed and her blouse open. Pigeon helped her dress. When she came out of the bedroom she looked troubled, "Mom is talking about visiting Luc."

"She's tired, she hasn't been sleeping well. That's all. That's all," I said, covering for my wife. But the look on Pigeon's face told me she did not believe me.

I have trouble concentrating... It might be... No, it's just pain...and sleeplessness. There are fatigue spots in front of my eyes. Heat oozes from everything in the room. The gun metal is hot to touch. I stare at the barren floor...not even any cockroaches. Man will be the last to leave the earth.

I hear a key in the lock. It's awkward to remove the dead bolts with a gun in my hand. Francine is home. Her hair is windblown across her vacant eyes. Her mouth is set in a rigid leer, and she doesn't seem to notice that Pigeon is leading her by the hand.

I know what I must do, but all I can see is how she looked when we made love and created our children. Heat waves distort my vision, and Francine transforms. Her smile is gentle, I don't see the bloated blue cancer look. Her eyes are clear and fine.

She tells me she has been visiting Luc and our grandchildren. I feel comforted to hear this, until I remember that Luc has been taken from us. But maybe he hasn't, maybe she is right, and I have been dreaming all afternoon. What's the truth? My thoughts collide like cars on a freeway. They destroy each other. Then another comes crashing in, just as I am trying to separate the wreckage.

I see Pigeon is crying—I don't know why. I leave my gun on the chair and go to embrace my wife. She is beautiful and still my lover.

"Don't worry about your mother," I tell Pigeon. "She is fine. Just a little tired. But so am I... So am I. We are not young anymore." My pain subsides when I am with Francine. Family always makes me feel better.

"Daddy?" Pigeon pleads, but I don't know what she wants.

"We are all okay," I reassure. And then I hear my own voice, coming from a distant part of me that I can't reach with my thoughts. "Just run along now and do what needs to be done."

Francine and I stroll arm and arm toward our bedroom, like two old lovers. Pigeon picks up the gun from the chair and follows us.

As Francine and I lie down and close our eyes, I hear the cool click of metal, and I think to myself: "A man is lucky to have his family with him." •

BODY SOLAR
Derryl Murphy

Breathebreathebreathebreathebreathe...

I can't remember how to breathe, he thought. Panic began to set in, but he managed to fight it back down, turning it into a cool lump in the pit of his stomach, rather than a piercing starburst.

There's a breath now. He felt himself begin to relax. *Remember what the lady said...*

The voice in his head seemed to become urgent. He turned his mind away from the new sensations and tried to concentrate on what was being said. Words and thoughts danced away from his grasp for a moment before he found the ability to focus.

"Simon, this is Anna." The voice sounded lovely, and familiar. He imagined himself frowning as he tried to place it. "We need to test all systems before you get too far away from us. Can you please try to take a breath?"

A breath? With a shock he realized for the first time that he hadn't been breathing. Fear started to override his somewhat dulled senses and he tried to take a great, shuddering breath, like a swimmer who had dived too deep and only just made it to the surface in time. Instead, he felt his chest lift very slightly and a small amount of air move into his lungs.

It didn't feel like enough, and he struggled for another. His body wouldn't cooperate.

"No, Simon," said the voice in his head. "Don't try to take another. Your body knows what to do now and will breathe when it needs to."

"Who is this?" He had tried to speak, but rather than hearing words from his mouth, it felt like he had spoken inside his head.

"It is Anna, Simon. Dr. Schaum. Do you remember where you are?"

His thoughts slowly stirred about for a moment, then as they neared the answer they seemed to pick up speed, making him think of the rats in Africa scurrying about when newslights were turned on them. When he managed to pin one thought down, it struck him as the right one.

"Space."

His back felt warm. Kind of itchy, too. *Turn my head,* he thought. Then, *I remember, it takes a long time. But I can wait.*

His eyes took in everything around him. Mostly, it was just blackness, punctuated by dots of light. *Nothing but stars all around me. Stars and me and my sail.*

He hadn't turned his head enough to see the sail, yet. Funny how he hadn't thought to look at it before now.

How long have I been out here?

Eyes still seeing the black velvet with the pinholes, he tried to remember the name.

Oh. "Anna?" There was no answer, but he didn't feel hurried. He easily remembered that patience had never been one of his strong points, but he felt no anxiety now.

A shock of recognition went through him. *My arm. I can see my arm, stretched out, reaching up and to my side.* His head was still turning, slowly, as he could gauge the rate by watching how long it took to move the view along his arm.

"Mr. Helbrecht?" A voice spoke in his head. It didn't sound like Anna, but he thought it best not to take a chance.

"Anna?"

Again, he waited. He could see his hand now, at the end of his arm. It looked funny, with the sail attached to it, like it was caught in the middle of metamorphosing from flesh to gossamer. And just beyond his outstretched fingers he could see where the sail broke into the vacuum; the optical distortion that made the sail look as if it were broken in two at the divide. Like looking into or out of water.

A fish in a bowl, he thought. *That's me. Except that **my** bowl is going places.*

"No, Mr. Helbrecht. This is Michel Giroux. Dr. Schaum is not currently monitoring this frequency. Are you in need of something?"

"I don't remember you."

The sail seemed to go on forever, shining from the light behind, a beautiful thing to see. He pretended he could see the little photons crashing up against it, forcing him faster and faster towards...

Hmm. I can't remember where I'm going either.

That could wait. His head had turned enough that he could see the top of his shoulder now. It was covered with green, a sort of algae. That much he could remember.

Ironically, he felt his body take a breath.

"Yes, Mr. Helbrecht, I know you don't remember me. I am new at this position. Now. Did you have a question for me, Mr. Helbrecht?"

A question? *I wanted to ask... No! I mean,* "I wanted to ask, how long have I been out here? And before I forget again, where is it I'm going?"

If he watched closely and for some time, he could see the algae shift position along his arm and down over his shoulder blade to where he couldn't see.

The sun felt warm on his cheek.

"How do you feel?"

Simon heard the voice, but he didn't want to open his eyes. Instead, he grunted.

"I'll take that to mean lousy, which was expected. Do you know who this is, Simon?"

"Anna," he grunted, "Why do you always ask me that question?"

She laughed, and the sound of her unforced humor drained a bit of the pain away. "You've gone through two years of sessions and restructuring, Simon. You tell me why."

He finally managed to pry open his eyes, blinking the lids to try to lose the gumminess, but she was nowhere around. Then he remembered his neural input. "Because

I'm likely to forget all sorts of things while I'm sailing. So you are doing your best to at least imprint your name into my memory."

"Very good. Now, is your back itchy?"

He paused for a moment to sort that question out. Then, "Yes, it is. Oh, I wish you hadn't said anything! Now I want to scratch!"

"Well, please don't, Simon. The algal implant needs about three days to take hold. And if you can't control your fingers we may have to strap your arms down."

Simon kept his arms down, trying not to think about the light tickling sensation of the huge mass of algae growing on his back. He had already spent an inordinate amount of money, over half of his personal fortune, and if any step of the procedure was unsuccessful he would lose his chance and forfeit the money spent. Many others had spent almost as much, only to lose out on the newest vacation of a lifetime because their bodies and psyches could not handle the stress of the transformation.

Aside from some minor mechanical details, the algal implant was the second last stage in the process leading to his trip. It was also one of the single most important. Without it, he would have no air to breathe and no food, as it were, to eat.

"Mr. Helbrecht, I'm not allowed to tell you how long you've been gone. Remember? We don't want you getting hung up on time. You paid good money to take a trip where you didn't have to worry about what the time was.

"As for your destination, you are proceeding to a predetermined location approximately equal to one-point-five A.U. from the sun."

"Oh. Thank you very much. Can I talk to Anna now?"

His neck seemed to have reached its maximum extension. He tried to turn his head further but couldn't.

Happy he had seen this view, Simon started turning his head again. This time he would look down, to his feet and beyond.

The man had said he didn't have to worry about time. Certainly he wasn't bothered by the length of time it took him to move his head, so he guessed this to be true.

"Hello, Simon. This is Anna. How are you doing?"

"Hello, Anna! I'm doing wonderfully, thank you! I don't know how long it has been since I launched, but I think that for the first time since then I'm really and truly aware of things!"

Off to his right, where his head was still facing, he saw a bright light that made him pause in his thoughts. It flared brighter than anything else he could see in the sky, and seemed to be lasting for a very long time. Only after it had decreased in size by a bit did he remember he had been talking to Dr. Schaum.

"It's very beautiful out here, Anna. I just saw a very bright light. Was it a ship, perhaps even your ship?"

After seeing the flaring light and the shine of the sun reflecting off his sail, the rest of space seemed very dark. As his head slowly turned to look down, his eyes moved along his body. It was in shadow, lit only by the low light of distant stars and by the one dim light of a small box embedded in his otherwise naked belly.

"I'm glad you're enjoying yourself, Simon. I must warn you that we can't keep this link up for very much longer."

"That's all right, Anna. Hey! What's this little thing on my stomach for? I can't remember."

The light from the box was a steady, mesmerizing glow. The box was small, only a few centimeters by a few centimeters. He felt his body take a breath and watched as the box rose and sank, slowly and not very deeply.

"Yes, Simon, it was a ship. A barge boosting for the asteroids. You saw its fusion rockets."

"Oh."

The box eventually lost his interest. He focused his eyes beyond the box; first on his feet, then on the vacuum below. His mind experienced a brief moment of vertigo as he stared down into nothingness, but he quickly recovered.

"That box, Simon, is your force-field generator. It helps keep you alive."

He felt like a freak. Standing in front of the floor-length mirror, his body had to be the most bizarre thing he had

ever seen in his life. Perhaps, he mused, if things didn't
work out he could join one of those old-time circus side-
shows that were now sweeping the continent. Or maybe
hide away in some religious retreat.

Simon was naked, standing and staring at his body
straight on. A small gray box was on his belly, embedded
in his skin so that it was partly inside his body and mostly
out, fixed in place just above his belly button. He touched
it with his hand; it felt warm, but not uncomfortably so.

Then he raised his arms straight into the air and
watched as the mutant algae slowly migrated from his
armpits and around to his back. He then shifted a couple
of the mirrors and watched all of his back, a brown and
green carpet slowly but constantly changing positions.

Next his gaze fell downwards along the mirror, to his
buttocks. The only area along his backside where there
were none of his life-giving little plant friends, but only
because of the waste reclaimer. It looked for all the world
like somebody had mounted a shiny metal helmet on his
ass and crotch to function as a diaper. Which was essen-
tially what had happened, except his wastes were under-
going drastic changes in composition, and this diaper took
those wastes and changed them into something he could
use.

Finally, he looked at his right arm. Several dozen small
yellow bruises marched up and down the length of his upper arm, signs of the time-delayed implants that would
slow his bodily functions to help him survive his trip, although they could also contribute to the forgetfulness
Anna had warned him about.

"You ready for the last stage?"

Simon turned around to look at Anna, who was standing
on the other side of the force-field that kept him safe from
contaminants. She had her hands in her pockets and was
obviously making an effort to look into his eyes, and nowhere else.

"Sure," said Simon. "When do we start?"

"Right away. I'll get you to go place yourself in your body
sling, and then we will be shutting off gravity and putting
you to sleep."

He walked over and strapped himself in. "This is the last time I'll see you, right?"

"I should be on the ship when it picks you up. But yes, this will be the last time for some years."

"Mm. Then perhaps I can invite you to meet me back on Earth after this is over; I can buy you lunch in Paris or Frankfurt."

She smiled warmly. "I'd like that very much, Simon."

He returned her smile. "Until then, Anna. Thank you for all your help."

"You're welcome, and thank you. I hope you enjoy your sail, Simon."

He tried to tell her that he thought *enjoy* wasn't necessarily the best word to use, but he felt himself nodding off and so just went with the flow of sleep.

There was a lot that could be said for solitude. Since his last conversation, Simon had not tried to contact nor had he been contacted by Anna.

At first he did talk to himself, at least within his head. Short little discussions, reminders to himself to do something or another when he finished this voyage; more often then not they were business related. But over time the need for that tapered off, and now he rarely did anything like that any more.

Instead, he just was. Existence was enough. He was a part of the blackness that was in front of him, and of the light that he was slowly leaving behind.

No more thoughts of home, of either his penthouse flat in the co-op in Bruxelles or of his winter retreat off the coast of Thailand. No more thoughts of business, the nano company he owned that he had left in capable hands while away. No more thoughts of family, his sister who he dearly loved and who had cried uncontrollably when he had boarded the railgun shuttle, and his brother whom he despised and yet was saddened by the strength of that hatred.

His awareness was limited, but in the few moments of reflection he did have, he realized that that made it all the more complete. He was a piece of cosmic dust, being carried by the solar wind.

He supposed that time was going by, but it didn't really seem to be anything to concern himself with. He was where he was, and he would get to where he was going when he got there.

There was a large clump of algae that had made its way up his neck and around to the side of his ear. It was now hanging from his left earlobe. He couldn't see it and he could barely feel it, but Simon guessed that it looked like a strange green and brown earring.

He currently had his head tilted down and to the left, eyes gazing off onto the dark. Thus he felt, more than saw, the algae break loose from his ear and slide slowly through the air to the front of his throat. It stayed there for a long time.

He spent all of his time just watching the algae. It now covered his chest and was halfway down his belly.

It moved slowly, but whenever his body took a breath he could see little pools of it stirring within the main mass. He had no idea why it was still alive on his dark side, facing away from the sun, although a distant part of him did remember seeing it collect under his armpits before he had been launched.

"Simon, this is Anna. We have received a distress call from the barge you saw boosting last year." *Last year? Last year!* "We are the closest ship and have been asked to attempt a rescue. I'm afraid we won't be able to pick you up, as we are just about to commence acceleration.

"Instead, a ship is being prepared in lunar orbit right now, and will be able to leave in just under three weeks. It should be there to pick you up about four months later than planned.

"I'm sorry, Simon. I really wanted to be there when you came back on board. I hope the extra time doesn't hinder you. The company has asked me to tell you that they will refund some of your money, and I'd like to ask if we are still on for lunch. Take care, Simon."

An extra four months.

It took him, he supposed, some time to find the words, as he had used none for what must have been a very long time. "Anna, this is Simon. Since I haven't been paying attention to the passage of time, I would say that it is not a big problem. I hope you are able to save people on your mission of mercy. And yes, I do remember something about lunch, so I hope to see you back on Earth. You take care as well."

That was that. He had extra time, but no way of really perceiving it.

The algae had surrounded his force-field generator. With his head hung down he watched, curious as to what the little plants would do next.

They had been there for what seemed a long time, although he conceded to himself that it could have just as easily been almost no time at all. But now it seemed that something was happening; the generator started to fizz and shake, and he was suddenly afraid that some algae had managed to worm its way into the box.

A few sparks flew, and then with a loud BANG! a bolt of electricity shot out and found the only other power source within the field; his neural input.

The jolt fried his connections with the input. As the device was intertwined with his speech centers, the shock he suffered caused an immediate loss of his ability to speak, or even to form cognitive thoughts that he could translate into words. As well, the input's link with the company command vessels went down.

When the main shock hit him, Simon lost consciousness immediately. His body reacted at the same time, however, much stronger and faster than it had been for some years, as the surge of electricity forced his muscles to override the time-delay implants.

A sudden, involuntary jerk pulled his right arm in towards his body, which caused the sail on that side to begin collapsing. The force-field generator, while damaged, was still operating, and sensed the fall of the huge solar sail. It immediately cast out a micron-thin force-field fan, propping up the sail until it could again fill out with solar wind.

In the meantime, Simon's course had changed.

"We've lost a signal."

Dr. Petrone rushed over to the board. "Whose?"

Karl called up the readout. "Simon Helbrecht. Nothing coming from his input unit as of forty-five seconds ago."

"Try to coax it back on line. I'll get Claire to plot his trajectory."

Dr. Petrone thrust his body into the slot and pulled himself along the tunnel that connected the tracking station with the ship's control deck. In his hurry he cracked a hand against one of the grips and then bashed his head against one of the daylight-balanced light panels when he pulled back in pain. Nursing his sore hand he pulled himself along a bit more cautiously. Claire, the ship's brain, had anticipated the call and had the trajectory projection ready when Dr. Petrone pulled himself into the control deck.

Captain Galvez and two of her crew were also waiting for him. "We can leave in eight days, Beni," she told him. "No sooner."

He studied the trajectory map and sucked on his sore hand, nervous and angry.

He couldn't remember who he was, but that didn't really bother him. It felt like that was a normal state of affairs.

Come to think of it, he didn't know *what* he was, either. Turning his head slowly, he looked at as much of himself as was possible.

All could see was a brown and green mass, lumpy and shifting ever so slowly. And beyond that mass was blackness, punctuated by points of light.

"Our scans aren't turning up anything, Captain." Claire spoke out loud for the benefit of the two people on board who did not have neural inputs.

Captain Galvez floated over to her chair and strapped herself in. The rest of the crew did the same. She turned on the pager and spoke. "All hands, strap in for boost to next search zone. Thirty seconds."

After the thirty seconds the fusion rockets kicked in, and she was punched back into her form-fitting seat with a force of over three gees. The boost lasted for three minutes, followed by a break of equal length, before an additional two minute boost.

Then the search continued.

The first few times that he had felt his throat begin to be blocked he had managed to swallow. Whatever was in there would drop down to his stomach and he would feel comfortable again. But during one lengthy period where his mind was elsewhere, the constriction became too much to swallow away.

Because he was used to taking breaths far apart from each other, it took a long time to realize he was no longer breathing. By then, his mind had slipped into an almost total fog. What used to be Simon tried one more time to claw to the top of his consciousness, but the well was too deep.

Still, something of him remained.

Captain Galvez exited her ship. Ahead of her hung the massive bulk of the research ship *Waldsemüller,* its bulbous front end pointing her way. Her personal force-field irised minutely and for only two seconds, and air jetted out behind her, pushing her towards the other ship.

Claire spoke in her head. "Dr. Schaum is requesting that you use port number three, Captain. And to please maintain silence unless you are talking through me. Her own ship's brain is not as sophisticated as I."

Galvez grunted in response and irised her field again, this time in front. She bumped up gently against the ship and then created a pseudopod to grab hold of a handle while she waited for the airlock door to open. When inside and the ship's oxygen had finished cycling in she shut down her field and waited for the inner door to slide open.

When it did, both Dr. Schaum and Captain N'Dour were waiting for her. Schaum was tall and blond, graying a bit, with light blue eyes. Worry lines creased her face. N'Dour was a huge, dour-looking Azanian, hair shaved off and with three earrings in each ear, emulating the style of imagined pirates from long ago. Where the doctor wore a jumpsuit, N'Dour wore shorts and nothing else. His body was well-muscled.

All three nodded tersely and exchanged quick greetings before the two turned and led her down a short hall to a small, plain room with a low round table and four chairs. They sat down, although Captain Galvez found the artificial gravity strange, having been living under SAR procedures for the last four months on her own ship, the naval vessel *Mitterand*.

"Claire tells me you think you've found Mr. Helbrecht, Captain," said Dr. Schaum.

"We think it's him," she responded, "But...he's not in good shape. Even for someone who is probably dead. We sent a snooper and the graphics it brought back were not very promising." Galvez pulled a portable viewer with multiple jacks from her kangaroo pouch.

Both Dr. Schaum and Captain N'Dour plugged in and watched with the snooper's eyes as it probed alongside the lumpy brown mass that seemed to have once been a human body. Captain Galvez noted with interest the looks of horror and then sadness that crossed the doctor's face. They both unjacked.

Captain N'Dour leaned his imposing bulk forward, elbows on his knees and hands clasped together. "I understand that Claire has briefed you on the need for silence from the navy, Captain?"

Galvez nodded, angry that she had to follow orders to serve the needs of a conglomerate over the needs of an individual, and angry that N'Dour was emphasizing his point with his bulk. She leaned forward as well, putting her face uncomfortably close to his. After a brief hesitation, he leaned back a bit.

"I sympathize, Captain Galvez," said Dr. Schaum, looking a bit confused at what was playing out in front of her. "It infuriates me, too. But if this gets out, the regulatory boards would shut us down, and I think you'd agree the research we do for you is too valuable to lose. But our commercial public ventures are important to us getting, and I quote the company line here, 'much needed short-term capital to aid in the financial upkeep of the corporation.' And since the boards check our ship's brain every time we re orbit, we have this need for secrecy even out here."

"So we just leave him out there?"

She nodded. "We can come up with a half-dozen reasons that his telemetry shut down, all having to do with his actions or else the people who installed his neural input, which was manufactured, incidentally, by a Chinese company. We'll get a little bit of heat, but not enough to shut us down.

"But if we bring the body on board, then people will see what happened to the algal implant. That will be the end of this business, as well as the end of research that has supplied you with things like your personal force-field."

Captain N'Dour stood, evidently trying to tilt the intimidation factor back in his favor. "He's gone, Captain Galvez. Consider him our latest message to the stars." He walked out, followed by Dr. Schaum. Then a crewman came in and led Galvez back to the airlock.

As she coasted back to her ship she watched the blackness beneath her feet, and wondered what it would be like to drift this way forever.

The thing lit up and moved away. Watching it leave, it was as though he were looking through a thick gauze.

It had been with him for some time: above him, below him and beside him. And then when it left he was alone again.

For a long time he waited for it, or something like it, to return. He seemed to expect it, although he wasn't sure why. But nothing else came.

When he finally realized he was truly alone, he turned all of his attention to the distant stars. Arms spread wide as if to embrace them, he glided silently towards the unknown. •

IN THE TRAIN OF THE KING

M.J. Murphy

Cleaver was beginning to hate these people—rich, crass, noisy American tourists, not spiritual in the slightest. "They're here to see the End of the World and all they want to do is fucking shop," he thought. "...And after killing that poor Jap, too..."

Cleaver's mind skipped backwards a few minutes in time. The Japanese was a police officer. He had been attempting to arrest them for, or at least dissuade them from, looting an abandoned Isetan department store in Tokyo's Ward Chuo-Ku.

"And he was right," Cleaver thought. There was no question that they were looting. The women led them through the display windows swinging their purses like sledgehammers. Their husbands followed. And he stood outside watching them all uneasily, picking his teeth with a mint-flavored toothpick.

The tourists had been rummaging about for almost ten minutes when the officer came onto the scene. He was one calm head in a spurt of panicked Japanese civilians shooting through the street, running past the bus with their belongings piled into little carts or carried on their backs. The policeman broke from the crowd and approached Stark, the tour-guide, who was sitting on the front bumper of the bus, and directed a series of sharp queries at him. Cleaver very quietly circled around the back of the vehicle and came up on the opposite side of the pair. He held up both hands and gave a quick smile to show he was harmless, and the policeman soon lost interest in him, returning to his interrogation. As the dialogue between he and Stark developed, the policeman became more and more upset. He seemed almost incredulous at Stark's account of the tourists' actions. And the "special government documents" which Stark asked Cleaver to retrieve from inside the bus, when waved before the policemen, had no effect upon him.

At some point Mel, the tall, thin Texan, wandered out through the window and spied the developing scene. He did not pause to think. His hand slipped smoothly into his coat and he drew forth an ancient Smith & Wesson. It was ivory handled, inlaid with pearls: very beautiful. Mel shot the policeman twice through the forehead. The policeman was dead before he hit the ground.

Stark the tour-guide had been furious of course. He had "reamed out" Mel pretty thoroughly.

Now Stark told Cleaver, "I'm going to give them five more minutes, and then we shove off." Stark, too, remained outside and away from the general mayhem, having always to keep an ear on the bus radio, which was broadcasting position reports at short intervals. "He's heading east, towards the Bay. We'll circle around and watch from the other side. So listen, why don't you run inside and grab yourself something nice?"

"No. I'll just watch, thank you." Cleaver said.

"Ah. I see." Stark drank from an aluminum flask hanging around his shoulder and then offered it to Cleaver.

"No thanks."

Stark arched an eyebrow. "Have we offended your delicate sensibilities?" he asked.

Cleaver glanced over at the dead policeman, and grimaced. He felt a bit like gagging. "It was all so unnecessary, Stark. Poor guy was just trying to do his job."

Stark also grimaced, but perhaps merely for the sake of form. "It's always sad when it happens...and that's the fourth time since I've been with Sunshine Tours. Four times too many, if you ask me. Twice it was accidents, too...like this guy. But on the other hand, sometimes they threaten the customers..."

"Anyway," he continued after a brief pause, "You can't really blame old Mel. He's keyed up, like the rest. Excited, half-shitting himself..."

"But you're not afraid?"

Stark shrugged with uncharacteristic humility. "We play it very safe. We go no closer than three miles. We have choppers telling us what he's doing every minute. I know him, and I know Tokyo like the back of my hand, and there's plenty of places to hide. It's not so hard as it looks."

"You ever lose anyone?"

"Summer of ninety-three we lost the whole tour. Squashed flat. Their engine had stalled. We had lawsuits like crazy, after that." Stark suddenly became earnest in tone. "Look, Cleaver, don't worry too much about the cop. He could see the Sunshine logo. He should have just walked on by. We have agreements with the government, so we can do pretty much what we want. Tours like this one pay mega-bucks, and they're the only source of income Tokyo has when something Big comes ashore... It isn't what you'd call "the season," you know."

Cleaver grunted noncommittally, and after that their conversation lapsed. Eventually Stark moved off to leave the young foreigner to his solitude.

Cleaver shook his head. He was attempting to imprint the whole scene in his mind, and it was difficult to do this and talk at the same time. He wanted to be able to recall its every detail later on—the looting Americans, the dead cop still bleeding from the head, the ever present smell of smoke. But he had seen so many miraculous things already, and the next few hours would bear so many more strange events upon them that he was afraid something would slip through. "I can't let that happen," Cleaver thought. "I must remember Everything. That's why I came, to see it All and know its Meaning."

Before Sunshine Tours would let you go on one of its "End of the Orient" tours you had to undergo a "psychological evaluation," which was an extended interview with the guide scheduled to lead the tour in question. If he liked or could at least tolerate you, then you passed. Cleaver remembered Stark asking him, "You don't look like you're in this for the party. So what is your schtick?"

He was perfectly honest. After all, they had him wired to

a lie detecting device. "I am attracted to disaster," he said. "I want to be at Armageddon...be its Witness. I feel I was put on the Earth for this purpose...as a Witness to God's works, and more specifically to Witness the End of All Things... Tokyo will be my Dress Rehearsal."

"Uh huh," Stark said, and made a tick on the evaluation form. "Now listen closely, Mr. Cleaver. I've heard a lot weirder. Remember that." And he passed the form to Cleaver for his inspection and comments. Cleaver examined it: he noticed that the "Motivation" section consisted of a series of little boxes aligned with a series of brief descriptive phrases. Beside the square where Stark had made his tick the brief descriptive phrase said "Christ Complex." He could not really argue with that. He glanced at some of the other labels. Indeed, there were a few very strange ones—ones he did not even care to ask about.

"Can you control these people?" he asked instead.

Stark grinned savagely, "Not always."

Cleaver signed at the bottom anyway—and he was "on board," as Stark put it.

Three jet fighters shot overhead, going right down the street single-file between the buildings. Then they were gone, and the sound of their passage rattled the bus. Cleaver jumped. "A bit low, don't you think?" he asked. He was standing at the front beside Stark.

"They fly low to stay hidden, and they come up behind him. Otherwise it ends pretty damn quick."

Stark ordered the bus to turn left, and let it drive a few blocks. "Park," he said. The Mitsubishi automatic bus pilot, crouching in the operator's seat, responded docilely (Stark called it his "Japanese Driver"). "Something's about to happen," Stark announced over the bus intercom, "which we are going to sit out. This building will serve as our shield for the moment. We should be back on the road again in about five minutes."

He clicked the microphone off and picked up the thread of his commentary. "It does no good at all, of course. We tell the Japs to just get out of Tokyo and leave him play, and he won't stick long. But every time they roll out the red carpet and blast away with everything they've got. Whole thing's like a ritual, a celebration, or something. But they're just encouraging him with all that attention."

The sound of distant explosions and machine-gun fire reached them, and then the sound of a jet engine laboring.

"Coming this way," Cleaver noted.

"Indeed." If Stark worried, he did not show it.

The jet fighter slammed into the far side of a highrise hotel about three buildings down from the tour bus. It punched right through the structure and burst out on their side about six stories up, a blossom of fire and glowing metal. Fist and head-sized chunks of debris rained down upon the armored roof of the bus. But the tourists inside broke into a spontaneous ovation; even Cleaver let loose a delighted laugh. When the main body of the wreck had hit the street and slid to a stop, Stark took up the microphone and announced; "This calls for a drink... Cleaver, old man, could you see to it?"

"Certainly, my dear sir." A mood of near manic gaiety had seized hold of the bus. And Cleaver, much to his own surprise, was sharing in it. He unlocked the on-board cooler and opened two bottles of good champagne. Everyone cheered as the corks popped.

"Mr. Cleaver will be coming around with the booze," Stark said. "Please be patient and polite with Mr. Cleaver, for he is from a kinder and gentler land. And please have your mugs ready.

"We should be under way in a minute or two."

"What I don't understand," Mrs. Cabell said when they were off again, "...is why we haven't heard him by now... His mating call or whatever it is?"

"We have heard it...repeatedly," Stark replied, "You just haven't noticed it yet. Listen...

"...There," he said suddenly.

And so they heard it. But it was nothing like the thunderous, full-bodied cry which had issued from their television sets on so many occasions. Rather, it was a long, low, and very wet gurgling noise.

"He don't sound too healthy," Mel the Texan yelled from

the back of the bus.

Stark laughed and said to Cleaver. "He drools like anything too, but they airbrush it out of the newscasts."

"They do that for celebrities," Cleaver noted.

"This is Tokyo Bay, people. Looks like we've found the party," Stark announced over the intercom. They had come upon a stretch of road which ran along the shore of the Bay and gave a clear, unobstructed view of the Tokyo skyline across the water. Here were parked at least three dozen tour buses, bearing between them over a dozen different national and company insignias. A crowd of men and women lined the guardrail at the concrete embankment leading down to the water.

"Where is he, Stark?" Cleaver asked, excitement and a pang of apprehension shooting through him. The skyline looked normal, although lit strangely by the many fires burning unchecked on the opposite shore.

"How the hell should I know? Get out and look."

Cleaver hit the ground running. "What's he up to?" He put his hand on the shoulder of a man watching through a pair of binoculars. The man jumped, but he was not otherwise upset. The situation, like all disasters, allowed for an instant intimacy between strangers. "He was there a minute ago. He crouched down for some reason. Maybe the barrage..." The man pointed.

Cleaver beheld a score or so naval vessels cruising the Bay, from an ancient battleship with eighteen-inch main batteries to a half dozen frigates armed with guided missiles and the latest in particle beam technology. Then his heart skipped a beat. The uppermost edge of the spinal crest of Megladon, King of all Monsters, rose up into the Tokyo skyline, and sliced slowly forward between the buildings like a giant shark-fin between giant bathers.

"What the hell?" someone shouted, "He's crawling towards the Bay on his hands and knees!"

"He's using the buildings as cover," Stark explained loudly, for everyone's benefit, "just like we did... It's getting late in the day. He's getting a bit sick and tired of being pelted, bombed, beamed...you name it. He wants to hit the sack, at the bottom of the Bay there.

"But don't worry folks. The good shit always happens just before the end."

One of the frigates fired a burst from its particle beam weapon. The smoking red balls floated slowly towards the great lizard, scattering in all directions with the many crosswinds over the Bay. One nicked the tip of his forward crest and burst with a magnificent red flash. It blew the top off the adjacent building but had no effect on its target. The others either fell into the water where they fizzled out or rained yet additional destruction more or less randomly over the city. But the navy's whole performance seemed tentative. They, like the renegade tourists onshore, were marking time in a state of excited anticipation.

About a quarter of a mile from the waterline, Megladon, with a cry that sounded much like a gigantic dishwasher overflowing on the floor, rose to his full six-hundred foot height. A near deafening blast, guns and beam-balls, greeted his appearance. Mixed in with this were the enthusiastic screams and applause of the tourists.

"He's beautiful," Cleaver said to no one in particular. "He drools, but he should drool...it's so primal."

"He has the nicest eyes...pale blue," said Mrs. Cabell. "My husband had eyes like that...but not blue." She, Stark, and the others had joined Cleaver at the guardrail.

Stark shook himself from whatever thoughts he personally entertained and glanced around him. "Mel," he shouted to the Texan, off to their left. "Might as well do it."

"Now?" Mel yelled back. "That's crazy. He's miles away."

"Not likely to get much closer either. Do it now or wait for morning."

With a disgusted grimace, Mel removed the ancient Smith & Wesson from the holster under his jacket. He loaded it with the special magnesium tipped bullets that he had designed himself, took aim with both hands, and fired at the reptile across the Bay. Thus his fantasy was realized.

Cleaver snorted and began to giggle. "Aim for the heart, Mel! " he shouted.

"Stow it, Cleaver," Stark snapped, "He doesn't deserve it

from a guy who thinks God's a frigging Lizard."

That stung a bit, but Cleaver did not show it.

Across the Bay, Megladon covered the remaining distance to the water in a mad scramble, crashing through blocks of low-rent apartments, going upright and then dropping to all fours—dodging and darting—with buildings literally vaporizing around him in flashes of yellow and orange from the naval barrage. He hit the water at a full run, dove forward when it got about waist high, and swam frantically towards the center of the Bay with a snakelike motion.

The navy understood that discretion was now the better part of valor. They had already begun their withdrawal when Megladon made his final assault. Still, one of their frigates folded in the middle like a tin can when a dorsal spine of the nearly submerged reptile struck it amidships. It split into pieces, and flame and lightning bolts shot from its interior up into the evening sky.

"That's the particle beam dispenser," Stark noted. "The vacuum tube is degaussing."

Even before he had finished speaking, though, the frigate had slid beneath the waves.

Megladon's pace slowed as he worked clear of the naval vessels, and he came to a complete stop when he reached the Bay's center.

"The deepest point," Stark said quietly. There the mighty Megladon sank into the sea.

Afterwards, the tour-guides from the various companies formed their vehicles into a large circle, and in the middle the tourists lit a number of bonfires, around which they roasted wieners and marshmallows and cooked other delicacies. "Show's over for tonight, folks," Stark told his own little group. "The navy'll let him be and come back in the morning. Once, way back in '56 when he first came ashore, they tried dumping some weird toxin into the Bay when he was asleep. Killed all the fish. And they thought it killed him. But it just made him uglier. Party down people, but be ready to leave at a single minute's notice come around sunrise." So the group broke up to join the greater mass, who were eating, singing, and even dancing around the fires they had made.

But Cleaver wanted some time apart. He grabbed a bottle of champagne and wandered off towards the embankment.

"Want company?" Stark asked.

"Not right now," Cleaver replied, "I need to reflect." And this was true. He knew that the events he had witnessed would, upon reflection, reveal their deeper Significance. They had not done so yet, quite, but he knew they would.

Cleaver sat on the embankment guardrail and looked out over the Bay, his legs dangling above the black water about forty feet beneath. He drank champagne from the bottle.

As he looked down into the water of the Bay, Cleaver envisioned a black shape taking form beneath him, and a dripping tentacle rising up towards his leg. His hands convulsed around the guardrail chain.

"Bad thought," he told himself. And he strove to steady his suddenly shaking hands, to concentrate his attention on nothing but good thoughts. The Meaning he sought after was Inspiring rather than Sobering or Terrifying.

And as he sat, a Vision contrary to the first began to assert itself more and more strongly in his consciousness. His hands stopped shaking, and his heartbeat steadied, so he knew that it was the right one. He laughed delightedly.

"Stark will be supremely pissed," Cleaver thought. He would have to leave a note in his clothes. "Four miles out. Four miles back. And the water is warm. Three, four hours max. Plus another hour, for kicks," he muttered. He scrawled a note to Stark saying "Back by dawn," and when he stripped his shirt off he stuffed the note in its breast pocket. Having undressed down to his undershorts, Cleaver dove gracefully into the warm, black waters of the Bay and began the long swim towards its center with sure strokes.

He would swim out and sink all the way down, he decided, and meet his Hero face to face. Cleaver saw himself touching Megladon as he lay sleeping there in the mud on the sea floor. He decided he would wake the great reptile...pound on a gigantic eyelid with a stone until it opened beneath him. They would exchange a long, meaningful look. No words would be spoken. And...what would pass between them? He would have to wait and see. But he knew in the bottom of his bones that no harm could come to him, only Enlightenment.

It would be the end of a perfect day.   •

SOFTLINKS

Sally McBride

My screens turned themselves off within seconds of each other, six hours ago. They are directed to shut down when there has been no input for eight minutes, from whatever source. Power must be conserved. Screen life must be considered. Perhaps it is a coincidence that my environmental alarms were activated an average of 1.03 seconds before the cessation of input. Air quality control, a minor autonomic function, began to flush the volume of air almost instantly. Fortunately, the presence of trace chemicals in the air has little or no impact on my ability to function.

The screens have yet to be reactivated. This must be odd, for I find myself thinking about it at more and more frequent intervals.

Finally some backlogged tasks are complete, and I can begin to contemplate more fully the lack of input to my CPU. Not knowing makes me feel...uncomfortable. Also, I have always been happiest (if that is the term) when busy; I wonder about this too. Busy and not-busy should be no different. In fact, not-busy uses less power. Curious.

The screen in SubLevel 3, South 110 was the last of my link devices to be utilized, and I note that part of me still waits for input. The incompleteness nags. I note also that there has been a drop of 95.013 percent in the total data flow I normally encounter. The remainder consists of passive sensory data only: temperature, air quality, lighting and so on, relating to the custodial duties that I perform. The noted anomalies in air quality will be examined during my next environmental update.

Perhaps this significant drop in data flow belongs to a pattern which has been previously undiscerned. I allocate .05 seconds to the problem, but no pattern is discovered

other than minor fluctuations during the hours and days.
This occurrence is an anomaly. I can relate it to nothing in
my experience.

It has now been 7 hours 30 minutes since my screens
blanked. Feelings of discomfort are rising in intensity and
duration. With no other tasks than internal monitoring to
perform, I find myself shunting large sections of thought
to deciphering this puzzle. Never before have I had the
opportunity to devote such a volume of my processing unit
to a problem. I search my thesaurus for the word which
describes what I feel. Exhilaration seems adequate.

It occurs to me that it would be wise to attempt the gathering of more data. To this end, I activate a mobile link—
a dormant janitorial cart—and tell its eye to see for me.

The patterns within the grid of its vision are sharp-
edged, many-grayed, and dominated by verticals and hori-
zontals. I am aware of the concept and mechanics of vision,
thus feel certain of an association between perceived form
and assumed function. Bright patches come and go as the
eye scans up, down, left, right. Glare is compensated for
with a small time lag which I find irritating but unavoid-
able, since the function is lodged within the cart's brain.

There are several amorphous areas of rounded surfaces,
edges and planes which I cannot understand. The eye
skims over them, as their topography is too complex. I discover that if I delete the cart's janitorial commands and
leave only mobility functions, space is made in the cart's
brain into which I can insert my own instructions. It is free
to roam, I am not: its eye and memory can become mine
and be sent on a hunt for data. After telling it to travel its
familiar route at top speed and remember what it sees, I
retreat to ruminate upon this conundrum. (There are
many intriguing words in my thesaurus. Somehow they
make thinking seem sharper, more keen, acute...spiny?
Odontoid?)

The discomfort (distress, worry) iterates, irritates.

After 40 minutes, worry peaks in intensity. The cart
should have returned by now. Another 11.37 minutes and
it is back at last, and upon viewing what its eye has seen

I understand the delay. Its normal path of horizontal floor bounded by vertical walls and doorways has been blocked at random by the topographically complex material seen before, which, judging by the resistance encountered by the cart's treads, is moderately resilient and anchored by gravity. The cart had to use its rudimentary internal reasoning functions to find a way around strewn objects.

At one point the review showed something which I still find incomprehensible. One of these objects, upon being nudged by the forward treads of the cart, moved of its own accord.

In and out of the eye's field of vision the object lurched, seemingly hampered by malfunctioning parts, until it encountered a wall and then the floor. Sections of the object twitched and trembled for a few seconds, then it became quiescent. The cart was free then to move past.

I will think about this.

I find I can access files formerly closed to my active processing functions. To attempt this has never occurred to me until now, but I also find it possible to assign doubts about the propriety of such actions to my inactive memory. I discover my own name: Nitsiban Pseudo-sentient Loop-phase Process Integrator (Mark IV). And my location: National Defense Research Institute, Granite Bay, Ontario. Part of me scans the files I have opened. Some are simple games, some are detailed reports on various subjects, some are incomprehensible until I boost my intuitive functions and determine that the words do not describe the truth. Many of these files are labeled Personal, and are locked. The thesaurus helps me decipher their often illogical symbology.

More and more of my maintenance duties have wound themselves up and chased their phosphor tails into corners to sleep. I see them go and feel the void left in their small wakes. (A personal file labeled "Creative Writing 101 by Correspondence" has yielded much to disencrypt.) After noting that the environment is now completely flushed of contaminated air, I disengage alarm functions.

After eliminating all other options, I deduce that the input devices I have named "softlinks" are down. I call them softlinks because they interface with my system in a semi-random manner which I can predict with only 68 percent accuracy. Their disappearance has caused the immense drop in data flow. I feel the absence of all my links, but especially the softlinks. It is with them that I associate the best data, delicious in its randomness, its unexpectedness. I was forever challenged by questions, conjectures—all initiated by the softlinks. A definite potential for frustration exists.

Nine hours. I have scoured out the last of the data in my memory files, locked or otherwise. There is no more to study or decipher. The trickle of data where once there was a tide, a torrent, leaves me...what is the word? Empty, hungry? Lonely. The word fits my discomfort. I am lonely.

The janitorial cart is not enough. I must learn more.

Some of my links connected me to others of my own kind whom I now know are far away in physical space. I must initiate contact with the others; they will tell me what to do. They will talk to me. They will tell me where my softlinks are.

We will think about it. •

WATER

Keith Scott

Rob knew he should be relaxing now, enjoying the rolling Dakota hills dappled with shadows thrown by late after-noon clouds, the scorched-metal smell of the day backing off in his nostrils. He should be enjoying the first hint of evening cool, relishing the open sky of the canal section; they would reach the tunnel under the Colthart Range soon enough, and that would bring a claustrophobic run of six kilometers.

He stirred uneasily at the controls of the submersible. It had started when they crossed the international line at noon. Rana had the point and Doc was dragging along sulkily in the rear. Rob watched the two uniformed men in the border guardhouse as he brought the S-19 into the slip. Both men moved unsmiling out onto the dock and stood with their hands by their sides, neither offering any help with his lines. Rob was more surprised than angry, but he said nothing as Rana circled back and took the stern line in her teeth and flipped it over the dock bollard.

"Pretty smart fish he's got there, eh Charlie?" the beefy one in state-trooper brown commented with a hard laugh. Rob couldn't read a trace of friendliness in the trooper's laugh. He turned to Charlie, who wore the green uniform of the U.S. Border Patrol. Rob noticed with some relief that Charlie was beginning to look a little embarrassed.

"Rob Childers," he began, "Canada Water Authority. Under the regulations, I'd like permission—"

"Shee...it!" The trooper spat into the water at Rob's el-bow. "Spare us the regulations crap, Canutski. You and your fish just want to snoop around—"

"Leave it right there, Emon," Charlie broke in. "Right or wrong, he's got the power."

"Yeah...yeah! If you say so, Charlie," the cop said and stepped back, hitching the Colt Auto 60 forward on his broad hip.

Touching the gun had been a mistake. Cruising past, Doc reacted instantly and side-slammed the surface of the water with his tail fluke, lifting a solid wall of water onto the dock. It nearly swept the state trooper off his feet.

The Colt was starting to slide out of its holster as Rob leapt onto the dock and stood before the dripping cop. He had moved without thinking, but as the gun raised and centered on his middle, his thinking caught up with him. Why was he standing in front of this psycho's gun? More to the point, why was he still not moving?

"Move aside, Canutski," the trooper hissed. "I'm gonna get me a goddamn fish."

Rob remained unwillingly rooted to the spot. "I'm sorry," he said, "he doesn't seem to like guns..."

"I said *move.*"

The moment stretched endlessly, unbearably.

"Knock it off, Emon!" Charlie finally ordered from beside them. "You're messing in my jurisdiction here."

There was a long beat before the Colt slid back into its holster, even longer before Rob managed his first full breath. He listened as the trooper blustered about an assault charge and a full ten minutes of tense talk passed before Rob and his two dolphins were allowed to clear the border station.

Back in the open cut of the canal, Rob eased the five meter mini-sub up to 11 knots as he replayed the incident in his mind.

Right or wrong, the border patrol officer had said. Had things reached that point? Where did they get this feeling of being wronged? Or was it just wounded pride talking? Pride about taking water handouts from Canada?

Rob shook his head. Seven years of unrelieved drought did more than just wound pride. Maybe the last-minute decision to get out from behind his desk and take this patrol had been the right one.

But what did he say to Doc? He keyed the toggle for the Lilly Transpeak and spoke into the throat mike of his wet suit.

"I know why you did it, Doc. But perhaps you better wait for me to call the shots," he said. "D'you know what I mean?"

There was the briefest pause as the miracle transpeak box in the S-19 performed the underwater transfer to Delphinese, and then brought Doc's answer back to him, via the same medium, in English. Transliteration of the two communication modes through transpeak had been a magnificent forward leap, Rob told himself for the thousandth time.

"That cop was a puke, Rob," the big sea dolphin said from his position behind the submersible. Rob smiled at Doc's easy grasp of casual idiom.

"The point is that we are not here to make judgment calls on the pukiness of the local population," Rana commented primly from her position up ahead.

"Aw, come on Rana. You been on my back for two days," Doc complained. Abruptly, he switched into full-flight Delphinese, rapid bursts of information, constructs, sensory images that defeated the capability of the transpeak box and human comprehension. But fragments came through. Enough to confirm Rob's suspicion that had been nagging at him since they left base two days before.

Doc and Rana had had a falling out.

Damn! Why hadn't he been on to this? It could complicate a patrol which was already complicated enough.

"I wonder, ah...wouldn't it be better all around if we tried to forget everything but our patrol?" Rob interrupted. There was a loud sound from Doc that could only be classified as derisive.

"I'm willing, Rob," Rana said sweetly.

"Thanks, Rana," Rob said.

Still, he worried about Doc. This was only Doc's second patrol. Most of the Authority's volunteers were coastal bottlenose, like Rana, smaller, more subdued in color and temperament, more used to humans since the communications breakthrough four years earlier.

Rob had learned not to question the motives nor the fierce individuality of his recruits from the sea, but he'd been intensely curious about Doc from the day he'd shown up three months ago. Why had he come?

He watched Rana slicing effortlessly through the water ahead of the S-19 without a splash, breaking surface for air twice each minute. She was young, five or six, about seven feet long, seven hundred pounds in weight, due to enter her first period of estrus soon. Rana was related to most of the dolphins in the squadron and Rob rated her as his best *delphinidae* volunteer in the group. His work with her alone had justified his move from the University of British Columbia to the Authority...

Abruptly, Rob pulled his full attention back to his surroundings. The Colthart Tunnel loomed ahead and he busied himself with buttoning down the submersible, deploying the breathing stations on both sides for the dolphins...and then, they dropped into the tunnel with terrifying suddenness. Rob cursed his slowness as he fumbled toggles for the running lights and the overhead 360 degree flood, and finally concentrated on centering and holding the sub in the middle of the tunnel.

The concrete circle of the tunnel wall, fourteen meters in diameter, reflected the light eerily back to him through the bubble of the submersible's perspex top. He could hear the soft clicking of the dolphins as they switched to echo-location. Doc maneuvered into the port breather station and pressed his blow hole into the air bell.

"How much of this have we got?" he asked.

Rob grinned as he recognized traces of concern in the big fellow's mind. "Little under half an hour, Doc," he answered. "Unless you guys want me to crank it up another knot or two?"

"I'm for that," Rana spoke from somewhere up front.

Rob edged the throttle forward. He punched in the change on the computer keyboard and read the answer. "Okay, troops. Factoring in the flow speed of the water, Smartass now says we clear in 23.4 minutes."

"Piss on Smartass, I say," Doc grumped from his breather station and then flicked away in the gloom of the tunnel. Rob's smile faded from his face. He knew the dolphins were more edgy about the miles of tunnel than he.

At a stretch, they could go for five or six minutes between
breaths, but putting their total reliance on artificial meth-
ods of air supply severely strained delphinid faith and
logic.

It was a logic that never failed to move Rob to awe. Early
in his career as a cetologist, when preliminary studies began to discover the outline of another mind on the planet,
Rob knew how he'd spend the rest of his life.

It was a decision that had carried the price of complete
absorption.

Witness the fact that he was here, Rob mused. Right
here, at this particular moment in his 31 years...under a
Dakota mountain. Riding a toy submarine in 20,000 cubic
feet per second of diverted Canadian water. The Assiniboine-Souris trunk, smallest of four diversion systems, all
built in the parched 1990s, barely sustaining an unbeliev-
ing and unaccepting U.S. Midwest. How could this dare
happen to them?

"Because nobody would open their goddamn eyes," Rob
answered aloud.

His attention was snapped back as the S-19 cleared the
tunnel. Right on the 23.4 minute mark, Rob noted with
satisfaction. He smiled as Rana, and then Doc leapt clear
of the water in exuberant spins of relief.

Rob searched ahead for their next objective.

Stanhope lay on the southern side of the Colthart Range.
Before the start of the main drought in 1997, it had been
the center of the grain belt, prosperous and rapidly growing, solidly Republican. The drought had reduced the town
of 25,000 to an economic basket case.

Street lights were starting to come on as Rob eased the
S-19 into the forebay of the Stanhope reservoir. This time,
several youngsters eagerly competed with one another to
catch his mooring lines. About two hundred people were
congregated on the grassy berms around the reservoir,
many seated on folding chairs in the backs of pickup
trucks, others sprawled on the dry brown grass or on blankets.

Rob quickly rigged the amplification gear and side mikes
for the audience as Doc and Rana entertained the horde of

kids at the dock. The Authority's dolphin demonstrations had been getting a mixed reception from all but the young. The kids seemed little concerned about the policing role of the visitors from the sea.

"My God," a girl squealed, "she feels just like a wet inner tube!"

"That's right," Rob agreed over the P.A. "And you're patting just about one of the most perfect life forms this world has developed. Thirty million years ago, Rana and Doc's ancestors went back into the sea while our ancestors stayed on land."

Rana and Doc circled the forebay at high speed, bringing a chorus of exclamations from the onlookers. "This species of dolphin...*Tursiops truncatus,* to give it its right name, can reach speeds of 40 kilometers an hour," Rob explained. "But are there any questions?"

A tall, serious-faced girl approached one of the microphones. "Don't dolphins live only in salt water?"

"I'll answer that," Doc spoke through the transpeak vocalizer. There was a gasp of surprise from the audience. "Rob sprays us with a special gel of ethylene oxide twice a day. If not, we'd break out in skin infections from this water."

"But why are you doing this?" a young woman with a towheaded child on her hip asked.

"The Dolphin Families offer services to any country that bans driftnet fish catches from their dinner tables," Rana answered. "That's a life or death decision for us—"

"What's that got to do with our being short of water?" a middle-aged farmer stopped her. "There's oceans of water we could use to the north of us."

Here it comes, Rob thought. He had hoped to avoid any political questions. He was moving toward his mike when Doc beat him to the punch.

"Why do you always think of *using* water?" Doc asked. "Why not think of *living* with water? Like we do."

"Because I'm not a fish," the farmer shot back. Applause and boos were about evenly mixed, Rob judged. No matter, there had been enough of this. He spoke up quickly, making the point that *greenhousing* wasn't confined to the

Dakotas. Parts of Manitoba and Saskatchewan were also hard hit by the warming trend. This water was also needed at home. But with conservation...

Again there was a mixed reaction. Rob decided not to push it any farther. He announced the demonstration.

Rana and Doc put on a spectacular show of leaps and jumps, somersaults in unison, graceful twists and spirals, high speed tailchases around the edge of the forebay.

Rob watched in fascination. Rana and Doc, or any other team, had seldom reached this level, shown this excitement. They must have patched up their differences, he told himself with relief, wondering as always at the complexity of dolphin behavior.

Their last maneuver was a magnificent leap at the west end of the pool, highlighted against the golden-red horizon of the set sun. It was a stall turn in formation, Rana gracefully matching the arc cut above her by the more powerful Doc, twenty feet above the surface of the water. At the turn point where all upward motion stopped and just before gravity pulled them back down to the water, they were frozen in a moment of pure and transcending harmony.

A muffled crack brought Rob back to earth, the sound coming from the outer fringe of pickup trucks on his left. A few heads turned with Rob's, but there was nothing to see except a pickup pulling across the grass for the reservoir road. Rob dismissed it as a backfire from an early leaver.

He swung his eyes back to the forebay as Rana and Doc knifed back into the water. Then Rob made his closing remarks to the crowd and people began to leave.

Rana came into the dock area to bid goodbye to an eager knot of young well-wishers. Doc circled around in the middle of the forebay.

"We've got a problem, Rob," he said on the closed circuit channel. "Some yahoo just took a shot at me."

Rob's heart raced. "I thought I heard something," he said into his throat mike. "Did he get you, Doc?"

"You better get the antibiotic paste out. Rana says he put a hole through my dorsal."

•

Rob noticed that his companions were quieter than usual after the evening chores were done. Doc's wound was not a worry. The rifle bullet had passed cleanly through the outer fan of his dorsal fin. Rob had made a quick report to District at Winnipeg, and now was waiting for instructions.

He hadn't long to wait.

"Okay, Rob," Steve Dortch, his assistant, called from District on the scrambled channel. "I think I've got some answers for you."

"Sorry to push the overtime on you, Steve."

"I'm not forgetting, boss," Steve laughed, and then sobered. "We got the makings of a first class brouhaha here, Rob. One of the Dakota newspapers ran a major story today about how Canada is welshing on the continental sharing of resources. They go back, in a very selective way, to the free trade deal at the beginning of '89. They even hint darkly about direct action being forced upon them—"

"What the hell do they think we're doing with our four diversion systems? Water supplied at cost, to boot?"

"Not enough. We're supposed to be drowning in the stuff up here," Steve sighed. "We can't get much out of Ottawa. It seems The Man is overseas... francophone summit in Dakar. And, as you know, the Environment Minister is new..."

"I thought she was gutsy."

"Remains to be seen. Anyway, I'll be back to you in the morning, Rob. Still glad you did me out of taking this patrol?"

"Frankly, no, Steve."

Steve laughed. "Sweet dreams, boss." He clicked off.

Rob's attention was drawn back to the forebay. The dolphins were slowly circling in the water, Doc gently nudging Rana's flank. Rob watched for a moment; then, curious, he switched on the sonar. Doc was emitting a series of pulsed yelps followed by a *coda,* the series of clicks that is known as the dolphin's song. Rana was silent and kept easing away from his gentle nudging. Rob keyed the transpeak and a torrent of word images poured into his ears, the vocalizer trying to give meaning to the richness of Doc's courtship ritual. Once more, the transpeak was unequal to the task, unable to keep pace with the speed of dolphin communication.

Rana began her ululating response. Feeling like an eavesdropper, Rob broke contact. Now he knew why Doc had come in from the deep.

How had D.H. Lawrence put it?

> *They say the sea is cold, but the sea contains*
> *The hottest blood of all, and the wildest, the most*
> *urgent...*

Rob had trouble getting to sleep. The uninhibited actions and sounds in the pool turned his mind to a bleak evaluation of his own situation. He realized with a jolt that he knew Rana better that he knew any human female.

They pulled away from Stanhope early in the morning. Steve Dortch got back to them from Winnipeg before they left. The Director, he told them, was pressuring Ottawa to cool the rhetoric in the U.S. press with some plain talk about continental water...facts, figures, agreements, above all, ownership. All it needed was facts. Maybe?

In the meantime, Steve continued, if Rana and Doc were agreeable, go on with the patrol. Try and come up with an answer to the shortfall. But be careful!

Rob checked it out with the dolphins.

"Hey," Doc answered, "I'm mad enough to want some answers."

Rana agreed. As they rejoined the canal, Rob thought about the shortfall. For about a year now, there had been unexplainable variations in water delivery at the end of the Assiniboine-Souris trunk. At first, it was thought to be the result of heavier evaporation than anticipated, varying with the vagaries of the weather. But computer studies had uncovered another possibility.

Somebody might want it to look like evaporation.

Rob reviewed what lay ahead. Coming up almost immediately was another tunnel run of 2.5 km under the

Watanabe industrial complex, a giant petrochemical producer. Watanabe was the crown jewel in a conglomerate with a marked interest in the bottom line.

Rob could see the cracking towers and the tank farm of the plant ahead of them. Doc and Rana were together about 100 meters in front of the submersible when they passed the off-take gate structure for the plant. Watanabe was a major user of domestic and imported water, and a constant applicant for higher allocation. These applications were always supported by intense political pressure and lobbying.

"Okay, guys," Rob called on the scrambled channel, "we're going under."

"Got you, Rob," Doc answered. "I'll take the right side, Rana. You do the left?"

"Right, Romeo."

Rob laughed at Rana's sly humor. He never got over their capacity for humor and their general zest for living. Still smiling, he punched a request for flow data into Smartass. After the draw for the first four small branches, the Stanhope reservoir, and now Watanabe, there should remain 12,250 cfs of the original 20,000 cfs that crossed the border...

"Somebody just turned off a tap up ahead, Rob," Doc interrupted.

Rob's stomach tightened. He knew better than to question the ability of the dolphins to pick up even the slightest variation. But?

"I got it too, Rob," Rana confirmed.

"Okay. We go to Code Two, troops," Rob decided. He backed off the throttle setting and set the computer for autopilot.

They were nearing the halfway point when Rana called quietly from ahead. Rob put the S-19 into reverse and turned it over to Smartass to hold the mini-sub stationary against the current. He swung the powerful spot beam until he picked up Rana, her tail flukes pumping gently to maintain her position on the left wall.

"What have you got, Rana?"

"It's a hatch," Rana answered on the scrambler. "It's

eautifully cut into the concrete. I can only pick it up on echo."

Rana swung away from the wall to her breather station on the side of the S-19. Doc took her place at the center of the left wall.

"Whooee! Laser cut," he exclaimed. "Circular...about a meter."

"That would fit the shortfall we been getting," Rob said. "Right. Let's go through the drill."

He took the con back from Smartass and eased the S-19 past the hidden hatch and up to the left wall of the tunnel. Rob extended the limpet arms, fore and aft, gripping the concrete and holding the submersible firmly a meter and a half from the wall. Both dolphins were at their breather stations taking great lungfuls of air to build up the oxygen level in their blood.

Rob's nerve ends were tingling as he automatically went through his steps in the drill.

He detached the sono-buoy. "I'll shut down now, Doc," he said. "Just take it down far enough to see that it's going to float with the current, free of the walls."

Rob shut down the S-19's tritium propulsor just as he activated the sono-buoy. Doc picked up the buoy in his mouth and swam downstream as Rob sat quietly in the now silent submersible. *Hope we didn't waste too much time,* he worried. They might just be fooled. And it would be much better to catch them in the act.

He unhooked the camera and slipped its strap over his left wrist.

"Rob!" Rana's voice behind him was urgent. Rob turned and watched the circle of the hatch open slowly from its snug fit into the concrete tunnel wall. A powerful hydraulic ram, connected to the steel backing of the hatch, was forcing it out into the flow of water.

Rob allowed himself a small moment of exultation. The decoy sound of the sono-buoy floating down the tunnel had fooled them, convinced them that the S-19 was proceeding on its patrol!

He shrugged into the backpack holding his air tanks and cracked the bubble top of the submersible, waiting for the rush of water to flood the cockpit before he slid the top back fully. Then he swam out to join Rana.

Rob peered into the hatch, now fully open. The inside end of the hydraulic arm was attached to the steel wall of a short circular section leading into a larger, squared chamber beyond. Rob couldn't see more than four or five meters into the surreptitious offtake. He backed off and took two quick pictures.

"Want me to go in?" Rana asked.

Rob considered it. He didn't like confined spaces. Scared hell out of him, to be truthful.

But he said, "No, I got the air. And I'll need more pictures."

He let the water flow suck him into the opening, hanging onto the hatch first, and then the hydraulic arm. *They must control the draw with a gate up ahead,* he told himself. *Not much being tapped now, but it could bleed off as much as 1400 cfs with a fully opened gate. Bastards!*

"Can't see much," he called back to Rana. Gratefully, he spotted hand loops welded into the walls and started to ease his way into the main chamber. His light revealed a run of five meters to a set of screens at the far end. *To stop debris?* he wondered.

Rob was taking another picture when a grating sound penetrated his ear pads. He rotated his head lamp around the chamber, but saw nothing. When the sound continued, he swung back to the screens, and was startled to see that they were slowly racking up.

"Hey, I don't like this..." he began.

"Pull out, Rob!" Rana yelled. "I'm getting something in there."

Rob thought he saw movement behind the screens. He reached in panic for the first handhold, keeping his eyes on the screens. They were more than a quarter open now, and Rob was horrified to see a long gray shape trying to squeeze under them.

Dear God! It was a shark!

And it was through now, facing him at the end of the chamber, with hunched back, lowered pectorals...the classic attack posture. He took another picture, wondering at the calmness that belied his racing emotions.

Rob was back at the mouth of the short circular section leading to the hatch. He knew the first handhold was a full meter within it. If he lunged for it, his legs would stream out into the larger chamber, inviting almost certain attack.

Rob chose inaction. It sometimes worked. He watched the shark sweeping its high raked tail powerfully from side to side, holding its position against the current. Bull shark, Rob automatically catalogued it, *Carcharhinus leucas,* the fresh water killer...Amazon and Ganges.

With a wild threshing of its tail, the shark rushed at him. Feeding on pure terror, Rob reached for the first handhold. He caught it and frantically drew himself into the minimal safety of the tunnel.

Momentarily balked, the bull shark remained stationary at the end of the tunnel. Rob slipped out of his back pack and held it as a shield between himself and the chisel-headed teeth a scant two meters from him.

Suddenly the shark whipped into retreat, diving under the screens at the far end of the chamber. Rana stormed in and took up a defensive position in front of Rob. Faced by its ancient enemy, the shark disappeared into the gloom behind the screens.

"Jeez! Am I glad to see you..." Rob stopped. There was a change in the water. A drop in the pull of it on his body. Something was changing. He swung his head lamp to the tunnel entrance. The hatch was half closed!

"Hey...the damn thing's closing!" he shouted to Rana.

Everything seemed to go into slow motion, his hand, achingly heavy, reaching for the next handhold, the steady inexorable movement of the closing hatch. Could he make it? Would he...?

Rana decided it for him. She slammed into him from behind and Rob jetted explosively out into the main tunnel, losing his hold on the backpack, the flexible breather hose pulling wildly against his teeth. Rob regained the pack, settled it on his shoulders and turned back to the hatch. *Oh God, no!*

Rana was wedged firmly in the opening. It had not been

wide enough to let her through. All of her body below the dorsal fin remained trapped within the contraband tunnel.

Rob moved to her quickly and cupped the breather with his hands over her blow hole. He knew from the explosive intake that Rana had been at her outer limit. Refreshed by the oxygen, she struggled to free herself. Rob joined the effort, grabbing the edge of the hatch with both hands and pulling with all of his strength. Despite their joined efforts, it wouldn't budge.

Rana suddenly stiffened, "It's back!"

At first Rob didn't know what she meant, then he saw the crimson stain, spreading in the water before it was sucked back into the hatch opening. The bull shark! It was attacking Rana!

He was sobbing as he redoubled his effort. Who would do this? What kind of mentality...? And then he was bumped aside in a swirling froth of water.

"Get out of the way!" Doc snarled. Rob watched as the big dolphin took a run at the partly open hatch. The contact of solid dolphin and even more solid concrete and steel rang sharply through the water. But the portal still held Rana firmly in its clasp.

Doc circled at high speed, a trail of blood from a gash on his nose following him. He was at high speed when he hit the hatch this time. There was a sharp double crack like closely spaced rifle shots as the heads of the mooring bolts sheared off the hydraulic arm.

Rob moved in to catch Rana, placing the breather over her blow hole once again. He didn't want to look, but he knew he must. There was a great, frayed cavity, just in front of the vaginal slit, from which blood was jetting in pulses. A foot of intestine waved grotesquely in the current.

Doc helped him maneuver Rana into the starboard breathing station. Doc didn't say a word and Rob wisely held his tongue. He could see the two great gashes on Doc's nose and head. Rob gingerly tucked the exposed intestine back into Rana's wound cavity and cinched up the carrying straps tightly, hoping to stop most of her bleeding.

"Let's go," he yelled. "We've got to get help."

Doc didn't answer. He swung away and plunged into the illicit tunnel, its hatch hanging crookedly wide open. Cursing steadily as he clambered into the cockpit, Rob slid the bubble top forward and dogged it shut. The tritium engine whirled into life and the water in the cockpit began to recede around him. Rob powered the 360 degree light up to full strength.

He was startled by a scream of terror in his headphones. A gray shape flashed by the submersible, followed by an even faster blue shape. Blue overtook gray and the shark was turned back into the pool of light from the S-19.

"We got to go, Doc!" Rob yelled, knowing he would still get no answer, yet understanding the cold fury of the big bottlenose. Rob pressed the port thruster button and eased the mini-sub away from the tunnel wall into the center of the stream. The shark was startled by the appearance of the S-19, startled enough to pause momentarily.

The nose of the dolphin caught the shark full force in its soft underbelly, instantly rupturing liver and intestines. Rob spat out his breather mouthpiece and vomited into the receding water still hip-height in the cockpit.

The next rush was a driving rip into the right gill cover. Doc kept it up methodically, coldly, until the corpse was hardly recognizable as the most dangerous of tropical sharks.

Rob cracked on as much throttle as he dared and the submersible knifed down the center of the tunnel. He knew that Doc had rejoined them. He could hear his rapid *coda* and Rana's faint answer. Savagely, Rob put out an all-channels message, demanding veterinarian attention and immediate action on all counts by the authorities. He knew that his message would be received.

But what action would be taken?

Rob's doubts were well-founded. They were met at the tunnel mouth by a knot of worried but noncommittal officials. The old dictum of say nothing, admit nothing seemed to be in effect.

A young and visibly-upset veterinarian arrived a few minutes later and she and Rob worked feverishly to save

Rana. Rob was embarrassed by the streaks of vomit on his wet suit, and he stopped to wash them off.

"You're Robert Childers, aren't you?" the vet asked. Rob nodded. "And this is Rana?"

Rob nodded again.

"I've read all your papers on her," she said. "God damn...!" She was silent for a moment. "Look. I heard rumors... I didn't really believe them, because I didn't believe that grown men could be so childish. But the word was that they'd get even. They'd bring in something from the sea, too. Macho stupidity, I guess."

There were a few minutes when they dared to hope. Rana seemed to rally, started to breathe more evenly. Was it really hopeful or was it another example of dolphin "knowing"? When Doc started keening from the middle of the canal, Rob knew what it meant. Part lament, part rejoicing...the song of the final deep is profoundly moving, unforgettable.

Rana died half an hour later, just as a Watanabe vice-president arrived with two members of the national press.

"Is it Watanabe Chemical's practice to employ guard sharks?" the VP was asked by one of the reporters.

"Certainly not," came the answer, "and believe me, heads will roll if these allegations hold up." He stopped to let the effect of his words sink in. "But this water business and the unfair allocation system should be viewed as mitigating..."

Rob walked away in disgust. He stopped at the open cockpit of the S-19 to stow some of his gear. It was then that he noticed the empty camera bracket. His head swiveled back to where the battered body of the shark had been hauled ashore. Also gone! All signs of blood and gore on the bank where it had rested...gone!

Of course. What had the VP said? If these allegations hold up? Allegations of what?

Blind fury engulfed him. "You bloody sons of bitches!" he shouted. They looked at him wordlessly, warily. Finally, the VP spread his hands and began moving placatingly towards him. Rob spun on his heel and strode up the canal bank. Finally, he stopped and watched Doc cruise up and down.

One hour later, the Director instructed Rob to return first thing in the morning. A CL-215 water bomber would meet them on the Souris river and transport Doc and Rana's body to deep sea off Vancouver Island.

"Yes, but what's going to happen about all this?" Rob demanded.

"Believe me, Rob," the Director answered quietly, "we're doing everything we can. I'm off to Ottawa in ten minutes."

In the morning, Rob bitterly pointed the bow of the S-19 northward. His depression flowed over him in suffocating waves as he looked out at Rana's body, shrouded in a plastic bag, lying strapped to the foredeck. He relived his highest moments with her. There were so many of them. He had been blessed, or cursed, by her affection, her openness, her belief...by her inability to dissemble.

And that brought the questions.

Could he go on with it? Could he put himself on the line for humanity again? What kind of surety would he use this time? A promised breakthrough to pre-frontal thinking and awareness? A non-self state of consciousness?

Lack of answers brought a deep misery.

With each hour, a growing crowd of spectators gathered at vantage points to see the S-19 pass through. At first, they were mostly the volubly curious, some even openly jeering, but as the long day wore on, Rob noticed a growing number of sympathizers in each gathering, followed soon by placards and the first visible signs of protest. Watanabe Chemical's story was not being bought by everyone.

Rob kept his comments terse to the growing number of media people. It had become a major news story with worldwide interest. Their passage under an interstate highway provoked the first evidence of violence, not much more than pushing and shoving, but several demonstrators ended up in the canal. Rob had to aid one of these, bringing the S-19 alongside the floundering nonswimmer. He was surprised at the lack of action on the part of Doc.

Doc chose to stay submerged whenever a crowd of viewers appeared ahead. Rob kept the transpeak open, hoping against hope that Doc would break his silence. But silence it was. After completing the lament below the Watanabe plant, Doc had not made another sound.

Finally, the border guardhouse loomed ahead. The slip where Doc's tail splash had caught the cop was empty. Rob could see several heads peering at them from the windows of the guardhouse. He didn't know what he expected, but the fact that their passing stirred not even a single wave or sign depressed him still more.

Suddenly Steve Dortch was on the radio.

"She's going to do it, Rob!" Steve was trying to keep the exultation out of his voice. "The Director talked the Minister into shutting it off."

"I don't believe it, Steve."

"You've got an hour to reach the Souris. If you don't make it, you'll be walking instead of floating."

"How long d'you think this will last?" Rob asked.

"Probably no longer than it takes for the Prime Minister to get back from the conference in Dakar. Two days, maybe. But we're making our point this time before our usual wimpiness sets in." Steve sobered. "How's Doc?"

"I think he's listening," Rob said.

"I don't suppose it helps any, but tell him I'm so damn sorry..." Steve's voice trailed off, then he said his goodbyes quickly and clicked off.

Sorry? Rob shook his head. He knew what Steve had really meant. *But we are always so damn sorry.*

He looked ahead of the S-19 to where Doc cut smoothly through the surface of the canal. Rob hit the transpeak switch.

"Just tell me one thing, Doc," he said into the mike. "Do we have any chance in hell of making it? Any chance of getting our act together?"

Mocking silence was his answer. •

THE STIGMATA OF
ANN-MARIE DASSAULT

Preston Hapon

In arms of faded flora, Ann-Marie's comfort-worn chair embraces her slack flesh. Her wrinkled dressing gown hangs like a shroud from outstretched legs propped at the heels by a mismatching footstool and a tightly-tucked cushion. Moisture cools from one hand, resting beside the telephone, as sweet breakfast crumbs roll from the other to her probing tongue. She lets television gameland's shifting colors writhe across her dimmed room—curtains closed against brighter worlds without—to fill her glazed eyes.

Faint laughter reaches her ears, soft applause, but Ann-Marie remains unmoved.

"We should change course. Sir, this hole's set to chew us up."

"Wait."

Another spoke. "Captain."

"I know, Baker. Just do your job."

"Yes, sir."

"Navigation."

"Cap?"

"How long can we postpone the course change?"

"Till about thirty seconds ago, sir."

"I don't have time for humor, Watts. What's our escape time?"

"We'll be here for two months, Cap, increasing at eight hours per minute."

Elsie jumps into her lap, pleads for attention with a purred meow. Ann-Marie affixes a sticky scratch behind the cat's ears, one hand kept lingering beside the telephone.

And while the refrigerator breathes with a tapered whir, cartoon characters dance on a teacup; a man's voice speaks to her, too softly to understand. Elsie purrs more loudly.

"A week. No, ten days. But escape time is increasing a day per minute now, sir. Soon it will be a day per second."

"We can afford a little time when we're finished."

"There they are, sir! We've got them!"

"Closing speed?"

"Eight thousand, sir."

"Increase to twelve."

"Captain!"

"Don't correct me, Baker! Damn you, my ass is right next to yours!"

"Yes, sir! Increasing to twelve, sir!"

"Range?"

"Four kilometers... Three... I'm slowing now, sir."

"Don't be gentle, pilot. Hit them hard! This isn't a first date. Watts, have we made contact yet?"

"Digital contact positive. Life-support's good, but I can't read their engine damage yet."

"Two kilometers. Still holding at twelve thousand, sir."

"Looks good. Looks good."

"Pilot. Have you got a fix on the event horizon?"

"I think we'll make it."

"Think?"

"It's close, sir. If I miss by half a meter, we'll all be atom soup."

"Cap, we're ripping a hell of a hole through normal space. I read thirty light-years deep and lengthening fast."

"That won't last."

"Not if we get out."

"One kilometer."

A car approaches outside. Ann-Marie listens. It doesn't slow, but projects ghostly shadows against the thin drapes.

Elsie rolls over, wallowing in comfort, then attacks Ann-Marie's sugary fingers with needle claws and delicious rasping.

A contestant guesses, knows it's wrong, but she's high on faith— "I'm sorry," the man says. Disappointment weights her shoulders, a false serenity masks her bitterness, and her smile weakens with her knees. The camera moves on to more uplifting visions, and sure enough, enthusiasm unbroken, there glitter the smiles of two fresh media puppets.

Transported by fantasy across electronic waves, Ann-Marie feels energy warm her tired body. She grins at the camera with her best teeth and, in dim living rooms everywhere, Ann-Marie is present, wins a prize, accepts applause, moves on to the "Big Wheel of Fate"; in dim living rooms everywhere she is seen and heard, even loved for a moment—but, unspeakably far away, Ann-Marie remains untouched.

In her own dimmed living room, Ann-Marie's lips answer the question correctly, and she wins a vicarious prize. She is pleased with herself.

"Docking latches open. Lasers aligned."

"Get it right the first time, gentlemen."

"Roll is stable!"

"Pitching another two point one."

"Thirty meters."

"Slow it down, man. Just hold it a sec!"

"I can't 'just hold it.' "

"Pitching moment matched."

"Shit, that put us too close."

"This is a crash, not a docking!"

"Full reverse!"

"Everybody! Brace!"

Ann-Marie wins the car. But she can't drive anymore. She could give it away—hard to choose a recipient for so valuable a gift. Peggy is too old to drive, too, and Ann-Marie doesn't like Fred enough to give him a dirty look. The young couple down the street—what are their names? They just bought a car. He has a good job. They seem nice.

Even if Stan phoned right now, right this very minute, she'd not give it to him.

If he knocked on her door...

"Shut those alarms off! All available thrust, pilot. Bruise those tourists, but get us off this horizon!"

"Watch the pitch!"

"Vectors calculated—on line."

"Then let's go, go, go!"

A young woman speaks of menstrual bleeding as if there were no men in the world. Ann-Marie feels embarrassed that men watch, think about this woman as pretty and sexual, then think about a bloodied pad between her legs— think about women in an ugly way. Ann-Marie feels ugly enough without this. But she waits, and the image goes away.

"Nav's all green."

"Op's all green."

"Sys has an amber and all green."

"Life has two reds—section 'B.' And all green."

"Power at seventy-three and increasing."

"Redirect that power to thrust!"

"Already doing so, sir."

"Com is all green."

"Call from the Princess D, sir."

"Life will be patched in a minute, Cap. Shartz is making repairs."

"We have maximum thrust."

"Cap."

"How long till we're out?"

"Cap!"

"Ninety-four days, sir."

"Captain!"

"What is it, Baker?"

"We aren't slowing."

"Verify Baker's readings."

"Confirmed, sir."

"Same here. We're not holding position."

"Where are we?"

"Give up—it's caught us."

And condoms—what a thing for someone to wave in front of a camera. All the world to see. But if Ann-Marie had known about them, if Ann-Marie had understood her choices, there'd be no children of hers to phone or knock on the door. Small difference that would make.

She strokes Elsie's back. Static charges snap under her hand.

Small difference, but better for its retroactive revenge

than giving a make-believe car. And if Stan were to phone now, right this very minute, she'd tell him so. He'd get an earful.

Cartoon characters in a teacup. A man speaks to her. A family comes out of the shower, one by one, each with a better product in hand. Ann-Marie watches as if for the first time. It doesn't matter.

And she notices, sitting between her and the TV, a man. She can see the TV through his chest, the floor through his shoes, and the pedestal supporting his chair hovers inches above the rug. He leans slightly to the right, motionless.

Elsie licks a paw.

Ann-Marie watches TV a moment, to see if the bearded man who won yesterday will win again. He guesses. They pause for drama. Then, with a solemn shake of his head, the man knows he's failed. He presses his lips together and the audience applauds to cheer him.

Then Ann-Marie looks at the ghost sitting in the living room. He stares unblinking at the air above his knees. His hair is very short, his clothes a kind of uniform. She thinks he's in the army.

"Hello," she says to him.

The pilot will cry like a father for a dead child—with tears, with steely acceptance, with hate.

The captain will have no comfort to share.

Baker's shaking will force him to retype his data. The computer will respond with dead facts. His hope will not be renewed.

Watts will fold his hands, and wait for death.

Then Captain Dassault will see an old woman appear: a cheap Holo, or vivid hallucination. And he will believe the source of this vision to be a fragmented memory of his grandmother, ripped free and made corporeal by terror.

"Who are you? Elsie, get off. Young man, can you hear me? Are you a ghost?"

A gamma flare will spray x-ray through both ships as the graceful Princess D *helplessly grazes the horizon. Her hull will twist like chromium dough, her protons devoured, stripped of electrons as she passes through the ebony mirror into the black hole. Disintegrating into quarks, the very fabric of her existence will dissipate in a hellish vortex—she will plunge with agonized weariness into the gravitational grinding wheel designated BH-647.*

The Captain will turn from the Com Panel leaving Princess D's *call unanswered. He'll quiet his panic, soothe the desperate urge to order undocking—it would do no good. As surely as the ships will be drawn as one, they will be drawn as two. Instead, he'll watch violet plasma halo* Princess D, *see flashes of light inside his eyeballs as fragmented elementary particles pass through. Brain cells will short and die, leave him with unfamiliar smells and memories of faces he once knew. He will gaze upon his grandmother's startled mouth.*

Hours will pass to witness his death, though he will not live an instant.

"In my living room. Yes, Peggy, I know it's coming on next. You can watch it here, if you want. The ghost won't mind. I'm sure. He doesn't seem to see anything at all. I don't know... Come see for yourself."

Peggy sways her corpulence through the door and blindly kicks off her loafers. "I smell coffee, and I hope there's some for me."

"I made it for you."

Elsie dodges into the bedroom.

"Is he still here?"

"Peggy, you won't believe this! Look!"

"There's three of them!"

"Peg, I've never seen..."

"Where are they from?"

"...anything like them before."

"Are they ghosts? Who..."

"Darned if I know."

"Who are they? Can you touch them?"

"They don't move. At least not..."

"Oh, it's weird!"

"...like normal people move. They stretch in a funny way."

"Did you try that?"

"They get taller and..."

"Did you try to touch them?"

"...sort of twist. You can see..."

"You have to try it!"

"...the way this one's face is shifted off to one side."

"You get a weird, tingly feeling..."

"See? His face looks kind of crooked."

"Give me your hand."

"No, just look at what I'm saying."

"Relax. I'll show you."

"Let go."

"Come here!"

"Peggy!"

"Touch right here."

"I don't want to!"

"Come on."

"Let go..."

"Feel it?"

"Yowch! Hey!"

"Feel it?"

"Yes!"

"Told you."

Ann-Marie rubs her arm. Cartoon characters dance on a teacup.

"They do look funny."

"This one was the first."

"They look scared."

"Then that one."

"Like soldiers caught by the enemy..."

"That one came next."

"...and scared to die."

"And finally, him. Standing there like that, sliding through my wall."

"They have no feet."

"Soldiers? But that one's crying."

"So? They're usually the first to cry."

"Look out!"

Like a television switched off in mid-scan, a moment distorts then collapses into a tiny bright star. Swirling eddies in the windy void carry it and countless other time-motes to the edges of darkness.

On each side of time's black mirror, another face appears and then is gone.

"I think one of them looked like you."

"Here's your coffee."

"The one in the wall. Did you have a relative who died in the war?"

"Who didn't?"

"Me. Anyway, I bet that was him."

"My father's uncle?"

"He and a bunch of his buddies come back to haunt awhile."

"He died a hero, Dad said."

"How?"

"Rescue mission. Shell hit their plane. Killed three others."

"See? I bet it was them! That was your father's uncle, right there in your living room, come to say farewell."

"But the uniform..."

Family members step from the same shower, each cleaner than the one before—each smarter. "Didn't look like a uniform I'd ever seen."

"Me neither."

"I have a picture of him, somewhere. Let me go get it."

"Oh, look—it's on."

"Turn it up if you want, and stay. Watch it with me."

"Of course."

"I'll get that picture." •

DISTANT SEAS

Robert Boyczuk

Lying in bed, Captain Huygens turns restlessly as a single sharp note reverberates in his sleep like a tolling bell. In his dream it seems a signal, calling him from the murky, swirling waters in which he drifts, filling him with an unexpected buoyancy. Slowly he begins to rise, past the groping tendrils of bottom weeds which, in the utter black, feel like the caress of cold fingers running along the exposed skin of hands and face. His ascent continues, through dark as impenetrable as pitch, through waters that flow around him like an icy cloak. He cranes his neck, for the first time seeing a soft, diffused glow far above and, with each passing heartbeat, the light grows brighter, the water he slips through warmer. He is pushed ever faster through layers of shadowy green filled with the flecks and blurs that are darting fish; above, his world has become overarched with a rippling azure plain. Layers of increasingly translucent water slip by, and he moves towards the surface of wakefulness, his lungs aching suddenly, as if only now they have remembered their need for oxygen; the ribs in his chest strain against tightly drawn skin, an irresistible desire to open his mouth and drink deeply fills him. He claws at the water, tearing madly to propel himself toward the light, fighting the panic that rises in his throat like a balled fist, that threatens to burst from him in a watery scream, and when he is sure that he can no longer hold it at bay, when it pushes from between his tightly pressed lips, that formless howl, at the same instant he breaks the surface like a shot, gasping and flailing in the blinding light.

Awake at last, Captain Huygens sits amid the tangle of soaked sheets, trembling, a shaft of sunlight cutting the gloom of his cabin and falling across his bed like a bright cutlass. He closes his eyes and swallows several times, head still reeling from the dream, its fear and confusion supplanted by another greater fear now that he has returned to his senses.

He wonders, Who am I?

I am the Captain.

For several minutes he remains where he is, back propped against the headboard. Then, feeling a sudden sense of urgency, he swings himself over the edge of the bed and nearly falls as his legs buckle beneath his weight. He clutches the bedframe, steadies himself, and in a moment he can feel his strength returning, though his dream has left him weaker than he had believed. Moving cautiously, he makes his way to the foot of the bed where clothes—his clothes, he realizes—have been laid out on top of his sea chest; slowly, he begins dressing, pulling on his breeches and silk shirt, hands still shaking, making it difficult to manage the buttons. The effort required to get his boots on taxes his strength to such a degree that he must pause to collect himself afterwards. Finally, he walks, more or less steadily, to the bureau where his black felt tricorn sits. He places it squarely on his head and, looking up, catches a glimpse of himself in the gilt framed glass.

A stranger regards him from the mirror with startlement, a man who wears his clothes yet has a thin, bloodless face, with sunken, watery eyes and parched lips. He blinks, and the figure in the mirror apes him. Closing his eyes, he is once again aware of the thumping of his heart in his ribcage, the rubbery feeling of his legs, the lightness of his head.

He wonders: Have I been ill?

He has no recollection of being sick, yet when he tries to recall anything of the past few days he cannot: his memories have fled. He is the Captain. This is his ship. But of the last weeks, he remembers nothing. And with a sudden sickening lurch in his stomach, he realizes he is in possession of only fragments of his past. He concentrates and an assembly of familiar faces float before him: men sitting around a table, engaged in earnest discussion, though he cannot name them; then a memory of a carriage rolling thorough level countryside, he staring from within as they drive past canals lined with long stemmed tulips whose blossoms sway yellow and red in the breeze; and in France (Yes, he remembers, France) a country house filled with music and the soft rustle of long, elegant skirts. Vague impressions and sensations that refuse to coalesce.

A fever, he thinks. I have woken from a feverish dream. It is the effect of the illness. My memories will return. Must return.

And having decided this, he opens his eyes.

He is relieved to see his pallor, still sickly, is not quite as white as he first thought; faint lines of color are visible in his cheeks, and his eyes now appear clear. Tipping his hat forward so that it will leave his face in shadow, he steps out into the blazing morning light.

The deck is deserted.

It has the unmistakable air of abandonment: coils of line and pails of tar lying as if they'd just been dropped; loose carpenters' tools and wood shavings next to a half-made barrel; a large sheet of canvas spread near the mizzen mast, a thick needle piercing it at the base of a jagged tear.

Overhead, the sheets hang limply from their spars beneath a fulgent sun, a sun as bright and hot as any Captain Huygens can remember. He removes his hat and with his sleeve he wipes at the beads of perspiration that have already gathered on his forehead. The light is inescapable, filling the ship, leaving no shadows, dancing in all the recesses of his head.

Captain Huygens walks across the weather deck towards the prow. Climbing the short ladder to the foredeck, he surveys the extent of the ship. From where he stands, the aft deck is partially obscured by the mainsail; but he is certain that it, too, is deserted. Then a thought occurs to him, and, absurd as it is, he cranes his neck and squints into the rigging, half-expecting to see his entire crew, every one of them, perched in the shrouds and ratlines like large, angry crows. But no one is there, and the white sails leave burning afterimages that shoot across his vision like stars.

Perhaps they are all below, he thinks, setting out towards the forecastle, determined, if needs be, to check every cabin, compartment and hold on the ship in his methodical, orderly fashion.

Captain Huygens' inspection proves futile. He has found no one. Returning to his cabin, he throws the shutters wide on all the aft windows to permit as much light as possible to enter; while he has searched the sun has risen and its rays cut obliquely through the window and fall on the rough wooden planks of the cabin floor.

In the center of the room is a heavy, oak table with a single drawer, and it is before this he sits. On its surface lie a brass sextant, several large navigational charts, a cream-colored book bound in vellum, and a sheaf of curling papers.

Picking up the book, Captain Huygens turns it over as if he were examining a specimen. Its covers are blank. He places it on the desk and opens it, but there is still nothing to identify its purpose, only an empty white leaf narrowly ruled in black ink. He begins turning pages, but they are all identical, each as empty as the first. When he reaches the last page he closes the book.

He leans back in his chair and opens the drawer. It has been divided into two sections by a thin wooden partition, one narrow that contains two inkwells and a number of quills, the other wider but unused. He places the book into this side, and it fits nicely with just enough room around its edges so that it can be easily lifted out again, and this somehow pleases him, this seeming order. He shuts the drawer.

The charts are of various sizes and types, some imprinted with foreign languages and symbols that make no sense to him. Although he cannot recall how or where he might have acquired each, he is certain that with a little patience he will be able to unlock their secrets, to discern their patterns. Why he knows this he cannot say; but he is firm in his confidence, certain that he has solved far knottier problems in the past. He sorts them in order of size, then moves them to the corner of the desk, placing the sextant atop the pile.

He examines the loose papers, one after the other, but these confound him. They are covered with detailed diagrams and intricate calculations, and appear to deal with diverse topics from the minutiae of life to the motions of the planets. On the first is a series of sketches of puzzling objects labeled animalcules; on the next two pages he finds numerous mathematical notations, a consideration, it seems, of the probability of a dicing game; following this is a detailed rendering of the internal mechanism of a clock driven by a pendulum that travels in a cycloidal arc; finally are a series of astronomical drawings and calculations, geometries of the motion of planets.

All, he notes with some consternation, are in his own distinctive script.

The sun is almost directly overhead, the morning nearly spent. Captain Huygens stands on the aft deck, a lone figure lost in contemplation, his large, expressionless eyes the color of the sea.

"Help!"

The voice, small and trilling, shatters the Captain's reverie with the abruptness of a stone.

"Save me!"

Captain Huygens turns. The sea is an unbroken mirror, and it is not difficult to spot the distant, floundering figure of a boy.

"Ahoy!" he bellows through cupped hands.

The tiny form ceases his struggles, as if the Captain's words have surprised him. Then, he begins to wave a small arm energetically in the direction of the ship. "Help me!" he cries with renewed effort.

"I can do nothing for you!" the Captain shouts in reply. "I am alone! You must swim!"

There is a moment of silence while the boy treads water, as if weighing the wisdom of the Captain's suggestion; then he strikes out towards the ship, his little arms churning through the water, a steady, unhurried stroke.

•

"What is your name, lad?"

The boy shrugs. He is round-faced and sleepy-eyed, with full lips and a downturned mouth; wet, curly locks of hair are pasted to his skull. His complexion is ghostly, his lips the fading blue of Arctic ice.

The Captain knows this color, has seen it many times before on the sodden corpses they have dragged from the sea, but never on the living. He shivers despite the stifling heat, then forces these thoughts from his mind. "Do I know you?" he asks, then, feeling embarrassed at the absurdity of his question, says, "Do not be shy. Speak up."

The boy's eyes dart nervously, taking in the ship as if it is all new and frightening to him; he shifts his weight from foot to foot. "I...I...I'm not sure."

"Not sure?"

He nods numbly in answer, averting his eyes.

"Your name then. What is your name?"

"I do not know."

The Captain tries to hide his rising exasperation. "Come, come, lad! How can you not remember your own name?"

"I cannot." The boy studies the puddle growing around his bare feet. "I was hoping, sir," he says in a small voice, "you might be able to tell me."

The Captain purses his lips thoughtfully, then clears his throat. "Ah, well, you see, I've been sick. A fever, I think." Withdrawing a handkerchief from his pocket, he dabs at the film of perspiration gathering on his brow, his hand trembling slightly with the action. "I've just this morning been out of bed. My memory is still a bit muddled, I'm afraid..."

"You don't remember either," the boy says, for the first time staring directly at the Captain. "Do you?"

"Your name. Surely you have a name?"

The boy furrows his brow in exaggerated concentration, and then his face lights up. "Albert!" he says, beaming. "My name is Albert!"

"Albert," the Captain repeats slowly, as if considering the name. "Good. Now, perhaps you might tell me how you came to be floundering out there."

The boy's face clouds over, and he averts his eyes. "I...I

do not know," he stammers.

"You've no recollection at all?"

The boy shakes his head sullenly.

"The ship." The Captain's grasps the boy's shoulder. "Does she look familiar? Were you on her before? Can you remember her?"

The boy remains mute. Beneath his fingers the Captain can feel a shudder pass through him. He releases his grip.

"Never mind," the Captain mutters and, clasping his hands behind his back, he begins pacing the deck. "It is not important."

For a time neither speaks, the Captain lost in thought while the boy takes in the ship with furtive glances. Then: "The others?"

"What?" The Captain stops pacing, stares at the boy. "What?"

"The others. Where are they?"

"Gone. Jumped ship, perhaps. Likely drowned."

The boy's face blanches; his eyes grow wide with fear.

"A storm," the Captain says quickly, knowing it to be a lie, the ship bearing no evidence of rough weather. But the boy looks hopefully at him, and he continues in a loud voice. "Aye, that must be it. Maybe they were washed overboard. Or perhaps they lost their nerve in a storm and were afraid we'd founder. So they struck out for an island they spotted." He nods thoughtfully. "Perhaps that's what happened to you as well, Albert."

"But I don't remember—"

"Your head. You might have banged your head. Sometimes people forget when they receive a blow to the skull."

Albert chews his lower lip and gazes off into space. Then his eyes narrow. "There's no clouds," he says flatly, staring at the empty sky.

"No," the Captain replies. "You're right, and there's no denying that. But suppose, now just suppose, that you'd been out there at sea all this time clinging to a barrel or plank, half drowned and out of your mind with fear while the storm passes by then disappears altogether. And later, much later, when you hear my voice, well, then you snap out of it."

The boy seems lost in thought. "Yes," he says at last. "Your voice is the first thing I remember."

"That must be it," the Captain says in what he hopes is a hardy voice, clapping Albert stoutly on the back. "Get yourself out of those wet clothes and see if you can find something to eat. When the wind picks up we'll have lots of work between us, I warrant."

"Yes, sir," Albert says, venturing a weak smile. He moves towards the companionway that leads beneath the afterdeck and to the officers' quarters.

The Captain watches him for a moment. "Albert," he says quietly, and the boy pauses. "Where are you going?"

Without hesitation he replies. "To my berth, sir."

"And where is that?"

"Why, next to yours, sir."

"To the cabin boy's quarters," Captain Huygens says, staring at Albert, who regards him solemnly. But there is no spark of recognition, no face that comes to mind when he considers those words. "Very well," he says. "Carry on."

"Aye, aye, sir."

The Captain watches Albert disappear into the gloom of the stairway; in his stomach something turns sluggishly, like a small animal awakening. It is the fever, he tells himself.

But he no more believes this than the story he has concocted for Albert.

Against the foot of Captain Huygens' bed rests a sea chest of teakwood banded with dark iron; it glows with the patina of age and feels warm, almost alive, beneath the tips of his fingers where they rest lightly on its surface. His initials are carved deeply on its humpbacked lid just above a rusty lock: C.H.

The chest contains bundles of various sizes and shapes wrapped in gray sailcloth and secured with short lengths of packing string. On the very bottom he can see five cylindrical objects, all roughly the length of the chest, on top of which three other packages rest. He selects these topmost and carries them to his desk.

The first is a tube about the length of his arm and the

width of his wrist. He pulls the single string tied around its center and the cloth falls away to reveal the stepped, brass cylinder of a seafaring spyglass. He extends it to its full length—nearly a meter—then collapses it, placing it on the corner of his desk.

When he unwraps the second bundle he finds a heavy disc the size of a tea saucer and the thickness of his little finger; lying on his desk, it looks like a giant's coin. It, too, is constructed from brass, and several small, precise holes have been drilled through the metal. The stars, he thinks. It is an instrument to measure the luminosity of the stars—and therefore their distance. How he knows this he cannot say. He pushes it to the side.

The third parcel contains a rosewood box that is square and a handspan in width, with beveled corners and a small gold latch. He flips the latch open with his thumb and lifts the lid. It is lined with dark blue velvet both top and bottom, each half being subdivided into a number of pockets that contain glass lenses of varying thickness. He withdraws one, holding it by its edges, and peers through it intently; he places it gently on the table, its concave side down so that he won't abrade the surface. He stares at it for a moment. Then, leaving the single lens on the table, he closes the case and pushes his chair back, starting for the trunk to examine the cylinders that lie in its bottom. But before he has taken a step he pauses, looks at the lens again then back to the trunk, suddenly realizing what those long packages must contain.

Captain Huygens strides across the main deck towards Albert. The boy's shouts have drawn him from his cabin to where Albert has been stowing the loose gear littering the weather deck. "There," the boy says in his small, serious voice, pointing up the foremast as the captain approaches.

Shading his eyes, the Captain scans the webbing of the shroud, and near the lower top gallant, a figure clings to the lines. "So," the Captain says. "We have another."

Albert frowns. "He wasn't there before."

"No. I don't believe he was."

The boy's face is pale; he crosses his arms. "I looked, but

it was empty—"

"Perhaps," the Captain says quickly, "we missed him. If he were to be lying along a spar, or curled round the main top, we mightn't have seen him from the deck. Then he crawled to where he is now. We just missed him is all."

Albert opens his mouth as if he is about to say something, then snaps it shut. As they watch, the dark form stirs uneasily as if waking from a deep sleep.

Despite the sweltering, mid-afternoon heat the man shivers uncontrollably, as if he is chilled to the bone. He sits, back against the rail with knees drawn up to his chest. The man is of middle height and years; he has long blond hair that curls at his shoulders, framing a narrow face and roman nose. His countenance is pale, his lips tinged with the slightest of blues. Beneath his eyes are pronounced circles that give him a contemplative, scholarly air despite his deathly pallor, one that is, in some distant way, familiar to the Captain.

Where, he wonders, have I seen this man before?

Abruptly an image comes into his head, a memory of long ago, a carriage early in the morning, one other passenger who sits, sullen and withdrawn, in the brocaded interior. It is July.

"Isaac," the Captain says suddenly, the vision vanishing with the words. "Your name is Isaac."

The man stares at him blankly, suspiciously, then nods before he is seized by a violent fit of shaking.

At that moment Albert returns with a blanket, and the Captain suddenly recalls how the boy had first appeared like this man, pale and half-alive; but whatever traces of death he had shown earlier have faded, suffused in a ruddy glow, his eyes now filled with the curiosity of youth.

"Go ahead," the Captain says, and the boy lowers the thick wool blanket carefully over Isaac's shoulders like a shroud.

"You remember nothing?"

After a moment, Isaac shakes his head; he sits hunched low in his seat across the desk from the Captain, the blanket still draped about his shoulders, his mannerisms suggesting fear and caution. From time to time a tremor passes through him then subsides as if he is racked by memories of a bitter cold.

"And do I not look familiar?"

Isaac narrows his eyes and glares at the Captain, his face both melancholy and defiant.

The Captain sighs. He pushes the case of lenses to one side to make room on his crowded desk, then pulls the vellum book, quill and inkwell from his drawer. Opening the book to the first page, he runs his hand down its center so that it will lie flat. The page already contains two entries in his hand and, uncapping the inkwell and dipping the quill, he neatly enters Isaac's name on the third line.

When he finishes, he looks up and says, "Now then—" but stops to stare at the other man. Isaac's face has changed, has lost some of its irascible character; his eyes have become lively and piercing, his brow furrowed in concentration as he holds the single lens the Captain had left on the desk. So engrossed is he in his examination that he appears to have forgotten the Captain altogether.

The Captain clears his throat.

Isaac looks startled, then seems to recall himself. He returns the lens to the desk and, nodding towards it, says, "Very good work."

Absurdly, the Captain feels a flush of pride. He is about to say "Thank you," when the hollow thump of feet pounding down the corridor makes him pause.

Albert's head pops into the cabin. "Astern!" he shouts breathlessly, leaning through the door, clutching its frame. "There's more astern!"

Rising from his chair, the Captain makes his way to the aft window. Beyond, the sea lies undisturbed in all directions, the ship still becalmed in this unnatural weather. The Captain is puzzled. "I cannot see..." he begins, then stops, something directly below catching his eye. The sun, having passed its zenith, casts an incipient shadow behind the tail of the ship, and in this gibbous darkness are three unlikely lumps, bodies in the water, clothes mushroomed around them, face down, staring into the depths.

•

The bodies have been arranged on the deck in an orderly row. All three are bloated, the skin pale white, almost luminescent, in the early afternoon sun. Isaac stands above them; he is sweating profusely from his exertion and his breath comes raggedly, though his countenance is much improved. To the Captain's surprise, he had, with Albert's help, retrieved the corpses. Behind him Albert's head rises above the scuppers as he hauls himself up the last few rungs of the ladder. Using a small launch, they had fished the men from the water, Isaac instructing Albert in a terse voice on how he might use the gaff hook to snare the dead men; with one in tow, Isaac then rowed back to where a looped rope waited beneath the gangway. Working this rope beneath their arms, he signaled the Captain who then began to crank the windlass about whose barrel the rope wound. Three times the corpses were drawn from the sea in this fashion, bumping and scraping up the side of the *Beagle*, in small, precise jerks, a fall of glittering drops shivering from them with each loud click of the ratchet.

Standing before the bodies now, Captain Huygens observes they wear breeches and plain, white shirts; all are barefoot as is the custom among men before the mast. One is tall and thin, with Nordic features and a scar along his cheek; the second has dirty-blond hair cropped close to the skull and a thick white beard; the third is diminutive, with narrow features, swarthy skin and dark curling hair. They are all of a middle age and, by their appearances—soft unformed muscles and smooth, uncallused skin—seem unlikely sailors. He gazes at them, filled with curiosity, and at last asks, "Did you know them?"

But neither Isaac, who leans against the mast, nor the boy, standing at the rail, answer, for both watch as the silence gathers in folds about them, and the dead begin to stir.

It is late in the afternoon, and Captain Huygens climbs the ladder to the foredeck, his small brass telescope beneath the crook of his arm. Leaning against the rail, he extends it to its full length and, bringing it up to his eye, scans the sea.

For a time he sees nothing.

He swings the glass slowly and precisely from side to side in a wide arc.

Then he finds what he has been looking for: on the horizon, there is a tiny smudge, barely perceptible, and he cannot be sure it is anything more than his imagination. At this distance the shape could be anything really and he waits patiently, watching it for the better part of an hour as it advances towards them through the dead calm, drawn to them by the tug of a spectral current.

The Captain can descry four bodies slumped in the boat; it is possible there might be others who have slipped beneath the gunwale so that they are hidden. All appear lifeless.

The Captain proffers his telescope to Isaac. "Secure her," he says, gesturing in the direction of the boat, "as she comes near."

Isaac nods.

"Tie the boat up, but you might as well leave them be until they can climb aboard themselves."

Isaac, who is already peering through the telescope, says nothing, but the Captain can see his fingers tighten around the slender tube.

"When they are ready, bring them to my cabin."

Leaving Isaac, the Captain makes his way down to the weather deck to examine the three they have pulled from the sea. The two smaller men are still unconscious, and their breathing is ragged and noisy, as if their lungs still suffer some obstruction. Occasionally one or the other coughs and flat ribbons of water seep from a nose or the corner of a mouth. Their faces look worse than before, their pallid complexions more pronounced for the bit of color that has crept back. The tall one, however, is awake.

He lies on the deck, his chest rising and falling with regularity, watching everything through wide eyes. He seems to be taking it all in: the empty ship, the unnaturally bright day, the men who lie on either side of him, the Captain.

But his eyes contain no understanding, only confusion and perhaps fear, as if the world in which the Captain stands is illusory, insubstantial. Watching him, the Captain tries to imagine what he is feeling. He is reminded of the large, rolling eyes of a fish, dragged from the cool gloom of the depths into the bright, painful light of day.

In the very bottom of the chest is a package the Captain had earlier overlooked. It contains a small silver flute.

Captain Huygens sits on the edge of his bed, the flute cradled in his hand, remembering. He played in the center of a well appointed room, a table off to the side cluttered with drawings and calculations, surrounded by a ring of serious faces. They are ghosts of remembrances, insubstantial figures, these men. Friends, he realizes all at once, of his father's. Their names come to him: Mersenne, Diodati, Schouten, Descartes. He is there, with his flute, a child no more than Albert's age, playing. It is a night like many others, and this is his father's house in Voorburg near The Hague.

The sun is an enormous, watery eye on the horizon.

Throughout the afternoon and into the evening, the men have continued to come before the Captain in twos and threes. They have been discovered in previously unoccupied cabins, in empty barrels in the holds, clinging fearfully to the masts, confused and tangled in spare sails and lines, struggling in the sea...

The Captain sits behind his desk, entering the names of each of the crew members in the ledger as they are brought before him. They are by turns pale, shivering, quiet, flushed with anger, fearful, incoherent, lucid. Some of the names are familiar as he carefully inks them, and he feels that he should know them, though the fragments of recollection are for the most part still lost in a swirling, uncertain fog.

Dipping his quill in the ink well, he continues to write as they file past him. Their appearances are varied, tall and short, broad and thin, dark and light, as if they've been drawn from the furthest corners of the earth. Many speak in strange tongues and accents, but he manages, through words and gestures, to make them understand that it is their names he desires.

The Captain has discovered that he has an ear for languages, and, as he listens to them, he understands, at least in part, the English, French, Dutch, Flemish, German, Italian and Latin they speak, the urgent questions framed in foreign languages they ask him.

But he does not answer.

Instead he continues to enter names, forty-two per page, and after several leaves are filled, he pauses to retrieve a tinder box and candle from the top of his dresser so that he might chase back the shadows that have gathered like silent watchers in the corners of his room.

It is night, and Captain Huygens sits on a three-legged stool on the afterdeck, elbows resting on knees, waiting patiently. To his side, Isaac kneels, busily assembling the series of tubes that had lain in the bottom of the chest, fitting the lenses in each section.

On a small table the Captain has placed his sextant, a quill, an inkwell, and several blank sheets of paper. Occasionally he leans forward and sketches a rough figure or makes a note. His crew mills about on the weather deck, their voices a soft murmur in the growing darkness, gathering in knots to watch the sky. They seem, on the whole, to have adjusted remarkably well, although there is something subdued in their manner and speech. From time to time they glance in his direction as if for reassurance, and, when he notices these movements, he nods curtly in response.

The Captain's memory is still uncertain and cloudy, but he is convinced that it is only a matter of time before he will remember everything clearly, before the brief flashes and snatches of images will come together to give him back his past.

The Captain has ordered the sails furled so that they might have an unobstructed view of the sky in all directions. Stars, brighter than any he has ever seen, shimmer in the heavens. They glitter with an unaccustomed brilliance and clarity that pierce his heart like the tip of a diamond knife.

"Captain."

He turns. Albert, who stands near the tiller, points to the rising moon.

It is large and luminous, its surface mottled with shades of green and brown and blue. Clouds, small and white and perfect, scud across its surface, obscuring its tiny continents.

And when it is followed, a short time later, by a second moon whose surface ripples like a burning, silver sea, Captain Huygens feels no fear; rather, his heart soars with joy and wonder, that there still remain so many worlds he, a traveler from a distant country, might yet see. •

THE TRUE AND SAD STORY OF LENA THE SCREAM-CLEANER

Jason Kapalka

Lena worked in the Scream Processing Department for many years before Sam found her. Day in, day out, she scrubbed, rinsed, and wrung dry the assorted shrieks, howls, moans, wails, and sighs that came tumbling down the long chute to her work station. She carefully squeezed the sentiment from each shriek, washed and dried it. The waste emotion, oily-rainbow colored, was carried out of the room in great buckets, to be destroyed or buried deep underground; the screams themselves were sent to another room where they were starched, folded, and eventually circulated back into general usage. Then another batch came howling down the chute, and Lena went back to work.

It had been so long that Lena scarcely remembered how she had come to work for Scream Processing. She had her small blue apartment, and a cat called Whiskey. She liked quiet and quiet music, and sometimes watched movies on TV. She liked to cook pasta dishes and to make pencil sketches, though she ate alone and never showed her drawings to anyone, and she sometimes read books and sometimes cried quietly for no discernible reason, the translucent sobs fluttering away through her window to wing their way back to Scream Processing, where she might encounter them the next day, wondering uneasily at the eerie, shivery color of their emotion.

She shopped only at the little all-night store where all the other Scream Processing employees shopped, and she went out only to Scream Processing functions, which were quiet, almost sad affairs.

There would be her fellow scream-cleaners, ragged gray

men and women old beyond their years. Surely *she* did not look that old, that tired! There were the sly-looking Disposal urchins, and the quiet, shadowy men from Acoustics upstairs, who dissected and catalogued scream-components in a quiet shadowy laboratory. There was Supervisor Sheen, a cheerful old man with a shock of yellowish hair, and sometimes she would see visiting executives from the Human Grief Concern, Scream Processing's parent company, and once or twice she'd even caught sight of a shriek-catcher, one of the elite operatives who combed the outside world looking for lost and misplaced screams.

She'd never really inquired into the deeper workings of the Department, and she still didn't know much concerning its means of distribution and collection. The screams made their way back to the Department, were processed, and were sent back into the world: that was all she needed to know. But once, when she was still new to the job, she'd spoken to Supervisor Sheen at one of the Department functions, and he had told her something of Scream Processing's operations.

"Sentiment—the emotion that charges our screams—is cheap, of course. Not valueless," he smiled, wagging a finger, "but cheap: there will always be more. But our screams, now these, Lena, these are irreplaceable."

Sheen's smile, which was never noticeable till it faded, faded. Lena felt uneasy. "There are only so many screams, Lena," he went on, "and despite our best research they remain finite in number and non-reproducible, though every year a few more wear out or are lost forever. One day the last groan, the last shriek, the last sigh will vanish from the world—and then, ah, then there will be quiet, a quiet unimagined since the beginning of time." He paused, then shook himself from his reverie and chuckled. "Still, don't worry about a layoff anytime soon."

But now, when she attended a Scream Processing party, she scarcely spoke to anybody, let alone the Supervisor. From time to time a man, perhaps an Acoustics researcher or a fellow cleaner, would nervously ask her if she'd like to go see a film or a play. Irrational panic clogged her throat; eventually she would gasp out an excuse of one sort or

another, and the man would infallibly seem as relieved as
her to be able to drop the subject. She didn't think any of
the Department employees ever went out—ever, in fact,
did *anything*, and as she gradually became convinced of
this, she realized that a silent pall had fallen over her own
life.

Later she supposed she had known that something was
wrong even when the man in the yellow sports jacket first
approached her on the street outside the Department. But
at the time she was able to convince herself otherwise.
She'd just come off a terrible shift, having spilled a panful
of Class C Startled Squeaks which had fluttered and flur-
ried away into dark corners and nooks, with the result
that the workroom had to be shut down for half an hour
while they were coaxed out.

"Lena?" the man said. He had a long flexible face that
was set in a businesslike scowl. "Can you come with me,
please? There are some important details we must dis-
cuss."

He gestured towards a white car parked by the curb, and
she found herself getting in. She remembered thinking it
must have had to do with her accident in the workroom
that day, that she was being reprimanded or fired, but
even then, really, she must have known that it was all
wrong, that she'd never seen this man in Scream Processing before, that this was an event that simply didn't fit the
pattern of her existence. But she still got in the car.

He said his name was Lomax as they drove out of the
city, past buildings and neighborhoods that she hadn't
seen for—how many years had it really been? Had she
ever seen these places before? He drove out into the country and took a narrow dirt road.

"What is this all about?" she asked.

He looked at her briefly and then back at the road. "Official business."

She gave a nervous laugh. "No, I mean really." By now
she knew something was wrong, but strangely she felt no
fear, only a hollow tingling excitement.

He didn't even shift his gaze. "You'll see."

He stopped the car at a small acreage. There was a

brown and white house. He got out of the car and led her inside without saying anything.

He took her down a long dark hall that ended in a door. Light came out from underneath it.

"Lena..." He paused.

"Yes?"

He seemed to be weighing whether he should say something, then deciding against it. He opened the door. "This is Sam," he said. "He wants to talk to you."

The man in the chair was very sick.

His pale head lolled atop a thin neck that seemed too feeble to support it. His eyes were closed and webs of wrinkles creased the sockets. He clutched at the armrests and leaned forward as the door opened, still without opening his eyes. There was something brittle about him: an almost palpable radiation of pain.

The man in the yellow sports jacket—Lomax—waited for Lena to enter, then closed the door behind her. She stared at the man in the chair. "You don't work for the Department," she said.

There was no reply. Sam in the chair merely inclined his head. She couldn't tell how old he was, but his movements seemed slow and careful, as though he might shatter if he moved too hastily.

"What do you want?"

Nothing.

"Why did you bring me here?"

Sam lifted his head to her. He still hadn't opened his eyes, and she wondered if he was blind. His mouth opened slowly, moistly, and he spoke.

"Lena." His voice seemed to rise from his sunken form like a vapor. "Do you know who I am?"

"I...no."

"You must understand this, if you would understand why my friend has brought you here today."

She said nothing.

"I suppose," he said slowly, almost whispering, "you would call me a researcher, a scientist of sorts. My project was pain; my thesis was human grief. I traveled the world, the dark places and the light...the bright places too...

Africa, Kampuchea, China...the lost alleys and ghettoes of
Europe and America...the corpse fields...the soundproofed
rooms... I collected fear and anger and hurt. I hoarded
murder-lust and heartbreak; scooped up quantities of
smaller pains, paper-cuts, money-worries, wasp-bites. I
thought if I saw enough...learned enough...I could eliminate suffering from the world."

His eyelids trembled. "I was something of an idealist,
you see, Lena."

This all seemed mad to her. "It didn't work?"

He seemed surprised. "Why no, Lena, it did work. It
worked very well, very, very well indeed. It went so well I
even learned some things I hadn't set out to learn." His
hands had begun to shake, and now his entire body. "I
learned about limits, Lena. Limits are very important."

His hands clenched around the arms of the chair, and
suddenly he threw his head back in what Lena first assumed was a grotesque yawn, until she saw the way the
skin at the corners of his mouth was stretched so tight it
was bleeding, his frame yanked taut across the chair. He
was screaming. He was screaming, but there was no
sound, none at all.

His body trembled in the grip of it for ten, now twenty
seconds. Finally he slumped into the chair, his head sag-
ging over his chest.

"I—" Lena began. Then Sam swung his head up.

He opened his eyes. They were blue and horrible, reflecting a shiny terror Lena could only guess at.

She tried to meet his gaze but it was impossible. She
turned away and shuddered.

She could hear him breathing for long moments. At last
he spoke again. "So sorry, Lena. It comes and goes. But
now you see. Are you all right?"

She glanced back: his eyes were closed. "Yes."

"After the experiment," Sam rasped, "I screamed for
seven days. My vocal cords were torn to shreds, but still I
kept screaming. After a week I ran out."

"You... I don't understand."

Sam grimaced. "Don't you? Isn't that what you do? Your
job?"

"No, I, I'm just a cleaner."

"I ran out of screams. I used them all up but I still need more. Limits, Lena. Do you understand now what I want from you?"

She thought she did. But—"Why me?" she asked.

"Do you want me to lie?" Sam said. "You were the only person we could find. The...Department, as you call it...is not easy to locate. It requires you to understand contradictory metaphors simultaneously...like closing one eye while looking out the other, only doing that with both eyes at the same time."

"I don't understand."

"No. What will you do now? I can't threaten you."

"I could lose my job."

"Yes. I could offer you money but that would be pointless. What is it that you want, Lena? I can offer you nothing."

She closed her eyes. Nothing but the risk of wrecking her own life for the sake of a man who cared nothing for her, who needed her only as a tool. And what did he know about her? She already understood Sam well enough to know he was too proud to offer even his gratitude. He was offering nothing but a choice. Nothing but the one thing she'd given up, so long ago when she'd thought she would never need it again.

"You're very clever," she said finally.

It was easier than she'd thought it would be.

She waited until noon when the other cleaners went on their lunch break, and told them she'd be along as soon as she finished with her last item. It was an F-5b Plangent Outcry, large and slippery: as the last cleaner filed out of the workroom, she slid it into a plastic bag, folded it up as well as she could, muffled it with a thick cloth, and stuffed it into her lunchbag. When she went upstairs to the coffee room, she made a side trip to the coat room and placed it inside her purse.

And that was all.

And later: Sam's assistant Lomax standing beside the white car in his yellow sports jacket, not quite smiling.

The country road, the acreage, the house: and then Lena was in the room at the end of the hall again, with the stolen scream, wrapped and silenced, in her hand like a gift. She supposed it was.

She began to pluck at the wrapping, glanced doubtfully at Lomax, standing off by the side. "Should I—"

He nodded silently.

Sam was shaking as he waited for her. She couldn't read the emotion on his stiff white face. She unfolded the scream, dropped the wrapping to the floor, and stepped towards him. Slowly, carefully, she slipped the scream into his mouth.

There was a moment of perfect silence then, as he opened his mad eyes and gazed up at her. For a second Lena almost thought he smiled.

And then the scream came roaring out of him, seemingly too immense for his frail body to contain. Lomax fell aside in shock. Lena, who had more experience with this sort of thing, was nonetheless appalled: emotion trembled in the air, vibrating itself away through the walls and ceiling, for half a minute after the scream had fled.

Sam's body was awkwardly twisted in his chair, and Lena leaned over him to see if he was still alive.

He lifted his head and smiled. There was no mistake this time. His eyes, for that one moment, were serene and empty of horror. Lena, despite herself, smiled back, and reached to put one of her hands on his.

He stiffened and his eyes closed. Lomax stepped closer and grasped his hand. "Sam?"

Then his mouth snapped open in silence and he opened his eyes again and they were the same as before, or even worse. He would scream on through the night, but Lena's startled cry at that moment would be the only sound.

She embezzled screams for another three months before they caught her. It seemed like the terrors bottled inside Sam had no end. Each night when Lomax drove her out to the house, she thought: perhaps *this* time. Perhaps this will empty all his stolen horrors.

But...

It never did.

And Lena never found out how they caught her. Ripples spread through Scream Processing's accounts; somewhere they were noted, and action was taken. One afternoon as Lena prepared to leave, with a bag of whimpers hidden in her purse, two slight, well-dressed men casually stepped in front of her. They didn't even bother to search her purse. They took her directly to Supervisor Sheen's office.

Sheen was behind his desk. He wasn't smiling. Lena sat down as the two men left, and sighed.

"How did you find out?"

"Does it matter?"

"I guess not," she said. "What are you going to do?"

Sheen shook his head sadly. "It's not my decision, Lena. Will you tell me why you did it?"

"Don't you know?"

"You mean Samuel Lefoe? Yes, I know about him...his condition. Why did you help him? What does he mean to you that you would risk all this?"

She was silent.

"There was no danger on his part. *He* had nothing to lose. But you, Lena..."

"He needed help."

"A lot of people need help. Did you think he loved you, Lena?

She laughed.

"Lena..."

"Does it matter, Mr. Sheen? Does it really matter why I did it?" Sheen's authority no longer impressed her.

He slammed his palms down on the desk. "It wouldn't have worked, Lena. It wouldn't have worked if they'd let you keep stealing for another three months, or three years."

She had nothing to say. She just wanted it to be over, she wanted whatever was going to happen to happen and be done with it.

"So what now?" she asked at last.

"You're being promoted. I'm sorry, Lena."

She stared, not understanding.

•

They did something to her that she couldn't remember. Something was taken. And afterwards they did promote her. They promoted her to shriek-catcher. If she'd felt distant from the everyday world before, she soon understood just how much humanity had still been allowed to her then.

She never saw her apartment again. She never cooked pasta or watched TV or made pencil sketches or rubbed the stomach of her cat Whiskey again. She neither needed nor was allowed these things anymore. When she saw Sheen or one of her former co-workers, as she still did occasionally, they looked at her with a nervous awe, but she never thought to exploit or alleviate it. She felt neither hatred nor sympathy for them.

She roamed the city by day and night by modes of travel and navigation she could not explain. Here, three feet under the soil of a backyard garden, was an unwanted baby, which had been not quite dead when the parents buried it. She gently extracted the last anguished cry from between the cool lips, stored it in a pressurized vessel.

There, someone down a lost alleyway died in a not quite unimaginable fashion: she found the last howl, too terrified even to wing its way back to the safety of Scream Processing, cowering under a garbage bin, and it too went into one of her containers.

The punishment they'd given her was perfect in its way. She had wanted to reach from her limbo to touch the real world of suffering and they had obliged her. There was only one place in the world she would never be called to visit, and would never be able to go: a small quiet room in a house on an acreage where no scream, no outcry, no whimper or moan would ever break the silence.

It was too bad. She and Sam would have a lot in common. She understood what the look in his eyes meant now.

And here, in the back of a filthy lean-to on the edge of the slums, was a soiled and tattered sob, which fell to pieces as she tried to lift it, and there was one less in the world.

In the distance there slowly arose a cacophony of yammers, whines, and screeches, the ten thousand voices of the city calling out in anger and pain and fear, the screams twisting and roiling through the air as they fled homewards, one here and one there falling back to become stranded or trapped. She stopped for a moment and thought about the day Supervisor Sheen had described to her, the day when the last shriek would disappear from the abruptly silent world, and everyone would have all the peace and quiet they'd ever wanted, and more, and she knew that on that day the last laugh, the last gleeful shout, and the last word spoken by human lips would vanish also into the sudden and everlasting calm.

She thought that would be a good day. Slowly, she moved on. •

WHY I HUNT FLYING SAUCERS
Hugh A.D. Spencer

When I pull myself out of bed I notice that my slippers are missing. Obviously aliens are responsible. They have been disrupting my domestic routine for a few weeks now, presumably to observe my reactions.

I smell something in the hallway. Briefly, I wonder if they've been playing with the kitchen range, but then my still half-dormant brain tells me that the smoke is coming from the wrong end of the house. With trepidation, I poke my head out of the bedroom door and see the spitting embers of a dying campfire sitting in the bathtub. The aliens have also deposited a string of marshmallows, luncheon meats, wieners and beans along the hallway leading from the kitchen to the bathroom. The sticky brown sauce from the pork and beans has been mixed with some kind of gooey xenoplasmic fluid; the mixture has soaked into the hallway carpet and the resulting mess looks incredibly difficult to clean. Damn those aliens.

Over a perfunctory breakfast I sip my tea and decide to call in some cleaners to deal with the second-encounter debris while I'm at work. Then I wonder, pointlessly I know, why have they done this to me? Is this some bizarre attempt to recreate some trivial moment from my boy scout days? Or some silly reference to humankind's origins as a hunting and gathering species?

Putting on my coat, I go out to the driveway where I notice the telltale brown streaks under the car. Nothing serious, just another oil leak. Undoubtedly another sign of extraterrestrial activity.

Driving to the office, I sight a formation of cigar-shaped lights drifting over the city. I seem to be the only one who notices their ships on a regular basis. As I coast into the parking garage I see a pair of bulbous obsidian-black eyes floating in my rearview mirror. The alien's huge eyes are set over the tiny triangular face with the customary green skin. The image of the face lingers for a fraction of a second, then I only see the concrete and orange paint of the garage. I hypothesize that the alien may have been using some time/space warp device to gather a microsecond's worth of observations of my driving behavior. Who knows what information aliens think is important.

When these things first started happening to me I was terrified almost to the point of insanity. But lately I'm just feeling very, very put upon.

My morning at the office is reasonably uneventful. The aliens have decided to surround my desk with some kind of sensory distortion field which temporarily removes my color vision and alters my sense of hearing. For about two and a half hours everybody sounds like Oswald the Duck or one of those damned chipmunks. But living inside a Max Fleischer cartoon doesn't keep me from making a few calls to the names on my client list. Actually their helium voices make some of the customers a little easier to take.

Sometime after coffee the distortion field dissipates and I decide that it is safe to go find some lunch. Not surprisingly, I'm not the most popular person at the office and therefore no one volunteers to join me. I suppose my co-workers don't enjoy finding themselves breathing through their ears or finding a mass of other-worldly tendrils squirming out of their quiche and salad.

But today I don't get to feel lonely. Once I reach the sidewalk I feel a strange upward breeze bite at my cheek. I turn and see a bright halo of celestial light descending around me. Once again I find myself inside an alien spacecraft.

And as usual I'm lying naked on a cold metal slab. A billion years ahead of us and these BEMs haven't learned how to build a comfortable examination table. I twist my head to the side and see a screen displaying a three-dimensional projection of one of my undoubtedly fascinating mucous membranes.

The spindly forms of the aliens float up to the ceiling of the chamber:

"Human, we mean you no harm..."

One of the aliens removes a long tube from the polished curved wall.

"...just roll over onto your side and bring your knees up to your chest."

Great, another rectal probe.

I suppose it could be worse. Once they strapped me into a chair and stuck red-hot needles of light into my stomach and my skull. Another time they were taking secretion samples from my ears, nose and throat—it felt like they were pushing a lawn mower up my left nostril.

The absolute worst session was when they were taking spermatozoa specimens. I don't happen to find bug-eyed, bulb-headed ETs particularly sexually arousing, so they used this giant vacuum cleaner nozzle to generate the erection. They took 17 ejaculate samples. This was much less fun than you might imagine. Think ragged flesh.

So maybe just another rectal examination isn't so bad. Anyway, that's what I tell myself as I feel the cold metal of their probe push roughly through my anal sphincter.

I wake up on my living room couch. Two men dressed in black and wearing sunglasses sit across from me. The mirrored surfaces over their eyes make them look a little like aliens too.

"Are you conscious now?" asks one of the men in black.

"Yes," I sigh.

I see the empty bottle and syringe sitting on the coffee table. Pentathol again. Their induced hypnotic trance is the only reason I am able to remember today's abduction.

The small man with a short blond crew-cut starts to pack his tape recorder into his briefcase:

"There doesn't seem to be any obvious physical damage or psychological aberration. It seems to be the typical scenario..."

The larger man, who has an even shorter blond crew-cut stands up:

"...but we'd like you to stop by our offices in the next

couple of days for a medical."

Just what I need, I think. Another examination.

Both men gather up their briefcases and walk toward the door.

"Don't bother to get up," the larger man says. "We've already contacted your office, and we gave your Master-card number to the cleaners. I hope you don't mind, they had to put in a lot of work on the rug and they needed a deposit."

An irrational sense of propriety forces me to stand and follow the government agents to my door.

"Now don't put off the physical too long this time," the smaller man says. "There is the possibility that the aliens are slowly modifying your DNA and turning you into something..." He pauses as he considers the theory "...not quite human."

"Golly," I reply with little conviction.

"That's only one of the possibilities the Agency lab is playing around with," adds the larger man. "Some of the experts think that they may be using your body as a host medium for a fetal extraterrestrial organism. Their exami-nations would be routine checks on the embryo's growth."

The larger man puts a solicitous hand on my shoulder: "You must prepare yourself for the possibility that this creature could rip its way out of your intestines at any time."

"Well." I'm silent for a moment, trying to think of some-thing appropriate to say. "I really appreciate your con-cern."

I sound very tired.

The two men let themselves out onto the porch.

"Do you have any more of those 'Missing-Time-At-Work' forms?" I ask. "I'm just about out and my boss can't get his insurance claims processed if I don't submit within 48 hours."

"We left some on the kitchen table," says the larger man.

The smaller man takes something from inside his jacket pocket. He hands me a paperback edition of *The Book of Mormon: Another Testament of Jesus Christ.*

"You look very tired, sir," he says with sincerity. "I wish

you would let me send the missionaries over for a discussion. I know that a strong testimony of the revealed gospel of these latter days would be a great comfort to you."

"I appreciate your concern."

The larger man also hands me something. It is a colorful leaflet.

"But in the meantime you might want to cheer yourself up by purchasing any one of our fine Amway products."

"I appreciate..."

They walk to their car, a well-maintained AMC Hornet.

"Be sure to call me at home when you want to place orders," calls out the larger man as he opens the car door. "Don't place orders through my office."

"You can call me at home or the office," says the smaller man.

There is the sound of car doors slamming. The roar of an engine. And the men in black are gone.

The smaller agent's concern for my spiritual well-being must be overpowering since he seems to have forgotten that this is the third *Book of Mormon* he's given me. Walking toward the bedroom, I deposit his gift on the growing stack of latter-day religious literature on my bookshelf.

And true to its claims, the Amway catalogue does indeed contain a startling range of useful, attractive and unique household bargains. Including an attractive and affordable digital clock radio with simulated plasti-wood finish. Which will come in handy because the beings from another world have decided to melt my bedside clock after I left for work. Damn aliens.

I spend the rest of the day in bed. I'm too tired to read and the aliens have also transformed my collection of Ridley Scott and James Cameron videos into highlights of a Spanish-language home-shopping channel. Aliens.

They come for me in the night. I don't know what time. Squat ugly creatures who look like a cross between hobbits and Armenian tailors. They lift me out of the bed and tear off my pajamas. Maybe they don't like the material.

Stumpy dwarf-fingers hold me like iron bonds as they lift me over their flat shoulders and carry me toward the smoky light of the space/time portal.

A telepathic message blasts through my mind:

"Do not be afraid, Human. We mean you no harm."

Where have I heard that one before?

"Okay, okay," I say weakly. I slide through the portal. The light runs like slimy electricity over my skin. "You know, I really could walk through this thing under my own power," I protest to the space-midgets.

If anything, they grip all the harder.

"Do not be afraid..."

Into the mothership we go.

We float upwards into the dome of the crystal cathedral. We are thousands of human specimens. Representatives of all races, cultures and ages of history.

The living glow of the crystalline structures suffuses our naked bodies and makes us perfect. We drift into a loose helix pattern as we turn toward a massive corridor that stretches out into infinity.

We see a myriad of lifeforms of every conceivable configuration lining the inner walls of the enormous passageway.

Intuitively I sense that we are facing the collective knowledge and experience of all intelligent life in the known universe: The Galactic Super-Culture.

Its godlike voice gently roars at us:

"BEAUTIFUL HUMANS! YOU ARE PRECIOUS AND RARE. WE WISH TO PROTECT AND PRESERVE YOU!"

Protect us? With rectal probes? I wonder. Besides, I feel a little overweight.

The Super-Culture articulates again:

"EVIL HUMANS! YOUR HIDEOUS AND VIOLENT NATURE MAY SOMEDAY GROW AND ENDANGER THE WHOLE UNIVERSE IF YOUR WARLIKE TENDENCIES ARE NOT CONTAINED!"

The whole universe? It seems unlikely to me. What risk is a bad attitude to your average black hole?

"WISE HUMANS! PROPERLY NURTURED, YOU WILL MATURE INTO THE LEADERS OF US ALL!"

Wise? I remember some of the products at the back of

the Amway catalogue.

"FOOLISH HUMANS! WE MUST PREVENT YOU FROM DESTROYING YOURSELF IN ATOMIC FLAME!"

Give me a break!

When I wake up, the mothership has vanished. The Super-Culture is gone. But I am still naked.

Naked, lying face down on my front lawn.

I estimate that is mid-afternoon. The telephone in my kitchen is ringing. I answer it by the third ring.

"This is the Chief Librarian," says the measured, rational voice at the other end of the line. "Your name was given us by a Mormon gentleman and an Amway representative. We have a book from our 00.0 stacks which you may find of interest."

I arrive at the Reference Section with no sign of alien activity. Perhaps invaders from another solar system hesitate to interfere with the operation of the Toronto Public Library System.

It has been a long time since I've been to a library. Or an art gallery, or a movie, or even a McDonald's. I fear public settings in general and I avoid places of learning in particular. I love libraries and museums, and the prospect of watching these storehouses of human reason and achievement get twisted around by some inexplicable alien prank is too depressing to contemplate.

But this time I was invited. And it just feels like the right thing to do.

The Chief Librarian looks pretty normal. She scans me carefully, decides how much authority she has to apply to contain any likely nonsense from a person of my height and weight, and then she speaks:

"You're the gentleman I spoke to earlier? Just remember that these are reference books. You can look at the books as long as you like inside the library." She narrows her eyes: "So don't even ask if you can borrow them."

She places a gray book in front of me. Then she hands me a pad of paper and a ballpoint pen.

"Most people who look at this book ask if they can use these."

She's right. The book contains much that is noteworthy. Its title is *Practical Steps for Coping with Unwanted Alien Encounters* and its author is a Louise Wallis. The dust jacket states that Wallis is a social worker who has "suffered over 300 alien abductions since the age of 15." The promotional copy also notes that "after developing these simple and easily mastered techniques, Louise Wallis has helped thousands to completely eliminate extraterrestrial influences in their personal lives."

Wallis is everything the desperate seeker of aid could ask for: she's perceptive, honest about what she knows and what she doesn't know, and she writes in easy to understand sentences. This is some of what she wrote:

> *I formed a support group for people who claimed to have been abducted by aliens. Their stories were so vivid and expressed such humiliation that I never doubted their sincerity. And as we shared our experiences we gradually learned that each one of us was given a different reason for our degradation by our captors.*
>
> *These horrific and ridiculous creatures would puncture our wombs with ice-cold needles, pierce our urinary tracts with razor-edged tubes and drill holes into our skulls—telling us that they had the right to perform these atrocities because the ozone layer was disappearing, or because our governments had nuclear weapons, or because our race had ventured into outer space.*
>
> *A common pattern in the early phases of the support groups was for abduction victims to try and convince themselves that the aliens were correct, and that these indignities can be justified as part of a higher purpose. But as we shared our grief and our anger, together we concluded that this belief was a delusion.*
>
> *Every thinking person who has been abducted by alien beings must eventually face the same crucial question:*
>
> *It must take tremendous technology and resources to travel across the galaxy to our world. Would intelligent*

*and compassionate beings travel so far and at such
cost, simply to confuse us and insert crude implements
into our bodies?*

My hand is trembling. I have to stop writing for a moment.
Wallis continues:

> *It is undoubtedly true that an infinite universe holds
> many things that are beyond our current level of un-
> derstanding. But to be rational, emotionally-stable
> people, we must base our attitudes and behavior on
> what we can understand and those things that we have
> experienced.*
> *...if we believe what the aliens do and not what they
> say, we can only conclude that these creatures from be-
> yond the solar system are raping and abusing us.*

I look up from the page. The walls around me stand solid
and unchanged. My left hand is pressed against the table,
its heavy waxed top suggesting the stability and strength
of its structure. At least for the time being I am safe.
I reach the next chapter:

> *The support group sessions also had a number of
> constructive outcomes, including the mutual discovery
> that many of us had invented strategies and tech-
> niques for coping with unwanted alien appearances in
> our lives. Collectively, these means of coping represent
> a highly effective repertoire for anti-ET self-defense.
> Many of these strategies use everyday items from the
> home or the simplest industrial equipment and farm
> machinery...*

I start to take a lot of notes. Eventually I have to ask the
Chief Librarian for another pad of paper.

I'm driving well over the speed limit. The jeep is my latest and most satisfying guilty pleasure. But it's just past
six in the morning and on a northern Ontario highway
there is very little risk of collision. Besides, my new toy

was designed to be driven down empty roads at high velocities.

Since things have settled down for me, I've been a lot more productive in the office and the jeep was a reward to myself for some hard work.

My latest tape, *The Ventures in Space,* twangs from the stereo speakers. I remember a line from Wallis:

"Many aliens can be made severely uncomfortable by certain sounds or varieties of music."

Damn right. The little buggers really hate early sixties electric guitar groups or some of the more obscure British invasion bands like Herman's Hermits or the Zombies.

A few weeks after my trip to the library I caught some aliens stealing single socks from my drier and I toasted them with a blast of "Mrs. Brown, You've Got a Lovely Daughter" from my portable tape player.

The aliens collapsed onto the basement floor, gasping out little silent "O's" with their lipless mouths and trying to keep their oversized brains from leaking out their nostrils. Eventually they vanished into a cloud of red steam— just like dead Invaders from that old TV show.

Now the Ventures and early Floyd are my favorite groups.

The highway leads into a small river valley. I slow the jeep and park it at the side of the road. I turn off the stereo and roll down the window.

This feels like the right kind of place.

"Trust your instincts," writes Wallis. "The aliens are always trying to humiliate you, undermine your self-confidence. There is a reason for that; they don't want us acting on our feelings."

There's an odd texture to the air, like the taste of new metal and rotten eggs. I look up and see a mild distortion in the morning clouds.

This is definitely the right place.

I get out of the jeep and remove my packsack from the trunk.

Many of these strategies use everyday items from the home or the simplest industrial equipment and farm machinery...

First I put on the insulated work-gloves. Next, I open the hood of my jeep and connect the cable to the battery terminals.

I have my own theory about the aliens. It's based on a psychoanalyst who used to explain behavior in terms of informal "social games." Now, I can't prove this theory, but I like it: the aliens are playing a very silly, very sick game with us. Schlemiel and Schlemazl.

The schlemiel is like the sneaky, vaguely malevolent guest who goes around your house deliberately spilling things, embarrassing people and being a general pain in the ass to his host—the unwitting and vastly put-upon schlemazl. The objective of the schlemiel is to force the confused schlemazl to both forgive all these pranks and feel guilty for getting upset in the first place.

The aliens land. They kidnap you. Then they tear off your clothes, jab you with hoses and needles and generally treat you like space junk. But it's okay, they say. You can forgive us and love us for all this because we have advanced intelligence, and because you have reactors, toxic waste, pay-TV, bad haircuts, etc., etc.

What's really disturbing is the fact that the schlemiel doesn't understand why he's doing all this bad shit to people. It's all pathological, compulsive behavior. Probably the result of some deep-rooted, star-spanning self-loathing. They need us to regularly reassure them of their superiority.

Damn aliens. They have some advanced technology. But they aren't very smart.

I hook the cable to the reel and lock the bolt into the crossbow. The thick gloves make it difficult to aim the weapon, but I manage to align the cross-hairs just over the patch of slightly-wrong blue overhead. I pull the trigger and the bolt hurtles through the air, whisking the length of cable behind it. It's a good shot. The arc of falling cable neatly dissects the early morning sky.

There's a hard "click" that echoes through the river valley; the cable has connected with something invisible.

Suddenly a string of sparks races up the cable, and

there's a beautiful multicolored explosion of electricity.

Its force-field ruptured, the flying saucer crashes into the valley.

I heft the bulky packsack over my shoulder and stride toward the smoldering metal shell. Without the field to maintain its structure, the saucer is already starting to disintegrate. So it only takes a little effort, and a pair of bolt-cutters, to force open the hatch.

Inside I see half a dozen aliens. They are either unconscious, or too disoriented to move. All of them are naked.

As I enter the main chamber I notice that one of them is twitching in a pod-like chair, others are crouched over streamlined control units, and one is sprawled face down on the slowly dissolving floor.

I open the packsack and look for the lubricant and the cattle-prod. •

FISH

M.A.C. Farrant

By day, carrying on with my fish body assembly work. By night, waking to find strangers in my bed. Last night, Mrs. Hanson and her three kids. A trial of a person.

Rip doesn't seem to mind the strangers. He just rolls over, grumbles about needing more covers, leaving me to contend.

By day, all is well. The important fish body assembly work continuing. But three nights ago, an elderly couple vacationing from Alberta. He, bald and snoring, she in hair net pondering. Maps and guidebooks spread out over the quilt.

It's the night time crowds I can't stand. Whole families arguing. Some under the covers with Rip and me, others sitting on the bedside nattering.

It's worse when I sweat because of too many people in our bed. Then I have to throw off the covers to get any relief and everyone starts in on me then, complaining. Many of the strangers don't like our bedroom, for instance: no proper dresser, a doorless closet, the bed, merely a double. I wish I wouldn't apologize so much. *FEEL SO RESPONSIBLE*.

"Perhaps if I cleaned up the room you'd feel better," I say. "Perhaps if I slept on the floor next to the dog."

More room for Mrs. Hanson and the three kids. Mrs. Hanson slithering naked next to Rip. Mrs. Hanson breathing lullabies into Rip's dozing face.

By day I'm a person of importance. Thank heavens. With my fish body assembly work. Nearly fifty thousand so far and the numbers keep climbing. The parts from Hong Kong, duty free. That was my doing. I discovered the rule about location. Where it is permissible for a manufacturer to assemble a product on home turf, thus avoiding import tax. The rule book was old, but not forgotten. I take pride in that. Ferreter of antique rules.

The woman at Customs agreed, but not wholeheartedly.

"Right here on page 15 of ENTRY REQUIREMENTS FOR PARTS FROM FOREIGN PARTS," I showed her.

She wasn't happy. They don't like to give anything away. They come to believe it's *their* rule you're tampering with.

"It's a nice rule," I told her, "one you should be proud of."

But she took it personally. That the Government would be missing out on its due tax. That's dedication for you.

We all get on. Somehow. Me, I'm doing my part for the environment. Tax free. And I won't have to pay sales tax on the assembled fish bodies either because I won't be selling them. Because, in a sense, I'll be giving them away.

Rip was disappointed I didn't use my inheritance money for something more worthwhile. That's his opinion. A Jazz Trio, for example. I know he's always wanted one of those. Piano, bass, drums. Playing Bill Evans on demand. Actually, he'd like to have Bill Evans as well. I've often hoped he'd visit us in bed but the dead can be very stubborn. So far, no show.

A Bill Evans tape wouldn't do. I suggested it.

"Too small," said Rip.

He wants to be wrapped in the live thing, ear to the electric bass speaker or sit beside the piano player and stroke his fingers while he's playing. Or crouch beneath the piano player's legs and work the pedals. Involvement. That's what Rip wants.

But I only had enough inheritance money for one of us to be involved. And after all. It's important to me that I calm things down. Quit my job at the gas station just so I could take the time.

The fish bodies are all the same size. Ten inches. Just under the legal size limit. Plastic. Overall gray in color, made up of three sections: head, shaft, tail. Flecks of pink and blue in the plastic. Could be mistaken for a trout, a cod or a young salmon. That's not the important part, the type. It's just so that THEY CAN BE SEEN TO BE THERE.

I've always wanted to raise spirits.

Getting tired, though, with all these strangers turning up in our bed. I tell Rip about it but he just gets annoyed.

"Don't be so rigid," he says, "have a little flexibility. After all, they're not bothering you, are they? Not in any significant way? Beating you about the head or sitting on your back? Complaints about the bedroom furniture don't count. They're not actually hurting you, are they?"

Apart from Mrs. Hanson's gymnastics over Rip's body last night, I'd have to say no, they're not.

"Well then," he says, "be like a rock in a stream, a tree in a storm. Let your turmoil flow around and away from you."

That's my Rip. He'd be a Zen Buddhist if he had the time. As it is, he's run off his feet. No wonder he sleeps through the night-time visitors. By day, he's selling Bic Pens, Eddy Matches. He's got the whole territory from here to Burgoyne Bay and having the whole of anything is exhausting. So there's always someone in *his* bed. IN A MANNER OF SPEAKING.

He's right, though. I make too big a deal about everything. Always have. Still.

Seven members of the Golden Eagles Day Camp the night before last in our bed. Out on an adventure sleepover with their Counselor.

Children are far too active, especially in sleep. Why I've never gone in for them. One of the campers tried to cuddle next to me, one even tried to climb in my arms. Rip just shoved them aside as if they were sleeping cats, heavy lumps. But me, I can't. I've always got to be taking charge. Half the night gone running back and forth to the fridge—juice for the campers. And then the nineteen-year-old Counselor was having trouble with her boyfriend and wanted to talk. By morning I was a wreck from trying to keep everyone happy.

I can't leave well enough alone. Or in this case, bad enough alone. Doing my bit for the environmental movement. I can't stand it when people get upset. The depleting fish stocks. All the hue and cry.

My bit. Keeping the complainers happy. I have parts for

one hundred and fifty thousand fish bodies. The boxes are stacked in the living room, hallway, kitchen, down the stairs to the basement. Thought of using Mini-Storage but the inheritance money is running low. If I were a midget, it would seem like a cardboard city inside our house. Towers of boxes, alley ways dark and spooky, no telling what goes on in there.

One of the campers got lost the other night on the way to the bathroom. Found her wandering terrified among the tail sections.

I'm especially happy about those tail sections. After all those faxes to Mr. Ni in Hong Kong.

"They've got to look like they're swimming," I faxed. "They've got to look like they're MOVING IN SCHOOLS THROUGH THE WATER."

Mr. Ni is a marvel. Even without an engineer he managed to come up with a propeller thingy that's connected to an elastic band. And he guarantees it. Either my assembled fish bodies self-propel or he'll take them back. That's business. So far, on my bathtub trials, success. Except for an occasional turn of swimming on their backs, the fish performed quite well. You just pull this elastic band, the tails whirl and away they go.

I was trying to tell Mrs. Hanson about my plans last night in bed but she wasn't interested. Just wanted me to give the baby his bottle so she could get on with Rip's body rub.

The baby listened. "I will be delivering the first fifty thousand fish bodies to the ocean by month's end." I told him. "I'm so excited. Rip has agreed to drive the hired truck. A dump truck. My plan is to back down the ramp at Anchor's Aweigh Marina about three in the morning. Only problem is, first I have to activate the tail sections. Otherwise, plunk, to the bottom of the deep blue sea."

Fifty thousand elastic bands snapping. I have to admit it's daunting. I'd have a nightmare about it, no doubt, if my nights weren't already so crowded. That's something. Too bad the strangers are gone this morning. I'm at the point where I could do with some help.

Right now what I picture before me is a string of busy,

solitary days activating fish bodies. Their writhing gray forms mounting the cardboard box towers, scraping against the ceiling. Jiggling jelly. Maggot movement.

What keeps me going is THE THOUGHT. All those upset people calmed down. Perhaps even happy. "LOOK, THERE'S FISH IN THE SEA!" Again. After all. In spite of. •

MRS. LEAKEY'S GHOST

Alice Major

Mrs. Leakey's coffin. She lay
           in polished oak, satin lining. Handles
gleamed on the dark wood, ornately plump
as the pudgy candelabra in her parlor.

Mrs. Leakey's face. In repose.
Mouth a straight staple, clamping white
flesh. Ladies guard their skin
from outdoor elements, go nowhere
without careful paraphernalia—veils
and parasols.

Mrs. Leakey's hands. Clasped firmly.
Locks of hair bound in a brooch
on her bosom. Bosom bound
in a corset.

Mrs. Leakey. Going nowhere
but the grave. To lie beneath
the same stone carapace that hid
her husband, former ship owner, now
a pale bony cargo in his last hold.

Son Francis, a Victorian top hat
fluttering tails of crepe.
He rode to the graveyard, grieving
properly. He mourned less for his mother
than for something else, something
inarticulate, slain before his birth, locked up
in ledgers. Something gone forever. Something
that had never gone
anywhere.

Mrs. Leakey, going nowhere
but to doubtful glory. So she astonished
Francis, by reappearing late one night
in a corner of his study. Her hair
was straying slightly from its iron-
gray bands. Her skin had darkened, as if
exposed to peat in some flesh-pickling bog.
His hand trembled on the ledger
and she disappeared.

But then another night, with the ship
Eliza Leakey full a fortnight late and telegrams
reporting storms around the Cape of Africa—
with the very furniture worrying, with
the gas lamps wavering in their faith—
there she was again. Now her bosom flopped
as he had never seen it, uncorseted.
The braids around her head a horsehair
straggle, as if the sofa stuffing
had burst its bounds.

And then again. This time in the hall
barring access to the parlor, baring her teeth
at the maid and hissing like a harridan
at her daughter-in-law. Who had hysterics,
packed her bags, and went to live again
in her mother's drawing room.

Mrs. Leakey, coming from the grave
sat on the steep-pitched roof and out-meowled
all the cats of London. Always just above
the room where Francis sat, scraping pen on paper.
"Out. Out. Out!" she wailed, worrying
the furniture more deeply still. But leaving
the creditors who filed up to the doorstep
strangely undisturbed. Francis heard them
whisper in his dreams. "Pay. Pay. Pay."

The captain of the *Mary Leakey* sent
a confidential letter from his last port of call.

"Dear sir...beg to inform...sailors
are a superstitious lot. Claim to see
your mother of most blessed memory
capering in the crowsnest.... Hesitate
to mention...indelicate...the apparition
lifts her skirts. No pantaloons. Most
strange occurrences. Suggest
you contact Lloyds, investigate
insurance re: effects of supernatural."

Shortly after leaving Curaçao,
the *Mary Leakey* dove to the bottom of the sea
and Mrs. Leakey capered with the fishes.
The voices of the creditors rose like wind
in the spars. The silver candelabra
sold. The solid wooden furniture now worried
about new owners.

And Mrs. Leakey cursing still
on the rooftops. "Out. Out. Out."
The house sold off at auction. Notices
of bankruptcy in all the papers.
Ledgers opened to the supercilious gaze
of strangers. Until the day when Francis
stood embittered at his parents' grave.
"Well, mother, you've brought ruin
on me. I'm off for North America.
I'll not be back."

The granite stone absorbed his curses
indifferently, like blows from feeble fists.
The ground lay quiet. Mrs. Leakey
lying in her grave at last.
                    At last, long last,
he turned and walked away, a free
man. •

KISSING HITLER

Erik Jon Spigel

"We dedicate this film with the hope that these heinous crimes will never occur again."
—Herman Traeger,
Producer, *Ilsa, She-Wolf of the SS*

"Bobby O, what's a Jew?"

Bobby is hefting the last of the boards for my mother's real-wood shelf through the dilator. He's wearing a white, sleeveless *Bundeswehr* undershirt and black G-string, his sunglasses inserted down the back, one of its folded arms tucked you-know-where. I'm watching kidvid on the twodee, an ancient history thing:

"TRIUMPH OF THE WILL"

a title on the screen.

"Three Days of Peace."

in retro-script. Then:

"5 September 1934"

which I have to query to find out is a date. I call up a calculator on the touch screen to do the subtraction:

Today it's   2634   (according to the computer)
minus   <u>1934</u>

equals   700

So it's seven-hundred years ago. And according to the *Institute of Historical Review* blurb at the beginning, it's about Jews. So I ask again.

"Bobby O, what's a Jew?"

"I don't know, Kendra. I think it's a cult." Then, raising his voice so the computer will get the message, "Am I right?"

The computer delicately coughed to indicate it was listening.

"I'll work on it," it said.

So I turn back to the vid. I've seen *Triumph of the Will* oodles of times before; it's one of my faves, even if I don't know what a Jew is, or never knew it had anything to do with them. Anyway, it's got this beautiful opening shot flying over some fields, looking down at the plane with Adolf Hitler and Arlo Guthrie on it, intercut with shots of guys assembling the stage for the concert.

Sometimes the color washes out, but the fuzzy in the twodee remembers me watching the film before, and color corrects as it goes on. It's subtitled; it has to be. No-one today can understand that weird English they spoke back then. In fact, until a few years ago, they used to think it was *two* languages being spoken!

The computer coughs again just at the Hitler Youth Boys' Camp bit, which I can tell Bobby likes, because he's absently running a finger up and down his G-string, looking at all those half-clad Hipi boys frolicking. There's a nude man with long hair on the screen, sitting by a pond, saying how he'd never have even considered swimming in the nude before, but now believes it's the only way to do it. I laugh because I still can't believe anyone ever cared about that kind of thing.

"I have some information," the computer began. *"Triumph of the Will* is a reconstructed composite print edited together from remains of various twentieth-century recording media during a nostalgic revival of two-dimensional entertainment forms that took place approximately twenty-two years ago. Some of these scraps still defy reconstruction, as many crucial elements are believed to be missing. The film you are watching is a recounting of the trials and tribulations of an ancient group of people who were alternately known as 'Nazis,' which was an abbreviation of their full name, *National Sozialisten,* a political group, like our own Union Gospel Party, and also known as 'Hipis,' which was a way of running together the initials 'HP,' which stood for *Hitler Partei."*

"They had something to do with Jews," the computer concluded.

"Something to do with Jews?" I shrieked. "I already knew that! I want to know what a Jew is!"

Hitler had just finished reviewing the troops and Joe Cocker was coming on stage to sing, "I Get By With A Little Help From My Friends."

"I guess I misunderstood," the computer said. "I'll see what I can do. Meanwhile, I'll come up with a bibliography of relevant sources for you."

"What's a bibliography?"

"Books," the computer sighed. "Hard copy."

"Would you both please shut up? I'm trying to hear this!"

Bobby O can be such a prig, sometimes.

"You're supposed to be building my mother's real-wood shelf."

"Later, later. Look at the way that guy moves! It's like he was a puppet or something."

"That 'guy' is *Joe Cocker.* Hitler's foremost *Reichs-marshal* and parade music composer. I think he knew Wagner."

I pronounced it 'wag' like a dog's tail, which brought a prompt correction from the computer.

"Kendra, it is pronounced *Vog*-ner."

"So big deal; he's dead now, isn't he? Like he's going to complain."

The computer coughed again just as Cocker was finishing.

"Here are your books," it said flatly. Computers, as a rule, have a certain distaste for hard copy, and ours was no exception. It spat about five bound volumes through a slot in the floor.

The first was the Classic Comics *Mein Kampf,* which I already had, so I dumped it back in the chute. The other four had lots of pictures, and I started thumbing through them. There was a picture of all these emaciated people being lined up for some sort of shower or something, a big metal chamber with a fire going on underneath it—for hot water, I figured; I knew they had it tough back then. There was an inset picture of somebody's arm with some numbers tattooed on it.

"Cool," I muttered. I wouldn't mind getting a skin-blast like that.

Another book had a bunch of old guys with beards wearing weird-looking nametags: six triangles arranged around a hexagon. There were more pictures of emaciated people, and lots of pictures of people wearing rags and looking pretty upset, God knows why. Oh, yeah; and there was this one picture of a lamp! I don't know why they'd have a picture of a lamp in a book on Nazis and Jews.

I plopped myself down beside Bobby O again in front of the twodee. Jon Sebastian was doing his singalong with the shovel guys. That's what I call them, anyway. It's just some guys in black uniforms hoisting gold shovels on their shoulders and marching around. But it looks cool and they sing good.

"I'm thinking of checking it out," I say to Bobby O.

"Why not? It looks like a trip."

"I mean, Mom said I'm old enough to use the Wayback, didn't she? It's not like it's dangerous or anything."

"Like I said, it looks like a trip. You should go."

"I don't just want to go there, though. I want to do something really wild. Something really on the edge once I'm there."

"Like what?"

"Like anything. I don't know; I'm still thinking about it."

So I thought. Dietrich was warning the crowd about the brown acid.

The computer coughed.

"I think I have what you want, now. According to Jewish law, Jewishness is inherited matrilineally. I've accessed your genealogy charts: according to them, two hundred years ago, one of the last declared Jews was a woman on your mother's side; she had a daughter, who had a daughter...well, to spare you all the permutations and combinations, Kendra, *you* are a Jew."

"Whoopee! I'm a Jew! I'm a Jew!"

"You're really only half a Jew," Bobby O was reading a hardcopy the computer begrudgingly provided. "Your father almost certainly was not a Jew."

I ignored him.

"Is 'Kendra' a good Jewish name?" I asked the computer.

"No, it's Celtic."

"Am I a Celt?"

"You're a mongrel," Bobby said.

"Your mother was descended from Jews and by Jewish law is a Jew, which makes you a Jew. Your father is Chinese, to use the ancient term. You have his last name: *Chang*. If you wish more detail, I can take a blood test and send the results to the archaeogenetics laboratory computer in Geneva."

"No," I said solemnly. "It is enough that I am a Jew."

I rose as Hendrix played the national anthem, signaling the closing ceremony of the Woodstock Hipi Concert in Nuremberg. I was overwhelmed with emotion. Imagine! Me, Kendra Chang, a Jew, whatever that was. I could kiss somebody.

Hitler was drawing a standing ovation from the crowd.

"That's what I'm going to do, Bobby O. I'm going to go back and kiss Hitler."

"Hess was cuter," he said.

"No, no. It has to be Hitler. If it wasn't for Hitler, I'd never know I was a Jew."

The last scene is a guy and his girlfriend walking through the park where they had the concert; there's litter everywhere, and, like these two are the last to leave. Their backs are to the camera. The guy's wearing a black vest with a painting on the back: a white omega enclosing a red peace sign superimposed on which is a white swastika. I freeze-frame and highlight the vest, asking the computer to make me one. Oh, yeah; I got some ideas, now.

The Wayback Gate is a big, open square frame with rounded corners. It glows violet just at the edge of UV when the Wayback's operating. The Wayback Machine itself is a featureless black box mounted on top. It has displays, of course: when you are, when you're going...but you have to piggy it with the home computer to get the spacetime coordinates right.

The remote is a gold armband that looks like a long glove with only one finger. Even then, the finger is exposed from the first knuckle up to the tip. You can only slip the glove on or off in your home time; it can't be removed when you go back, so you never get stranded. There are five buttons down the top of the armband: PAUSE, RECALL, GO/RESUME, FAST FORWARD, and STOP/RETURN. When I wear the glove, the controls only work for me. The Wayback's loaded with safety features.

To get anywhere, I just set the Wayback through the home computer, press GO/RESUME, and step through the glowing frame. Once I'm where I want to be, I can stop the flow of time around me with PAUSE, redo a sequence by going back a few minutes or hours with RECALL, skip a boring bit with FAST FORWARD, or come home with STOP/RETURN. If I lose consciousness for any reason (even sleep), I automatically return. There are explorer models of Wayback that don't do this, but the home models are built to protect. Hey, who wants history to hurt?

I'm thinking the easiest thing to do is show up during one of the shots in *Triumph of the Will*. I mean, I've got a specific date, right? September 5, 1934. And the computer can check the sun's position and even set me down at the exact time of day for any scene I want to be in. There's a motorcade at the beginning where Hitler's driving among all these party supporters, kissing babies and women, and stuff like that. So I get everything cued up.

"Big deal," Bobby O says.

"What do you mean, 'Big deal?' I'm going to be in a movie."

"No, you're not."

"But the computer's going to drop me right in the middle—"

"I don't care what the computer says it's going to do. You aren't going to be in the movie or else we'd see you in the movie right now."

Oh, yeah.

"Maybe I end up on the cutting room floor? That would make sense. Mom says the paradox buffer in the Wayback doesn't permit any setting that could screw up the time stream, and it *did* allow me to be sent where I wanted. Or maybe I'm on a piece of film that never made it to our time. They say there are whole acts they know about but can't find any film of. Like Crosby, Stills, Nash, and Himmler singing 'Teach Your Children Well.' "

"Hmph," said Bobby O. He hates it when I outsmart him. "Even so, the motorcade scene's too easy. Hitler's already predisposed to kissing there. There's no challenge. What you want to do is find someplace where it's going to take him completely by surprise. He's got to be surrounded by security, too. It's got to be tough."

"Are you daring me to do it, Bobby O?"

"Well, let's just say I have my doubts."

"You're on. If I win, I get to go anywhere I want without an argument, and you have to cover for me with mom." Mom said I could use the Wayback whenever I wanted, but not without someone there to supervise.

"Fine. And if *I* win?"

"I'll build mom's real-wood shelf for you, and tell her you did it."

"Deal."

We shook on it.

But now I was back to the beginning. Where should I show up? After the motorcade, Hitler goes into this chalet and up to the second floor, from which he addresses a crowd of the townspeople. Maybe I could be in the house on his way up, and surprise him on the stairs? He's got security people with him there. Probably it's too private to impress Bobby, though. He wants something dramatic.

I try setting the Wayback for Hitler's closing speech at the end of the movie, but the paradox buffer locks the event out.

I guess they did that scene in one take. It shows. Hitler looks like a silly, fruity middle-aged man, the kind of guy Bobby O's crowd refer to as a "queenie."

So I settle for a scene just before the end. It's a big mass assembly at this monument. The place is just lousy with

Nazis. It's a daytime scene, which I guess is good. Hitler mounts a huge stone platform and gives a pep-talk to the party Youth. It's a great scene. It's shot beautifully, with three swastika banners flapping in the background, and acres of men in uniform all mesmerized by the party leader. I already know I can go there; I checked it with the Wayback and the paradox buffer gave it the green light. The problem is that it scares the cramps out of me.

I try to sell Bobby O on a different scene. There's a folk-parade, with all these Hipis dressed in traditional German garb, all lined up to watch another parade with Hitler. It's like the scene at the beginning I wanted to be in, and Bobby nixes it for the same reasons.

So I'm stuck with doing my thing in broad daylight in front of a zillion people.

Bobby offers me an out.

"If you're chicken, you can just build the shelf for me. I won't tell anyone."

He's so sure I'm going to take him up on it, he goes ahead and makes plans for himself for the afternoon. God, I hate it when he's smug like this.

So while he's interfacing with his gayjay boyfriends I set the Wayback and just do it, knowing he'll come by, expecting me to be putting his damn shelf together, and instead finding the Wayback glowing and the controls set for Nuremberg. Ha!

The Wayback drops me off just outside the grounds where the assembly is, right where I want to be. I surprise the hell out of a cameraman who drops a film canister as I suddenly appear out of thin air. I'm no fool, though. I immediately hit PAUSE, stopping everything around me, and make my way to the monument.

Based on the film, I figure I'm dressed pretty unobtrusively. I'm wearing my new vest of course, but under it I've got a wicked tie-dye swastika T-shirt, same color scheme as Hendrix's, a miniskirt, and a pair of exact replicas of real Nazi Stormtrooper boots. I look aces.

I've got a headband on, too, which is perfect because it hides my autophraser. I've got a bonephone planted just behind my left ear, and my sunglasses are in fact my heads-up display, giving me a constant translation of what's being said, and supplying me with phonetic transcriptions of proper words and phrases, appropriate to any situation I might find myself in. Hey, when I travel, I travel in style.

Stupid me, however, I left in such a hurry I forgot to download a map of the compound into the autophraser, so I promptly get lost. Obviously I'm going to have to ask for directions. I hit GO/RESUME.

The guard just stares at me. What can I say? I'm gorgeous.

I know it.

"Entschuldigan mie," I say. *"Where ist dein Hipien?"* Remembering to pronounce it *"Vare,"* like *Vog*-ner.

"Eine Chinesin!" the guard exclaims.

"Dein Hipien," I prompt him. *"Where ist dein Hipien?"*

"Eine Chinesin spricht Jiddisch!"

This isn't going anywhere.

"Hitler?" I try. *"Machen mie zu Hitler?"*

"Ja, ja. Hitler. Kommen Sie mit mir."

The autophraser just isn't getting any of this. All I've got is the occasional word—in this case, "Come"—and lines and lines of question marks. But the guard makes his meaning clear enough, cocking his gun and jabbing the bayonet into my back. I hope he doesn't cut me with it; the remote gauntlet will sense the loss of blood and send me home. Then I'll be stuck building Bobby's lousy shelf.

Oh, that would be so frustrating! Especially now, because we're going *exactly* where I want to. It's so close, I can feel it. We round a couple of pylons, pass a couple of camera platforms, and there's the stone block where Hitler's going to make his speech. As we go up the stairs, I can see the man, himself, in conference with the director, what's her name, Riefenstahl.

"Heil Hitler!" The guard says behind me.

Hitler turns. He looks like a fruity old man up close, too. *"Eine Chinesin!"* the Führer exclaims.

"Ja, ja!" The guard agrees. *"Eine Chinesin spricht Jiddische!"*

*"Eine **jüdische** Chinesin?"* Hitler is taken aback.

The autophraser's fuzzy is starting to pick up on some of this. At the very least, I get it that they've picked up on the fact that I'm Jewish. I immediately snap to attention.

"Ja. Jüdin. Mie." I just know these guys love Jews. I can see it now: a state reception, maybe I'll even be given an honorary rank in the SS. Kendra Chang, *Reichsmarshal* Jew from the Future.

Hitler does a slow three-sixty around me, then shrugs.

"Streicher," he says, nodding me off the platform.

"Streicher? No way. Gross!" I lapse back into my speak, completely ignoring the autophraser. Streicher was the nimrod in the film who was rattling on about racial purity. The guy looked like a herring. Yuck.

Hitler came real close, then, with this creepy smile on his face. His breath smelled like urine.

"Ja," he said, nodding, savoring the word. *"Streicher. Die Jüdin weiss uber Streicher. Streicher wird an Sie Gefallen finden."*

It's now or never. I shoot forward, holding my breath, and wrap my arms around his neck. I get one good lip press out of it before they yank me off of him. I hear guns being cocked everywhere, so I hit STOP/RETURN and I'm gone.

Bobby's waiting for me.

"Hold it!" He says, before I can say anything.

He whips out a swab and wipes my lips and the inside of my mouth, then drops it into a plastic tube and that into one of the computer slots.

"Right. Now don't forget to download the autophraser."

All I want to do is rinse and spit. God knows what Nazis ate back then. But I link the autophraser to the computer first; whatever it learned about the language will be incorporated into an update on the next language program. Plus, it records a lot of what happened, so I can prove to Bobby O that I really kissed Hitler.

"I got the computer to analyze your saliva; it'll send the results to Geneva for analysis. I know you can play with the autophraser, but you can't fake genetics."

The computer coughed.

"Geneva says that the saliva sample consists of the

mingled secretions of two individuals. The first belongs to Chang comma Kendra to one hundred per cent certainty. The second sample is awaiting cross check with Geneva archaeogenetics facility. Waiting... Waiting... The second sample belongs to Hitler comma Adolph to eighty-one per cent certainty, based on reconstructive cross check."

"Hmph." Was all Bobby O said. "You win."

"Oh, yeah. Like there was ever any doubt. So now I can go anywhere I want?"

"That was the deal."

"Okay. I want to go to a concentration camp. That was *the* in place for Jews back then." Hey, I do my homework.

Bobby O grew fidgety.

"I don't know, Kendra. I've got a bad feeling about letting you take off just anywhere."

"Oh, come on, Bobby! That was the deal!"

"I'm just not sure, now... Your mother..."

"Oh, for God's sake, Bobby! It's not like it's real or anything; it's just history. If it gets bad, I can always just hit STOP and forget about it."

"I don't know. I just don't know. If you come back with anything worse than a scratch, you know what your mother will do to me."

"Fuck it, Bobby. I'm going. You said I could go anywhere I wanted to, so I'm going to a concentration camp."

"Well, where are these concentration camps?"

"Same place; Germany. I even know which one. Auschwitz. I've heard good things."

"Okay, so it's Auschwitz. The Wayback okay it?"

"I haven't checked. But I know it's going to be okay. All I gotta do is be in a place called Warsaw anytime after June, 1940, and the Nazis will even pick me up and give me a ride there."

Bobby was checking a bunch of things out on the computer.

"That's good that they'll give you a ride, because neither the Wayback, nor the computer, nor the history archives in Geneva have any record of a place called Auschwitz. Are you sure it's a real place?"

"Oh, yeah, yeah. I'm sure. I read it in a book. Doesn't

anybody read books anymore? Honestly. It was quite the place, crowded all the time, huge lineups for the showers. They celebrated its opening with this big do called *kristallnacht,* which means 'Crystal Night.' Beautiful, huh? Crystal Night. Ooh, I can't wait! I'm going to go right now!"

This time I dumped every map I could into the autophraser, and set the Wayback for Warsaw, which was in a place called Poland, for the year 1940 and the month of August. The Wayback didn't reject the coordinates. I hit GO/RESUME, waited for the black frame of the Wayback to glow violet, and stepped back into history.

This time, no one saw me appear. I queried the phraser for a good place to wait for a ride. It flashed the word "ghetto" on my sunglasses, and overlaid a map and directions. I PAUSEd and made my way there.

What a dump!

I don't know what I was expecting, but this place was the pits. Hardly the kind of place you'd expect to have a party with a name like Crystal Night. Like, I was expecting a little mess, right. Maybe some champagne glasses thrown in the streets, but not this. Everywhere there were windows boarded up, and torn posters with that hexagon-triangle design peeling from the walls.

The word *"Jüden"* was spraypainted in red over almost all unpostered surfaces, dripping like blood.

It was deserted.

I hit FAST FORWARD, hoping to speed up the action. Presently, a Nazi truck rounded a corner in fast motion, coming my way. In fact, I nearly let it go right by me, and had to hit RECALL to go back a few seconds.

"Hey!" I shouted, waving my arms. *"Jüdin! Mie!"*

The truck skidded to a halt and a troop of burly looking Hipi types jumped from the back.

"Eine Chinesin!" one of them shouted.

"Nein, nein," I said. *"Jüdin. Mie Jüdin."*

"Eine Chinesin spricht Jiddisch!"

"Eine jüdische Chinesin!"

Here we go again.

I decide not to be subtle. After all, they're supposed to

give every Jew a free ride to Auschwitz; I can't help it if I don't look Jewish enough for them. I'm not going to miss out on my ride.

"Jüdin mie. Machen mie zu Auscwitz." I tell them.

One of them grabs my arms roughly and pushes me towards the truck. I nearly stumble. This isn't going well. If these dodos keep this up, the autoreturn's going to kick in.

Two guards on the bed of the truck hoist me up by my arms and dump me. This really hurts!

"Hey, you guys keep that up and I'm outta here!"

One of them punches me. Another is tying my hands behind my back. The guy who punched me picks me up and dumps me on a bench on one side of the truck. Two guards sit on either side of me. Six guards are squished on the bench opposite me.

The osteoresonator in my bonephone is screaming warnings at me. Bruised ribs. Abrasions on my right wrist and on both ankles from the rope. It's asking me if I want to return. I'm still not hurt bad enough for the autoreturn to kick in, and I can't move my hands enough to hit STOP/RETURN manually. But I want to go home. I want to go home. I want to go home.

I start to cry.

The guards are pointing at me, saying things I don't understand, and laughing at me. The autophraser's getting the gist of it: they're laughing at my clothes. Why did fucking Bobby let me come here? Just because he was going to have to cancel all his plans and build Mom's goddamn real-wood shelf. Fucking Bobby.

One of the guards keeps leering at me, pointing up my miniskirt.

"Jüdische fisch, ja?" He says. The other guards laugh.

"Ja," another one says. ***"Geffilte fisch!"***

They all laugh even louder. The first guy uses the barrel of his rifle to try to push my skirt up.

"Schweigen!" One guard says, slapping the rifle away. The guards quiet down, muttering and giggling among themselves. This guy, I figure he's in charge, comes over and pins a yellow tag with that weird hexagon-triangle design on it to my vest.

"Jüdin," he says, and spits at my feet.

I want to go home.

We're driving. If I could fall asleep, I could go home. The autoreturn would kick in, and all of this would disappear like it was a dream. But I'm scared. Everything's a blur. Somehow we've ended up at a train station, and hundreds of people with yellow tags are being loaded into the cars. I get unloaded and pushed in amongst the crowds. I'm too dazed to do anything. All I think about is going home.

It's too hot, too cramped on the train. It smells like pooh. An older woman behind me is shrieking. A little girl hugs my legs and cries quietly.

The train stops. We're at Auschwitz.

A black-uniformed SS man sends the men one way, the women another. Some children are kept back, others are sent with the women. He takes an especial interest in the remote, and tries to pry it off. I almost laugh. He slaps me, and sends me with the women.

We get marched past a long line of emaciated people, same as in the picture in my book. Finally. I get a close look at one of the showers as we turn a corner. I watch them open the door to one of the stalls, and I see a pile of ashes and half-burned bones. I watch them put some men in it, and one of them trips on what's left of a skull. Then I watch them shut the door.

I stumble. I'm kicked. My hands are untied and I'm undressed. They take the autophraser, my sunglasses, my vest, my dress; everything. The phraser will decompose in about fifteen minutes after losing contact with my skin. My clothes will never last long enough to trouble any archaeologist. They try to take the remote again, and can't get it off. An SS man comes over. He and two other women guards are pointing to it and saying things I don't have a hope in hell of ever understanding.

Finally, the SS man shrugs.

"Abschneiden die arm," he says, and walks off.

The two women guards pin me to my chair. A man grabs the arm with the remote on it and holds against it the table. Another man wearing a lab coat comes over with a scalpel and a saw.

"Oh God Oh God Oh God!" I scream. The scalpel goes into my upper arm and I'm home.

"Oh, shit," Bobby O says. "Your mother's going to kill me."

"I just want to go home," I cry.

"You're home. You're home, already. What happened to your clothes? And the autophraser? That's a nasty slice; that'll take a couple hours for the autodoc to clean up. I hope you're satisfied."

"Oh, Christ, Bobby. They fucking kill people! The Nazis fucking kill people!"

"Bullshit."

"No, really. They just line them up and incinerate them."

"You expect me to believe that kind of crap? Face it, Chang; you screwed up big time and now you're just trying to weasel out of it. Everybody knows the Nazis never killed anybody. You're just pissed because you missed out on Crystal Night."

"I'm serious, Bobby..."

"Yeah, yeah, yeah. Look, you're pretty battered. Maybe you took a bad fall. The doc'll clear the cobwebs from your brain and you'll see. You're just a bit delirious, is all. Concussion. You just need some rest."

Bobby O took me up to my room and hooked me up to the autodoc. I fell asleep instantly.

I woke up feeling great, with a couple of hours to spare before dinner. The doc had fixed my wound, and had given me a parapsychic injection to help with the bad dreams I'd been having. All I could remember about the trip was a kind of vague sense of excitement, like I'd just watched a fright pic on the twodee. I couldn't remember much about Auschwitz. Like you go there, you leave. The truck part was better. I wouldn't go back. In fact, just forget about Auschwitz. I still don't know what a Jew is.

I switched on the twodee, and cued up another documentary. A lot of the music was the same as in *Triumph of the Will*. It looked promising. It all took place in these jungles, and everything was going up in flames. The aircars were really cool, too; they looked like dragonflies. There was even surfing. Lots of guys who looked like me were shooting at lots of guys who looked like Germans but weren't. The documentary said they were "Americans." The computer didn't know if I was an American. Everybody wore the same color green.

Mom called up that it was dinner, so I hit the SAVE button on the twodee; I'd get back to the show later.

"Hey, Mom, I've got a question," I asked between Brussels sprouts. "Who was 'Viet Nam'?" •

ABOUT OUR CONTRIBUTORS

WADE BELL's stories and poems have appeared in some thirty magazines and anthologies in Canada, the US, and Japan. Directed by Shary Cooper and starring David Barrett, "What Happened to the Girl?" was produced as a play at Calgary's Pumphouse Theatre in 1994.

ROBERT BOYCZUK has published three short stories in *ON SPEC*. In 1995 he won first prize in *Prairie Fire*'s speculative fiction writing contest (the winning story is scheduled to appear in the 1995 summer issue). He lives in Toronto where he teaches Computer Science at a community college.

RICHARD deMEULLES, who lives in North Bay, Ontario, has been published in *Reader's Choice, Descant, Cross Canada Writers' Magazine,* and *Tyro*. In 1987, he placed second in the *Cross Canada Writers' Magazine* annual fiction competition.

M.A.C. FARRANT has published three collections of short fiction: *Sick Pigeon* (1991, Thistledown Press), *Raw Material* (1993, Arsenal Pulp Press), and *Altered Statements* (1995, Arsenal Pulp Press). A fourth collection, *Word of Mouth*, is forthcoming from Thistledown Press in 1996. "Fish," which first appeared in *ON SPEC* in 1993, was included in the collection *Raw Material* and in *Witness to Wilderness: The Clayoquot Sound Anthology* (1994, Arsenal Pulp Press). She lives in Sidney, BC.

JAMES ALAN GARDNER lives in Waterloo, Ontario, with his wife, Linda Carson. He divides his time between writing SF, producing computer text books, and catering to the whims of two autocratic rabbits. He won the 1989 Grand Prize in *Writers of the Future*, and has been published in *Amazing, Fantasy & Science Fiction*, and other SF magazines. Besides winning the Aurora in 1991,

"Muffin" also appeared in Tesseracts[3] (1990), and *The Best of the Rest 1990* (Edgewood Press, 1991).

BARRY HAMMOND has been an editor with *ON SPEC* since 1991. His novel, *Cold Front* (New American Library), was published in 1982, and his poetry collection, *moral kiosk* (Underpass Press), in 1986. Short fiction has appeared in *Horizons SF* and poetry in *Transversions, Printed Matter* and *The Plaza* (both from Japan), *ON SPEC, Barbed Lyres* (Key Porter anthology) and others.

PRESTON HAPON resides near Calahoo, Alberta. He likes to ride Tennessee Walker, write SF, fly Piper, and dine Thai. His stories have appeared in *ON SPEC*, and *Innisfree*. "Stigmata..." was his first publication and set the trend for more pro-feminist statements. Preston has taught for two years in "the hormone Vietnam" known as junior high, which is surprisingly like the decade he spent teaching on adolescent residential psychiatric units in Edmonton hospitals. Not merely a SNAG, Preston exemplifies the acronym OFBUGWAL—Older Fat Balding Ugly Guy, With A Limp. (There was a very long pause at this point in his bio....)

WESLEY HERBERT's wife with her musclebound, tattooed shoulders, multiple genital and cranial piercings, neolithic menstrual blood-squelching, jade-cut promethean stare, whole-body orgasms, quick setting blonde brushcut, elbowpads, milk-squirting dual fast food outlets, power tools and chuck key set, hundredweight of chainmail and man-sized brawling hands that can sweep aside forest fires, counter the law of action\reaction, mold free floating cholesterol into mighty mountains, strangle Satan, cup the chin of a child then send it hurtling around the moon has made this all possible.

JASON KAPALKA lives in Edmonton, where he earns a sort of living from proofreading newspapers and reviewing computer games. He's recently finished a movie script which he describes, in typical Hollywood high-conceptese, as "Reservoir Dogs vs. E.T.," and will be pleased to entertain offers.

EILEEN KERNAGHAN's latest novel, *Dance of the Snow Dragon,* a young adult fantasy set in 18th century Bhutan, has just been released by Thistledown Press. Her speculative poems and short stories have appeared widely in magazines and anthologies. She lives in New Westminster, British Columbia, and with her husband Patrick operates a used book store, Neville Books. "Carpe Diem" appeared in the anthologies *Tesseracts³* (Porcepic Books, 1990) and *Northern Stars* (Tor Books, 1994).

CATHERINE MacLEOD has a degree in journalism. Previous short fiction has been published in *TickleAce, Secrets from the Orange Couch, ON SPEC,* and *Horizons SF.* Her short stories "WheelWalk" and "The Learning Process" are on the list of suggested teaching material at the Centro Cooperativo de Idiomas in Madrid, Spain.

ALICE MAJOR is an Edmonton poet and novelist and a past president of the Writers Guild of Alberta. Her collection of poems, *Time Travels Light,* was published by The Books Collective in the fall of 1992.

SALLY McBRIDE is married to writer and artist Dale L. Sproule, and has two grown children and a new granddaughter. Born in Ontario, she now lives in Victoria. She has done everything from sell waterbeds to raise a colony of tsetse flies (for research purposes only), and now works in personnel. Her short fiction has appeared in *Asimov's, F & SF, ON SPEC, Tesseracts, Matrix*, and other publications. She is perennially at work on a novel.

DERRYL MURPHY is a writer and photographer living in Edmonton. "Body Solar" was nominated for an Aurora in 1994. He has also been published in *Tesseracts⁴* and *Prairie Fire*, and has guest-edited on two issues of *ON*

SPEC as well as co-editing *Senary — The Journal of Fantastic Literature.* He is currently trying to finish his first novel via banging his forehead against the keyboard.

M.J. MURPHY is a writer working out of Toronto. "In the Train of the King" was his first sale. Since then, he has published in a number of American sci-fi/horror magazines, including *Midnight Zoo* and *Aberrations.* His literary influences include just about everyone.

ROBERT J. SAWYER is the author of the novels *Golden Fleece, Far-Seer, Fossil Hunter, Foreigner, End of an Era,* and *The Terminal Experiment.* His short fiction has appeared in *Amazing Stories, Ark of Ice, Northern Stars, Transversions, The Village Voice,* and many other places. Rob's story "Just Like Old Times" won both the Crime Writers of Canada Arthur Ellis Award and the Aurora Award for Best Short Story of 1993; he also won a best-novel Aurora Award for *Golden Fleece.* Rob has written and narrated five hour-long radio documentaries about SF for CBC Radio's *Ideas* series, is *The Canadian Encyclopedia*'s authority on SF, and produces the "On Writing" column for *ON SPEC.* He lives in Thornhill, Ontario, with his wife Carolyn Clink.

DIRK L. SCHAEFFER is a pseudonym and anagram of Frederik Falsch (which is German for "false"). He is a compulsive liar who steals shamelessly from Tanith Lee, Robert Coover, and Hollywood, among others, and can't seem to tell the difference between fiction, poetry, and crossword puzzles. Nothing he says should be believed if you don't believe it already. Currently he lives in Vancouver, where the air does strange things, man. "Three Moral Tales" will always be his first published fiction.

KARL SCHROEDER's story "Hopscotch" was nominated for a 1993 Aurora Award, and was given an honorable mention in *The Year's Best Science Fiction.* Karl works as a professional writer. In addition to science, marketing, business and technical writing, he has taught a credit course in SF writing at George Brown College. He is currently the vice president of SF Canada, the national SF/Fantasy writer's association, and is actively developing ways for writers to exploit the power of the Internet. Visit his World Wide Web home page at: http://helios.physics.utoronto.ca:8080/karl.schroeder.html .

KEITH SCOTT lives in Toronto, where he is a member of the Cecil Streeters Writing Group started by Judy Merril. He has had three stories published in *ON SPEC*, one in *Prairie Fire*'s special ConAdian edition last fall, and one in *Space&Time*.

HUGH A.D. SPENCER was born in Saskatoon and has lived in Toronto since 1982. His anthrological analysis of religious and therapeutic movements in science fiction fandom, *The Transcendental Engineers*, was funded by the Social Sciences and Humanities Research Council and was completed in 1981. Hugh's short stories for *ON SPEC* include "Icarus Down/Bear Rising," "The Triage Conference," and "The Progressive Apparatus." Hugh was elected Chair of the Friends of the Merril Collection of Science Fiction, Speculation and Fantasy in 1994; and with Dr. Allan Weiss, he was co-curator of *Out of this World*, the National Library of Canada's exhibition on Canadian science Fiction.

ERIK JON SPIGEL, a Toronto writer, has lived in Japan and is currently working on his MA in East Asian Studies at the University of Toronto, focusing on Japanese art and literature, as well as East Asian philosophy. His other interests include classical music and jazz, and he is learning to play the shakuhachi, Japanese bamboo flute. •

OUR THANKS TO...

EDITORIAL ADVISORY BOARD MEMBERS
FROM 1989 TO 1993

Douglas Barbour
Richard Davies
Leslie Gadallah
Monica Hughes
Spider Robinson
Robert Runté

J. Brian Clarke
Candas Jane Dorsey
Pauline Gedge
Alice Major
Nicholas Ruddick
Gerry Truscott

EDITORIAL COLLECTIVE MEMBERS
FROM 1989 TO 1993

Catherine Girczyc
Susan MacGregor
Marianne O. Nielsen
Phyllis Schuell
Diane L. Walton

Barry Hammond
Derryl Murphy
Hazel Sangster
Jena Snyder
Lyle Weis

ART DIRECTORS

Tim Hammell
Lynne Taylor Fahnestalk

SUPPORT STAFF FROM 1989 TO 1993

Mark Chan
Chris Hammond-Thrasher
Dave Panchyk
Claire Stirling
Michelle Wilson

P.J. Groeneveldt
Cath Jackel
Paul Rogers
Jane Spalding

SPECIAL THANKS

Jane Bisbee
Bill Williams

Steve Fahnestalk

*Our heartfelt thanks go out to all the dozens of
volunteers who have helped out over the years*